The Fall of Jaz

THE FALL OF JAZ

A Harrington Family Story

Tamara Martin

The Henry Mayberry Group
Adelaide

First published in Australia 2017 by The Henry Mayberry Group

www.thehenrymayberrygroup.com

Edited by Cathleen Ross

National Library of Australia Cataloguing-In-Publication data

Martin,Tamara, 1973-

The Fall of Jaz / Tamara Martin

1st ed.

ISBN: 978-0-6480250-4-7 (pbk.)

Cover Design: Kristyn McQuiggan, Drop Dead Designs

FOR NANNA

who saved her butchers paper and told a 7 year old to write her
stories
Thank you
I miss your hugs xoxo

Chapter 1

I ran the paddle brush through my hair, a gift from my late grandmother and one of the few things I took with me when I left home. It felt cool and heavy in my hand as I forcefully raked it through my black curls that tended to have a life of their own. If I'd cared more, I'd have gotten a haircut, maybe turned on the straightener and ironed the Harrington out of me like I did most days or gotten my favourite silk wrap dress dry-cleaned. But I didn't care enough for any of that.

Lying on the bed was the royal-blue linen shift dress I'd found in the back of Jay's wardrobe. I had a pair of nude pumps on the floor and the matching clutch on the bed beside the dress. Jay had found an old fascinator with blue and white feathers from somewhere, perhaps I'd worn it one Melbourne Cup. Maybe. He thought it would be wedding appropriate, look as though I'd made some effort. He cared more than I did even though it was my family. I'd have been happy to sit at home in my tracksuit pants and not bother with any of it. Not that this was home, this was Jay's home, but the same thing, really.

'Would you hurry up, Jaz?' Jay called from the next room.

Jay was already wearing his fancy pants and a dark blue shirt that matched his eyes. He looked handsome. Ridiculously handsome. He'd shaved off his usual multi-day growth. I'd almost forgotten what was underneath, the tanned, beautiful face he hid behind all that hair. The beard made him soft, understated, without it you got the full power of not just his handsome face but the power and strength he exuded. Women tended to stare like guppies, which I'd laughed at, but now I'd become desensitised to the full power of Jay, I was starting to understand why they turned to jelly when that power was directed at them.

He pulled the matching jacket from the wardrobe and shrugged into it. He rarely stepped out of his board shorts these days though he'd worn nothing but a Hugo Boss suit when we'd met. Now he spent his days on the beach, surfing, and running his beach front pub, there was no room for Hugo in his life anymore but clearly he'd kept one. The only sign left of my Jay as he knotted his tie was the salt caked hair he struggled to tame. My father would be impressed. Almost.

I stepped into my dress as his eyes crinkled with impatience.

'There, fine, I'm done. Let's go, then,' I moaned once I'd pulled up the zip and shoved the silly fascinator on the side of my head.

He threw his arm across my shoulders and pulled my head to his lips. 'It's going to be okay.'

'Whatever,' I smirked, turning to kiss him chastely before

grabbing the clutch and heading out to the car. It was going to be anything but fine and we both knew it.

I was getting antsy by the time we pulled into the dusty driveway of my parents' country house after an interminable drive. I'd forgotten how long it took. I really had moved a good hike away. I could have moved further, should have maybe, but Adelaide suited us. The beach suited Jay. The people were good people, we fitted and they didn't care about Harrington's or money or power, so it had been far enough.

'I don't want to go in,' I sulked, tightly clasping my hands together in my lap to control the raw fear rippling through my body.

We both sat still, staring out the front window of the jeep as people hustled around us, laughing, holding hands, carrying their oversized gifts down the long driveway to the back of the house, their footsteps crunching on the gravel as they went. We watched them silently for a few more minutes before there was a knock on my window.

I jumped, turned, mouth agape, horror movie style, staring at Margot, my parents' housekeeper, who was looking at me with the same kindness she'd shown me my whole life. No matter what I did, what happened, the chaos erupting around us, Margot always smiled at me with kindness and I knew everything would be okay.

'Come on. We have to go in,' Jay said softly.

'I don't want to, Jay. I don't want to see them. I don't want to see him. I just don't think I can.'

Margot jiggled my door handle until the door flew open and

again we stared at each other, the years of knowing passing between us unspoken.

'It will be okay, Jasmine, dear. He's still inside. If you hurry, you can be seated before he comes out,' she smiled sweetly.

I looked at Jay and he nodded. 'It's our best bet. We're here for Tom, anyway.'

'You're right,' I said, reluctantly climbing out. 'But any trouble, Jay and I'm outta there.'

'Deal,' he smiled, nodding a thank you to Margot when he thought I couldn't see.

We rounded the corner of the house and suddenly the familiarity was overwhelming. The pool sparkled in all its resort-like glory to our left, the tennis court beside it now covered in oak panelling, transformed into a gathering place where people were drinking from cocktail glasses and laughing haughtily while uniformed teenagers scurried between them.

Margot hurried over the spacious deck filled with people coming and going and into the house on our right, squeezing between the masses of people paying her no attention as though she were invisible. It irked me that they ignored such a beautiful human being but as I surveyed them, I remembered this world, these people in their finery, a who's who of the runways draped over their perfectly maintained bodies. Because in this world a misjudgement in diet or fashion could see you exiled. They had no time for the hired help. They exhausted me already.

We headed to the other side of the tennis court, to the grassed area on which we'd once played backyard cricket as children. Pale pink rose petals were scattered over the dark green grass, cared for and mown to perfection. Fairy lights twinkled above, hung through the tree branches and draped expertly above the chairs, from one side to the other as though they balanced by magic. White bamboo chairs sat either side of the aisle, facing the beautiful arbour draped in more of Margot's pale pink roses at the other end. More roses swept over the chairs as though they grew there, as though we'd entered our own fairy tale, our own secret garden. More fairy lights sparkled through the frangipanis dividing us from Margot's prized rose garden beyond and the marquees I could see set up for the festivities to follow. It was everything I'd always dreamed of, before it became an impossible dream. But the impossible was real. Tom and Alex had found it, or their wedding planner had.

Plenty of people had already begun to take their seats. I recognised some as my father's associates, too self absorbed to even look at me. I hurried past a few more familiar faces before they looked, before they saw my face and realised who I was. Traditionally we should have been sitting in the front row. I was having none of tradition. If we'd gone with tradition or what was appropriate then I'd be sitting alone and Jay would be inside somewhere helping Tom knot his bowtie. But Jay wouldn't do that to me, not even for his oldest friend. And to be honest I'm not sure my father would have actually allowed him over the threshold of his palace anyway.

We found a row towards the back already filling with people we didn't recognise and squeezed our way into the most inconspicuous seats we could find. We'd promised Tom we'd at least come. Well Jay did, I hadn't personally spoken to Tom in years. But Tom had contacted Jay's sister, begging to speak to Jay so they'd been communicating since with Jay doing what he could to keep our location secret, just in case my father was paying attention. Tom had been disappointed when Jay had declined the invitation of best man. I could tell by Jay's voice as he apologised profusely and even up to last weekend Tom had held the spot open for him just in case. But Jay had told him, 'I just can't leave Jaz,' and I'm sure Tom had understood the rest.

I sat with the afternoon sun warming my bare shoulders, people passing by and chattering around me as though I were invisible, of no importance to this event or the grand scheme of anything and it was perfectly fine. I stared off to where the path snaked between the frangipanis, the last time I'd been on the other side of those trees I'd been seventeen and running away from home. I'd run across the property under the glow of the nearly full moon heading to the creek and the dinghy we'd used to go up and down the creek when we were kids. That day it had held only a bag of my most prized possessions that I'd been sneaking out of the house for days. No more laughing children. First to go were Tom and Lydia, running to the other side of the world, Dad sent Christian to the far corners of the country and then the globe to manage properties and then there was just me. I'd read in the newspapers that as soon as Tom and Lydia returned, poor Christian was demoted and sent to manage the regional properties as though he were worth nothing. Typical Dad move, playing favourites, messing with people's heads, missing their potential. There was a light inside of Christian, a goodness that he hid but if you looked hard enough, if he let you in, it made you strong. But Dad never looked. Not at Christian, not at me, not even at Lydia, always in Tom's shadow.

That last night I'd run through the orchard ducking low hanging branches, fallen, rotting fruit mushing beneath my shoes. I rowed across the creek under the glow of the bright moon, the sound of fireworks cracking in the distance. Jay waited by his jeep on the other side, knowing once we drove away, I'd be disinherited and he'd be jobless. I had nothing but the few thousand dollars squirreled away in a zip lock bag in my coat pocket. Thankfully he'd been squirrelling away more than that for a long time.

Jay put his hand on mine, the warmth of him calming me, bringing me back to the now. Tom was walking to the front of the chairs with Johnno, always together those two, like musketeers. A deeply suntanned man followed. An unfamiliar face proving lives had continued on without me. I didn't know them anymore just like they didn't know me. It made me sad to know we'd drifted so far, that things happened, joyful things, sad things, fearful things and I wasn't there for them. I wasn't a part of their lives.

Michael and Moe followed the stranger proving there was no escape from being a Harrington, even on your wedding day. Although I supposed when your bodyguards had travelled to the far corners and done for you what Michael and Moe had done for Tom, it was possible they could actually be friends. Highly likely really when you considered mine was sitting beside me holding my hand, having defected from paid protection long ago but still protecting me none the less.

A small boy in white, carrying a satin pillow ran laughing

down the aisle, the entire gathering smiling in awe at his near angelic glow. Right behind him, calling him back to where he was supposed to wait for the bride, trying not to make a fuss, as he'd never make a fuss, was Christian, my brother, my anchor, who I hadn't seen in so long. His face was rounder, no longer haunted by shadows of expectations. He looked broader and stronger too, confident in a new way, not the son of a billionaire but happier, sure of himself, of who he was as a man. He no longer lived in the shadows of his brother. The angry, frustrated boy I'd once held onto, that had been the only one to keep me going until Jay, had been replaced with a man, a strong man so handsome he'd be worthy of any magazine cover but that would never be his way.

As though he sensed me watching among the hundreds also admiring his transformation, Christian suddenly stopped, catching my eye. As I quickly turned away I saw the smallest hint of a smile in the corners of his mouth. I don't know why I turned away. I'd hoped to see him, to meet his wife Ainsley, to hold his son, my nephew, Henry in my arms. Now I wasn't so sure, now it had happened, I wanted to run and go back to the quiet and safety of Jay's beach house. I wasn't ready to confront it all, who I was, what I'd done to my family when I'd left, the mess I'd left behind, the lost years, my father. I wasn't sure if I'd ever be ready.

'Is he coming?' I asked Jay, too afraid to look up.

'No,' he said, squeezing my hand.

'I don't think I can do it. Everyone will know who I am as soon as they see us together.'

'It's okay, Jaz, there's nothing they can do to hurt you.'

'But they'll tell him I'm here.'

'It'll be okay, I promise,' he insisted, but we both knew it was just wishful thinking, just a matter of time before I was face to face with my father.

Jay draped an arm across my shoulders. To anyone else we would have looked like a loved up couple about to witness another loved up couple say their 'I Do's,' they couldn't know this was how Jay kept me from falling apart. That without his arm holding me together I'd break into a billion shaky pieces and run for the hills.

Tom fidgeted at the front of the aisle. Christian got his son under control. Everyone took their seats and then, as a hush fell over the garden, my father walked my mother down the aisle and I had to hang my head between my legs in the small cramped space to avoid vomiting all over myself and anyone within the vicinity. That's the affect my father had on me.

'Breathe. He's gone,' said Jay, softly stroking my back, whispering in my ear as curiosity woke in the people around us.

I realised in time, smiled politely and quickly became a stoic Harrington. Jay smirked. I hated that somewhere deep inside I still carried the skills and the genes or whatever it was that made us who we were and in my case a bloody Harrington and all the pomp and foolishness that came with it.

The music began, a trio of string musicians buried in the corner played a vaguely familiar tune. Christian and a pretty brunette who I assumed was Ainsley, scurried quickly down the outside of the chairs to take their seats after having presumably secured their son for his duties. Then there he was, little Henry walking as tall and as steady as a small person could, his little suit making him the spitting blonde image of his father as he held his satin pillow high for all to see, a grin playing at the corners of his mouth.

Behind him, one at a time, came a beautiful, tiny redhead. According the printed order of events Jay had handed me. She was Andrea who I knew enough of from the glossy magazines to know she was my sister's partner. Next came an incredibly gorgeous brunette with tanned skin who was apparently Sarita. Another stranger who fit in to my family where I no longer did. Perhaps she matched the mysterious man in Tom's entourage named Rick. Then came Bex, minus the blonde dreadlocks I knew her for, replaced with a chic blonde bob. She was once a friend, a long time ago and now the wife of Johnno. According to an article I'd read online, they'd married on a beach in Spain a year ago before coming home so Johnno could work for Tom. Then came my sister Lydia, as radiant and full of life as ever. I felt my stomach flip and my heart ache at the sight of her, a million images of sisterly moments flashed before me and I'd never before wanted to reach out for someone as much as I did right at that moment, and as if on cue, Jay squeezed tighter.

I had no idea what kind of a girl could capture Tom's heart, who could mean so much he'd risk everything to be with her but when Alex, his bride, stepped into the aisle, somehow I was not at all surprised. She had a kind, sweet face and as her eyes caught Tom's she smiled so brightly she nearly glowed. Her dress, I'd read in a magazine, had been made especially for her by my sister, a talented designer finally finding her way and reaching success in her career after all the years she'd travelled with Tom hiding in the shadows. She'd made me a dress once, before she'd run to Europe, so I knew from experience how talented she was. I was glad Alex was wearing one of Lydia's gowns, glad my sister was finally getting to do what she loved. If people didn't already take her seriously, they would now because the dress, a satin A-line gown with a square neckline, Swarovski crystal belt embellishment and the slightest hint of a train was gorgeous.

Alex accented the dress with Swarovski crystal encrusted strappy sandals peeking from beneath the gown. Her long blonde curls dripped with more crystals as did her ears, although I'm sure those were diamonds. She was to be a Harrington now, after all, my mother would accept nothing less. But it was her face that struck me. She had a sweet girl next door look that drew you in. It would have even if she wore rags and as Tom watched her walking down the aisle, his own face full of so much happiness, my heart melted and for just a minute, it was as though they only saw each other, that the rest of us were unwelcome intruders.

I wanted to thank Alex for giving my brother that much happiness. I wanted to thank her for bringing him home and keeping him safe. It might have been a long time since I'd spoken to Tom but it wasn't because I didn't love him.

Chapter 2

The bride and groom left the area for their formalities and guests began making their way through the frangipanis and into the marquees. I didn't move. I couldn't move. I knew we had seating inside that big marquee. I also knew my father would probably be waiting beside my chair and I couldn't move.

'We have to stay, Jaz,' Jay said. 'We have to at least speak to Tom.'

'You have to. I'm happy to wait in the car,' I told him, already imagining the perfection of lying across the back seat.

'Hell, this is hard work,' moaned Lydia flopping into the recently vacated chair beside me as though we'd only spoken yesterday not five years ago.

I stared at her.

She stared at me.

Jay squeezed my shoulders.

Bex fell into the chair beside Lydia. 'Hey, Jaz,' she called and took a long swig through the straw in a piccolo bottle of champagne before handing it to Lydia. Lydia took a long draw on the straw and then handed it to me as though it were the old days. I almost considered drinking it too but Jay ripped it from my hands and passed it back to Lydia without a word.

'None at all?' Lydia asked.

I shook my head.

'Shit, sorry.' Lydia took another drink before handing the bottle back to Bex. 'So you best get in there before the old man finishes smiling for the camera if you want to avoid him. Your seats are under Angelina and Brad Jones,' she smirked triumphantly and without another thought, I pulled away from Jay and wrapped my arms around my sister as tears suddenly welled in my eyes.

'Hey,' she smiled when I pulled away and tears had begun rolling down my cheeks. 'It's not that big a deal, you know, I just rewrote your names on the seating chart. He doesn't even know you're going to be here,' she smiled, even though she knew that was only the smallest part of the tears. What she'd done was a very big deal.

Before she stood and went back to her duties she wiped a tear from my face, pulled me in for another hug and whispered, 'I miss you.' Then she was gone. Lydia and Bex hurried around the side of the house. I imagined them posing for photographs in front of the blue hydrangeas, their champagne satin dresses sparkling in the sunshine. I felt a pang of jealousy, of sadness, of something. I wouldn't be in the family photos. I wouldn't stand beside my brothers, my sister, my mother, their smiles bright and wide, their eyes proud and happy. But I wouldn't be there. There would always be a hole in the photograph. As though I never existed at all.

'See,' said Jay, trying to instil some courage into me. 'Are you okay?'

I nodded even though I wasn't yet sure if it was true.

'Alright, shall we go in then?'

I nodded again and he put a finger under my chin, turning my face to his and drawing my lips to his in a slow and lovely kiss. When he was done reminding me I wasn't alone, he playfully tapped my nose and we followed the masses through the frangipanis and into the enormous marquee. The sides were up to maximise the beautiful country breeze, the fairy lights glittered above us and through the flowers, making us believe in magic. Margot's work, no doubt.

Our seats were towards the back with some of Alex's family, perfect for maintaining our anonymity. I sat beside a snotty girl named Felicity who was too busy being educated to read the kind of magazines where my face used to appear. I smiled as her and her mother, Veronica, gave Jay a good once over as though I wasn't standing right beside him before giving me the familiar look of death that followed. Yes he was handsome, he was enigmatic, mysterious even, but I wasn't exactly a bland sack of potatoes. It always amused me though, never offended, particularly as I remembered the press that followed our disappearance. I'd been an 'it' girl, a former child star, daughter of a billionaire, everything supposedly laid at my feet and he'd just been a lowly body guard running off with a seventeen year old rich kid. We'd seen opinions change as time went by and people forgot who I was and I didn't mind a bit. I'd never loved being photographed and followed, it was an inconvenient by-product of the family I'd been born into. But as the conversation resumed around us, excluding us, I became more and more self-conscious. I hadn't changed that much in three years. I still looked like that girl who had millions of Instagram followers, who waltzed into nightclubs underage because she brought with her free publicity. I still looked like the girl they plastered all over the internet puking in the gutter, the spoiled, indulged, ungrateful brat they labelled me, The Princess of Party my friends labelled me. She no longer existed on the inside, but the outside hadn't changed that much.

'I should have done something with my hair,' I mumbled to Jay. 'They'll recognise my hair,' I added, surreptitiously glancing around us. It was easy to blend when we were in packed rows to watch the ceremony, but here at the table, we were out in the open where people looked for familiar faces, faces they wanted to become familiar. It was a be seen kind of wedding and I didn't want to be seen at all.

'Stop worrying, I've got you. What are you doing?' Jay asked as I began fishing in my bag.

'I'm looking for a hair tie. At least if I can get it into a knot, it will be one less giveaway.'

'You can do what you like with your hair, but you can't change your face. Stop worrying, we're down the back, we have the worst lighting and are sitting amongst the required family invites, no one will look here.'

But as the night wore on and the food came and went and people became bored and restless, I began to feel them, the eyes, the double takes, the warmth stretching up my neck. I'd managed to hide from my father, hiding behind menus, turning our backs at the right time as he passed but it wouldn't be long if rumblings began before he came looking. I was about ready to suggest we sneak out when dessert came with a note:

Behind the Orchard, 10.17pm

xxx

Jay looked at me with his eyebrows stretched high and a grin pulling at his mouth. I checked my watch and nodded, smiling, knowing the silliness of time was a reference to our childhood rendezvous when we'd meet to cause havoc on an unsuspecting world in true trust fund brat style. Even though I'd been younger than them, they had always made sure to include me. That was a long time ago now, before Tom joined the army, before everything fell apart, when the world was still easy and simple.

We checked for where my father was, he was deep in conversation with a man who looked like a barrel so we snuck out the side of the marquee. Jay held my hand as we raced for the orchard, unable to contain our laughter as though we were children. Although Jay had never been a child when we met, fresh out of his stint with Tom in the army, but still young enough, none-the-less and he'd been by my side since he was hired to protect me when I was fifteen and turning out to be more trouble than the other three put together.

We reached the empty orchard breathless and smiling. He gathered me into his arms and kissed me like he meant it, that he did often and it never failed to send my heart aflutter.

'Ahem.'

We stopped and I turned. Christian stood with his hands

deep in his pockets, a smile on his face, his wife beside him and his son holding her hand. I immediately flew out of Jay's arms and into Christian's.

'I missed you. I missed you so much,' I cried, tears and make up ruining the collar of his shirt.

'Hey, hey,' he soothed. 'I missed you too.'

'Are the rest of us going to get some of that?'

I turned to Tom, standing tall and handsome in his black tux and melted into the protective arms of my other brother, gripping him like a buoy in the deep ocean.

I eventually let Tom go and Lydia handed me a handkerchief, 'Really?' I asked holding it aloft.

'Margot made me,' she laughed. 'You know Margot and her blasted handkerchiefs.' And we laughed like only brothers and sisters can over shared childhood memories.

'How are you Jaz?' Lydia asked holding my hand after making the introductions to my sister's-in-law and my nephew.

'I'm okay,' I said, nodding.

They all looked to Jay for confirmation and he nodded, 'She's good. You don't have to worry.'

I shook my head at them.

'So you're in charge now?' I asked Tom, referring to the family business. Dad's retirement had been in all the papers but I'd never really believed it. It was hard to believe anything my father said when you knew every word came with an agenda.

'I am,' he smiled.

'And you quit?' I asked Christian.

'I did,' he smiled.

'I offered him a job doing anything he wanted any way he wanted to do it,' said Tom.

'Which was very good of him,' acknowledged Christian. 'And he is doing a far better job of it than the old boy. But I wanted something for myself. I needed it. I needed to do it for me, for my family and it makes me happy,' he said as his wife squeezed his hand.

'And he's good at it,' offered Tom. 'Tough competition, too,' he smiled proudly as Christian brushed off the compliment.

'So where is home now?' I asked Christian.

'I stayed in Adelaide after Dad sent me there to redo the Old Regent Hotel. It's where Ainsley's from, where her café is and we were happy there so we stayed.'

'Adelaide?' I asked. 'So when I thought I saw you on the street one time, it might have actually been you?'

'That's where you've been hiding?'

I shut my mouth and shrugged. Christian smirked and shook his head. He'd find me in a blink now, I supposed. Maybe. Did it even matter anymore? He was no longer a boy controlled by his father. He didn't even work for Dad anymore. But would Dad still be watching anyway? He'd know Christian was my weak link. That if I contacted anyone it would be him. I'd have told him everything right from the start otherwise. I wasn't that easy to find though. But I had a job, I paid tax, someone like my father could find that information or pay someone to. Clearly he'd given up and stopped looking so did any of it matter anymore?

'Where is your café?' I asked Ainsley, changing the subject.

'It's in an old bank, east on Wakefield. Mrs May's Tea and Toast,' she said.

'That's a very popular café,' I said. 'So I've heard. Must have seen it somewhere,' I added still not sure how much I wanted to give away without further consideration, without discussing it with Jay. Seems I couldn't keep my mouth shut though no matter how much I tried, giving away clues to where I lived left and right but I was suddenly wondering why it was so important. These were my people, my family, they loved me. They weren't my father. We were all grown ups now, we were our own people and we were strong and wise and he couldn't push us around anymore even if he did find me.

'It was a beautiful wedding,' I said, not sure what else to say, but needing to change the subject.

'Thanks,' said Tom. 'When I saw you guys there, everything was perfect, thank you. I know it wasn't easy,' he smiled, a tear in his eye.

'Well, don't you go crying you big baby,' I laughed, dabbing my own eyes.

I wasn't sure what to do next when Bex and Johnno appeared, sneaking through the orchard holding up a big white box. 'From Margot,' Bex declared as Johnno gave me a hug and shook Jay's hand.

'Cake!' cried Lydia, diving into the box.

'Cake?' piped up little Henry, his bored eyes suddenly interested.

Bex handed out plates of cake and Johnno pulled piccolo bottles of champagne and stubbies of beer from inside his jacket, along with a small plastic bottle of juice for Henry and a Coke for me. I smiled gratefully at him and he nodded before opening his beer.

And that's how we caught up, long lost brothers and sisters, old friends and new family, catching up on the details of lost years of love and loss and tragedy and strength and adventure.

'I suppose we should get back,' said Tom, regretfully.

We all nodded but no one moved.

'We could do this again, properly,' I suggested. 'There's always rooms at the pub,' I told them, suddenly needing more of them and no longer caring if they knew where I lived.

'You have a pub?' Lydia asked.

I shrugged. 'Jay has a pub.'

'You would actually have to tell us where that pub is,' smirked Christian.

Jay and I laughed and Jay gave them all the details, which was no small thing. We'd worked hard to keep that information a secret for so long, but now, somehow, it didn't seem important at all. These were not the people I'd been hiding from. These were the people I love and had missed every second we'd been apart.

'I'll sort something out for us all,' suggested Lydia as she pulled me to her. 'This isn't enough.'

I smiled and we left our mess for the poor unfortunate hired help to collect later and headed back to the festivities.

Christian draped his arm across my shoulders even though Jay was still sticking close to my side. 'Are you really okay?'

'Really,' I nodded, looking up into his handsome face and his happy eyes.

'So are you, it seems.'

'That I am,' he winked and we laughed.

'I'm sorry I dumped you in it that day,' I told him. The one thing I'd always felt guilty about when I'd run was Christian. He'd set up the meeting with Jay after Dad had banned him from the house. He'd never expected me to run though.

'It's okay. I knew Jay would look after you. I was given penance though, don't you worry and some day I'll make you pay for that,' he laughed.

'I'll pay up, I promise,' I giggled. It was nice, there was something about family, the good ones, that can mend wounds and heal hearts like nothing else.

We all looked up as we were nearing the marquee and two things happened simultaneously. One, a bright flash captured our laughing return from the orchard and two, my father appeared with Michael and Moe flanking him, as though they were holding him back.

I froze.

'It's okay, Jaz, he hates me more than you and I can take care of myself,' Jay said sympathetically.

'It's true, Jaz, it's okay,' soothed Tom from my other side.

'Just get me out of here. Please,' I begged breathlessly, fear rippling through every vein and artery in my body, choking the words as I spoke them.

'Just take her, Jay,' Tom instructed.

'Just go, we'll take care of him,' Lydia nodded.

I had no time to hug anyone goodbye, my father was breaking free from Michael and Moe who were doing their best to avoid a scene and Jay and I ran for the jeep while the others hurried towards my father. He couldn't get past them all.

We flew into the jeep and Jay roared out of the park he'd chosen just in case he'd had to do exactly this and before I knew it we were on the highway and I realised I hadn't even spoken to my mother. All I'd even seen of her was the back of her head, not a single look at her face, not a smile, not a hug, nothing. I looked at Jay horrified that I'd been there the whole afternoon and half the evening. I'd spoken to everyone, even seen my father but I hadn't been able to see just one smile from my mother and my eyes filled with tears and my mouth opened to speak but nothing came out.

'It's okay, Jaz, she'll understand,' Jay said, knowing what I was thinking. He always knew.

'No, no she won't.' But there was nothing I could do about it now. I couldn't go back and I couldn't go there again and she couldn't know where I was because I couldn't ask her to lie to her husband.

'Pull over,' I said as we were passing through a small neighbouring town about to pass their Seven Eleven.

I grabbed one of Jay's surfing hoodies from the back seat, shook most of the sand out of it, a by-product of him living so close to the beach and spending so much time in the ocean, and put it on over my dress and went into the shop. I found the small selection of cards and the man at the counter sold me a stamp and loaned me a pen. I stood at the counter and wrote my mother a note. Simply saying, *I'm sorry. I miss you. I love you. Jaz.* I was suddenly struck by the full circle of events. The last time I'd contacted my mother was when I'd run, by card, and as I looked around, from this same shop.

We'd always had a tumultuous relationship Mum and I but she was still my mother, she loved me in her way, had a good heart even if she was ruled by societal expectations, she'd done her best and she deserved more than road stop greeting cards. But that was the only option I had. It had to be better than nothing, I told myself as I put the card with two bears kissing in the envelope, sealed it, addressed it, stamped it and mailed it in the box the man had said was just outside the door.

I climbed back in the jeep and Jay asked, 'Better?'

I smiled and nodded. 'Thank you.'

'Of course,' he said, kissing the top of my head, then looking in my eyes, because he knew that's where the truth always lived. Happy with what he saw there, he smiled, kissed me and we began to drive.

We drove through the trees leading to the secluded lodge. It was a zero star kind of place. One of those bunkhouse buildings used a lot by scouts and Girl Guide groups. It was hidden amongst the trees, a little of the path making it easy to see if anyone had followed us. It would be just the thing my father would do. We'd spent days here after I'd run from the country house and the memories were filling me. Good memories. Happy memories. Memories of waking up in bed with Jay, devouring him with nothing but the sounds of the birds to keep us company.

The room held mostly bunk beds but there were two single beds on either side of the bedroom, which we'd pushed together. They were the plain, thin metal frame type you'd except to find in a place like this, or a convent.

'It hasn't changed a bit,' I said.

'Dirt and all,' Jay laughed.

'It's nice,' I said leaning in to him as we looked out the doorway into the night. After our quick getaway, we'd needed to stop, to take a breath. It had been a long day, still a long way home and this seemed as good a place as any. 'It's quiet and it smells like the country.'

'We had good times here, didn't we?' Jay said wistfully, scooping me to him.

We'd always fit together like pieces of a puzzle. It's where I felt safest, loved and no matter where we were, he felt like home.

'Are you okay?' he asked quietly as the night animals fussed outside.

'You know, I think I am. Thanks to you. Always thanks to you,' I added stretching up to kiss him.

'Mmmm,' he groaned happily as we pulled apart. He looked deeply into my eyes as only Jay could. 'See, now that's why I do what I do,' he joked.

'Well, I'd better settle my debt in full,' I smirked, stretching up to find his mouth again while I slipped my hands under his shirt.

We weren't going anywhere in a hurry tonight, not as my hands glided over his body, toned and muscled from surfing and bar work and living. My insides ignited as a fire of need, of desperate wanting to feel him move against me, with me, because of me, inside of me. I needed all of it, so any hovering wildlife would be getting a show tonight.

'Well that was a bit of something,' Jay smirked as he put his shirt back on.

'Well, I am a Harrington, we are not stingy people when it comes to paying our debts, you know,' I joked.

'It's why I'm always happy to have you indebted, Ms Harrington. As long as you find alternative ways to repay the rest of the fair folk of the world.'

'Of course,' I smiled, feigning shock. 'Besides, repayment would never be as sweet with the fair folk. No one can hold a candle to my man,' I insisted, kissing him like I meant it. Like his body, I never got sick of his mouth. There was a lot to appreciate about my man and I liked him to know. 'Let's go home,' I suggested, done with the memories and ready to get back to the little world we'd created for ourselves.

It had been a long day by the time we arrived back at Jay's pub, home, even though it wasn't my home, it felt like home because it was Jay. As we climbed into bed, I smiled as I snuggled into him. I would never get sick of sharing a bed with Jay and feeling him against me, the familiar beat of his heart, his breath and the rise and fall of his chest, his smell, as familiar as my own. There was nowhere else I could be and I missed him more than I'd ever tell him during the week, but I needed to prove to him I could be the kind of girl he could love, that he could spend his life with and that it wouldn't always be about

the Harrington's and my messed up life, that we could be more.
I could be more.

Chapter 3

Still groggy with sleep, I blinked into the sun already streaming in through the windows. Jay was already gone for his daily commune with the ocean. I stretched, feeling where he'd been and the great things he'd done to my body to clear my head the night before and padded out to make coffee. Through the floor to ceiling front windows overlooking the ocean, I could see Jay bobbing in the water with a couple of the young local boys. When my coffee was ready, I went out to the balcony, pulling one of the furry blankets that lived out there around my shoulders to protect me from the slight morning chill. I knew it wouldn't last long at this time of year. The sun would be up and warming the day before long but I found comfort in the warmth of the blanket.

I watched Jay catch a wave, my saviour, my strength, my protector, my everything as he whipped his board this way and that across the face of a wave. I'd never bothered with surfing myself, what with the suiting up and unsuiting, the having to get ready all over again and the waiting, so much waiting for a wave to come. But he loved it. It soothed his soul like nothing else could and if I was honest, I never minded how all that neoprene gripped his hips and the water glistened on his tanned body. It was never lost on me how lucky I was to have him.

Jay raised his hand in a wave from the beach and as he made his way back, I went inside to make us more coffee.

'Hey,' he said, kissing my cheek as he passed, heading to the bathroom for a shower.

'Hey, yourself,' I called after him. 'Where's the paper?' I never really read it but I liked to flip through and look at the pictures sometimes and read the creative headlines, it was an old habit, I guess.

He didn't answer. He always brought up the paper after his surf, so I followed him into the bathroom. He was just stepping into the shower as I pushed opened the door and I watched, as stunned by the sight of him as I was that first time, in disbelief as always that I got to play with the magnificence that was Jay.

'If you're just going to watch, you can join me, you know,' he called out, laughter in his voice.

I regained my composure. 'Where's the paper?' I really wanted to see what pictures they put in the paper from Tom and Alex's wedding.

'It didn't come,' he said and I could tell, I was probably the only person on the planet who could, that he was lying.

'Jay?'

'Aren't you the one who says it's bogus, lazy journalism, anyway?'

'That's beside the point. I wanted to see Tom and Alex's wedding pictures.'

'Why, you were there,' he said as he turned off the water.

He stepped out, water dripping from his naked body and he stared down at me for a second before reaching for a towel and it took every ounce of my strength to remember what it was I was saying and he knew it.

'What's going on?' I asked, once he'd finally covered himself, not sure if I was amused or annoyed.

'Nothing,' he smiled, drawing me to him. He smelt pretty good too, clean but still with a hint of the ocean that never seemed to leave his skin. 'Just thinking of something I'd rather be doing that doesn't involve talking,' he smirked.

I laughed. It was pretty tempting to just fall into bed with him for the day. We'd spent many a Sunday looking out over the ocean appreciating each other. You could do that when you lived on the top floor of a pub. You could see out but no one could see in. But I knew he was using his body and my weakness as a ploy and I wasn't so gullible that I couldn't see it and extricated myself from his arms.

Walking away shaking my head, I put on track pants and his hoodie I'd stolen the night before and ran down the internal stairs before he had a chance to put on pants and stop me.

The pub was empty and quiet. We wouldn't open for brunch for another hour or so, so the only light came from the big windows in all the rooms but it was enough. I walked barefoot through the front bar and unlocked the front door, reaching for one of the papers that waited there. We had five of them delivered every day for the customers who still preferred their news in paper format. One, we kept for ourselves because Jay was old school, but there was nothing on the ground. Maybe Jay was telling the truth after all and I was just being paranoid. A bird flew out of the big plant on one side of the walkway leading to the carpark and I saw just one paper lost amongst the palm fronds.

I dusted it off, ripping the plastic from the outside and unravelled it. I saw why the other papers had never found their way upstairs. Taking up the whole front page was a picture of my brothers, sister and me returning from our rendezvous in the orchard the night before, laughing, Lydia taking a swig of champagne from the bottle. The headline screamed, *The Harrington children back together and up to their old tricks?*

I sat on the floor cross-legged and began reading the article beneath the picture. The journalist started with: *Wayward Jasmine Harrington returns after years of exile and already champagne is being swilled from bottles. So where has the rebellious Jaz been all this time? Rehab? Jail? Family exile? The Princess of Party as she is known in the circles of the rich and famous, famously disappeared at seventeen after weeks of confinement at the family's secluded country house following a long teenage battle with booze and drugs, creating the kind of havoc that only a big fat trust fund can bring. The gossip pages have been quiet since her disappearance and there is a definite buzz surrounding her return. We wonder what fun we can expect from the beautiful, troubled, Jasmine Harrington now she's back.*

I couldn't believe it. After all this time, all this hiding and in an instant it was over. They would find me. That's what they did when they sniffed out a story with a fat pay cheque. It wouldn't take them long, for someone to give me up, a friend of a friend or a workmate or a client I'd passed in the halls once. They would give them a few bucks and that would be that. One lead would lead to another and then they'd be camping out at work, my home, in Jay's pub, waiting for me to screw up all over again.

It had taken us years to rebuild our lives. A long time for me to even get a job, for anyone to see me as anything other than spoiled, broken Jasmine bloody Harrington. We'd originally lived together, renting a little flat in the suburbs under Jay's sister's name but Jay needed the beach and he used all his savings to buy the pub when it came up for sale. I'd finally just gotten a job in the city working as a talent agent for Delia Edwards. It wasn't a dream job or a career I'd ever envisaged but it was the only job I could get and I loved the anonymity of living in the city, of being a number in a big office building where people often turned their heads to avoid saying hello.

I didn't mind being alone during the week. After living in a fishbowl all my life with maids and security watching my every move, it was nice to have some quiet, to finally be alone. And now it was all going to end. The media were going to take it all away and I'd have to give up my job and my own place and live under the protection of Jay inside the pub, again, looking out at a world in which I wouldn't be able to contribute.

It's no wonder I'd gone off the rails. Well, one of the many reasons but when you begin to self medicate with alcohol at thirteen, there's only one way to go and that was down. Not that anyone cared about the whys, especially my father. All he had cared about was the Harrington name and locking me up away from the cameras that were always waiting to ruin his stupid good name, which he'd ruined just fine all on his own by being an intolerable ass. He'd lost all his children at some point, in one way or another and even in the world I'd been raised in, that didn't go unnoticed. It had taken so long, so many tears, so much trust and hard work to creep out from the Harrington shadow and just be me, just be Jaz and now it was over. They'd come looking for me, looking for a story and using anyone they could to get it. Delia would never stand for it and my home, even though secure enough, wasn't safe enough to protect me from their incessant need for gossip.

The fact I wasn't that person anymore, I hadn't had a drink in years, no longer puked in the gutter or got groped by strangers, wouldn't matter to them. They were unrelenting and they wouldn't give up until they had something to report. They'd make it happen, manipulate the truth if they had to. It wasn't new to me. They had families to feed, drug habits to fund, whatever, everyone has something.

Slumping against the wall, closing my eyes, I let the finality of my life sink in and then Jay's arms were around me, pulling me to him, keeping me whole.

'Told you you should have just come to bed with me,' he said, only half joking.

I wrapped my arms around him and held on tight.

'It'll be okay, I promise. Tom says they're trying to find out who sent the photo.'

'It doesn't matter who. It's done. It's all over.'

'No it's not, Jaz. You're not that person anymore and they'll see it. When there's no story, they'll move on. You don't need to worry about your father, you're an adult now. You don't have to be afraid, he can't ship you off anywhere against your will.'

'I know, I know. But the journos, they'll just keep waiting, keep provoking until I crack. It's what they do. You remember how they were, always there, hiding in the bushes, waiting, twisting what they saw, what they heard, making everything bigger, worse.'

'I remember,' he groaned. 'I won't let them do that to you again.'

'You can't stop them. You couldn't stop them when it was your full time job. You have a life. I have a life. It's not like the old days where we could just pick up and hide or move on. We have responsibilities.'

'You didn't exactly help last time,' he smirked. 'And I have staff that can manage just fine without me. Come on, let's go upstairs,' he said gently, helping me up.

Jay sat me on the love seat on the balcony, brought me tea, wrapped the blanket over my shoulders even though the sun was now reaching across the deck and held me in our little piece of paradise. Up here, no one could reach us, no one could see us and as yet, no one even knew where to look. But even he knew this was borrowed time. I was big news once. They would be looking. We were both in the pub all the time. I'd designed the now infamous T-bar downstairs that served fancy tea during the day and martini's at sunset with Jazz on the deck. I'd spent many a Sunday afternoon there and if someone from my life didn't dob us in to the journos, a million tourists had passed through that bar, stopped and chatted and waved. Someone would put it all together and claim their reward. But all I could do until they did, for these borrowed minutes, was to relax into the arms of my man, love him for all that he was and wait.

Chapter 4

Monday I watched the sun come up while Jay surfed. I liked the quiet of the early morning. I revelled in it knowing it wouldn't last, knowing my picture perfect life was on borrowed time and about to come crashing down. I'd barely survived the last time my life crashed at my feet. I wasn't prepared to lose everything again. Wasn't sure I'd survive another crash. But I refused to go down without a fight. I wouldn't let them chase me into a corner.

My father had locked me away once. No one was ever taking away my power again. So I took the memories of our beautiful Sunday wrapped in each other on the balcony and I went to get ready to take on the world again. I wasn't that messed up teenager anymore. I'd taken on my father once, fought for my independence, I could take on the Australian media.

'Stay,' asked Jay when he returned from his surf and saw me dressed and making coffee.

'I can't do that. You know how hard this job was to get. I'm not going to be that person they expect me to be. I'm going to stand up and be the person I am. You were right yesterday, I can do this. I'm not the person that creates headlines anymore. And I am a Harrington, if that's what they want then they'll get my father's daughter which means stuffy, stoic and silent. He trained me his whole life to be that way. They're not taking this life from us. They're not. I won't let them.'

He wrapped his arms around me. 'That's my girl,' he said with pride and a smile. 'You could still stay though, I'm sure someone owes someone something for last night,' he winked.

I laughed. 'It was alright, hey?'

'Alright?'

I rested my hand on his bare chest still beading with water. 'Mmmm it was alright,' I said raising my eyebrows. 'We have another Sunday coming up though, you best start thinking about how we can top yesterday.'

'Is that a challenge?'

'Maybe,' I said, picking up the toast I'd just buttered, grabbing my handbag and giving him a peck on the cheek before heading for the sliding doors.

'You're killing me, Jaz,' he laughed from the kitchen.

I turned, laughing, 'Perhaps there's some of the old troubled Jaz Harrington still in me after all?'

'That there is,' he laughed, shaking his head as I closed the door.

I raced down two flights of metal stairs. It was quicker to use the outside stairs in the morning than traipse through the pub, unlocking, relocking and all that. My faded red beetle waited in the car park where I'd left it. I'd once driven a brand new Audi, a gift for my sixteenth birthday, but I'd left it behind along with the designer wardrobe when I'd left and now I'd had this, bought third hand or so for a couple of years. I really only used it to come out here to the beach, otherwise it sat at my apartment all week while I walked around the city. But I loved it because it was mine, all mine, not a gift, every cent of it paid for with money I earnt.

After parking the beetle in the carpark next to my building, I walked the ten minutes to the office, stopping for a coffee from Joe's cart and squeezing into a full lift just as the doors were closing. I'd half expected journos to be in front of the front office but so far it seemed I was still free, although the paranoia was already kicking in as I tried ignoring the whispers coming from the back corner of the lift.

When you're followed by journos every minute of every day, to kindergarten, ballet, the supermarket, people also start whispering when they see you. *Is that her? Oh look at what she's wearing. Oh my god, what is she wearing?* That sort of thing. You can't move without someone photographing you or whispering about it, speculating about it and before you know it, you begin to think every single whisper is about you. You start wondering who likes you for you and who just wants their photograph in the glossies and access to the VIP sections of the best clubs, even when you're years underage. Everyone wants something and the only person I've ever been able to truly trust is Jay. All he ever wanted to do was to love and protect me. Even when I was at my worst, at my lowest, the most miserable excuse of a human being, he was there to pick me up and dust me off and love me anyway. The man was a masochist. A saintly masochist.

'Hi Shannon,' I called to our receptionist as I walked through the big glass doors and into the shiny, glossy reception room. It was grand with shiny white tiles and intimate meeting rooms to the right and the boardroom to the left.

Shannon gave me a tight smile and bowed her head. It wasn't unusual for her to be busy, but it was unusual for her to not be warm and open and friendly, ask how my weekend was, comment on something, that was her way. Shannon and I shared many a laugh on a Friday night. It wasn't like her to snub me or anyone else. My stomach dropped as realisation set in. It was happening already. Obviously we weren't the only ones who received a Sunday paper and people would already be taking the headlines at their word, making their own assumptions and judgements and choosing a course of action. Do they jump on the crazy train with the troubled rich kid or run for the hills? They'd always been the only options anyone considered.

I dropped everything at my desk and was about to fall into the chair when Delia stuck her head out of her office, 'Jaz,' she called. 'Got a minute?'

Her tone of voice sent a chill up my spine but what could I do? She was my boss, she calls, you come. Those are the rules. 'Sure,' I said as cheerily as I could.

'Is this going to be a problem?' she asked holding up Sunday's paper.

'Nope. It's nothing.'

'That's not what it says.'

'Well, it's wrong. There was nothing in it, no trouble. I went to my brother's wedding, that's all.'

'This looks like trouble.'

'Things are rarely what they look like, Delia.'

'Where was Jay in all this?'

'He was right beside me.'

'Why isn't he in the picture, then?'

'I don't know. The same reason Tom's wife wasn't and Christian's wife wasn't and Henry wasn't and Andrea wasn't. I swear, I hadn't had a sip of alcohol, nothing more than a soft drink.'

'Well, I'll take your word for it. For now. But I hope this going back to being a Harrington isn't going to be an issue for your work.'

'I'm not going back to being anything. I was just there for the wedding, I promise.'

'Alright, then. Keep it that way. We don't need you distracted and we don't need the journos and the fans messing with our day to day and harassing our clients.'

'My head's down. Nothing's changed. If they call, I won't be engaging, I promise. It's not who I am. This is who I am, the Jaz you know is who I am.'

'Alright, then. We have a new client so your head needs to be in the game. Robbo's Chicken Delights are coming to town and they have a big opening day coming up and they need a chicken man,' she said with the heavy sigh that often accompanied my accounts. Chicken Men and the sort might have been a chore to everyone else, but to me it was my job and to the business, characters were a good, profitable earner that made them worthwhile. It didn't mean anyone but me had to like it though. 'An email has been sent to the suitable men in our data base. I've emailed you the suit measurements. Robbo wants whoever we hire to be available for all openings and various other promotional engagements. So that should keep you busy and out of trouble.'

'Excellent,' I smiled. It was no surprise I'd be in charge of the chicken man account. I got the chicken men, the dogs, the roosters, Santa, the Easter Bunny, anything that required dressing up as an animal, a clown or any other ridiculous costume. As a leading talent agency, we, of course, did all the good jobs too, organising models and actors for the big campaigns. I never got those accounts. I was always going to be a Harrington and I was always going to have to prove to everyone I was serious about my job, about working and not the spoiled princess they'd once seen wasted in the magazines. It would probably be for the rest of my life but I didn't care. I had my own money, I paid my own rent, put petrol in my own car. I relied on no one to support me but myself. Not even Jay. I didn't care what I had to do to keep it. And for the most part, before today, most people had actually forgotten I was a Harrington.

'Nice,' laughed Meg when she fell into her chair at the desk opposite mine, dropping a copy of today's paper on my desk.

'What's this?' I asked as I opened it to find a picture of Jay and I escaping the wedding with the caption: *Where's Jaz Harrington running to?*

'I go away for four weeks and I come back to this?' laughed Meg.

I shrugged. I didn't quite know what to do about it. I was out of practice, navigating foreign territory with people who didn't understand that most of it was inflated bullshit.

'Jasmine?' questioned our resident queen, Clary. Clary, a former local teen model that did a few parades in the local Westfields but never really gained traction beyond that so gained a business degree instead was in charge of the top models and who liaised with only the top companies and promotional campaigns. I looked up to see her smirking, not in an amused way. 'I suppose those journalists downstairs are here for you?' she questioned smugly with her plum voice I knew she'd acquired through years of practice and not from her average suburban upbringing. Not that'd I'd ever rub it in her face. She had the right to be anyone she wanted to be. I knew what it was like to reinvent yourself and choose who you wanted to be, who you wanted people to see. She'd long cut ties with her roots though. I guess we were the same. We just went in opposite directions, she ran to the status and I ran from it.

'They found me?'

'Of course they did. You get your face in the magazines two days in a row, of course they're going to find you. You're not hard to find, after all,' she added, clearly having no idea how much effort and planning had gone in to me being hard to find. But I suppose I probably wasn't hard to find here. It was a legal job, it wouldn't take much to find if you cared enough to look but by the time I'd got it, I suppose, no one had really cared anymore. 'Looks like that precious tiara of yours is about to slip,' she smirked.

'Shit,' I groaned.

'Well, just keep them out of my way. It was a nightmare

getting through the front door. Delia is not going to be impressed.'

I looked at Meg and we both rolled our eyes. We both knew Clary would love getting her hoity toity face in the paper, only she'd hate that it was because of me. Until I came along she was the 'IT' girl of the company, of the industry and liked to think of herself as the 'IT' girl in town. When I came along, a former real life 'IT' girl myself, I became a daily reminder that she lived in a dream world. She knew I was trying to blend though, leave my past behind so she enjoyed stomping around with her nose in the air as though in challenge. I think secretly she wanted me to crack, return to my bad, attention stealing days, just so I'd leave and she could go back to living in her daydream. The reality was, I had no intention of stealing her 'IT' girl status but more importantly, she would have been eaten alive in my world. But I let her have it because none of it mattered to me.

I hadn't chosen my family. I'd had no say in the money, the big houses, the lifestyle. People didn't care though. They judged me anyway. Made me pay for it anyway. I hadn't been a 'Harrington' since I was seventeen. But it didn't matter. Even though I hadn't spoken to him in years, I was still held responsible for the choices my father made, for the man he was. Even when I'd read in the paper about his heart trouble a couple of years ago, I'd felt nothing, no inclination to rectify old wrongs as some people did when faced with life threatening circumstances. I had nothing for that man, nothing but fear and hate.

He'd taken away my voice. He'd locked me up. Denied me my freedom. He'd kept me from Jay, threatened me with hospitalisation in a foreign country because he didn't understand me, because he was ashamed of me. He was my father, he was supposed to love and protect me but he hadn't. I'd fallen into a hole, into a world that was destroying me because no one had bothered to look beyond the façade, to see me, to understand me, except for Jay. If it hadn't been for Jay, I'd have died five times over. Even when I told him I hated him and even when I'd been so wasted I couldn't speak, Jay had scooped me up, wiped the vomit off my face, cleaned me up and taken me somewhere safe. He never let me down. He should have. He should have run for the hills but he never did.

My father did, gave up on me, locked me in my room, planned to leave me in a facility in Italy. And banished Jay. That was my father's solution to the drinking, the partying, to finding out Jay and I were sleeping together. By the time he tried to save me, it was too late. Jay had already done it and then Dad had banished the only person who meant anything to me, the only thing that was keeping me together and it had nearly destroyed me. I could have taken the facility, in hindsight I could see his desperation but he'd taken away my lifeline, my hope, shattered my soul. If I'd gone to the facility in Italy, I'd have been there until Jay had moved on with his life, until there was nothing for me to come back to. I'd have taken anything my father offered except for that. I couldn't lose the only person who'd ever seen me, ever bothered to look into the darkness and see the girl inside, to see someone worthy of love. He saved me. His love saved me. My father had taken that away and the only way I could have Jay was to leave. I'd never forgive my father for making me choose between Jay and my family. But even now, looking back, I couldn't see another choice. I'd have existed as a shell of a human in Italy. I'd have been sober but I'd have had nothing to be sober for and it wouldn't have stuck. But the pigheaded fool wouldn't listen to me. My words were of no consequence, just ramblings of a silly girl, a seventeen year old drunk who didn't know what love was. His words.

I'd had to beg Jay to run away with me, not because he hadn't wanted to, he only ever wanted to be with me, to protect me, but because he didn't want me to do anything I would regret. Discovering my father's plan though, that he'd planned for me to have an indefinite stay in Italy, Jay knew neither of us would survive. He was afraid of what would happen to me if I was all alone on the other side of the world with no one to catch me.

If Dad had just had a conversation with me, if he'd just seen me, maybe things would have been different but he managed, that's all he knew and I didn't need to be managed. I'd needed someone to see past my bullshit. I'd needed Jay. So we'd left and we'd started fresh, just the two of us, leaving behind our friends and our families and everything we'd known.

Since we'd left, I'd done everything I could, everything expected of me, to put that person and that life behind me. I committed to living a life of worth, for myself, for Jay, to be worthy of him and now it was over.

Clary was just the beginning. Delia had no patience for drama and even though she was the only person who'd given me a chance, it was only a matter of time and it wouldn't take much to push her over the edge and send me packing for being too much trouble, causing too much chaos. She had a business to run, staff to protect, I didn't blame her.

Chapter 5

I did what I promised though. I put my head down and got on with my day. I tidied up some details of another account, replied to some emails from clients and some from entertainers looking for more information on the chicken man gig. We stopped for morning tea to celebrate Lindsay in accounts birthday and eat the strawberry swirl cake Barb had brought in. Barb was Lindsay's boss and our resident cake baker. Usually, because her husband had a habit of disappearing on her for days at a time but sometimes just because she wanted to. Either way, we were grateful because they were good cakes.

'Lunch?' Meg asked right on twelve.

'I am not going out there,' I told her so she picked me up a sandwich from down the street and we ate together at a table in the lunchroom amid the chatter of weekend gossip. Everyone politely avoided asking me about my weekend, about Tom's wedding, the guest list, the fashion, the food and I was grateful.

'Tell me about you, about your holiday?' I asked Meg instead.

'There's so much to tell,' she smiled in that whimsical way

people do after a long vacation somewhere far away. 'I met lots of new people, saw lots of incredible things. It really was life changing. Europe is just beautiful, isn't it?'

'It is,' I smiled, remembering trips I'd taken with my mother, my sister, the good times we'd had wandering the cobblestone streets with nothing else to distract us.

'You've probably been loads of times, I suppose,' she said, a little deflated.

'The beauty is never lost on you. Where was your favourite place?' I asked, not wanting it to be about me or for my Harrington past to be marring the tales of her lovely holiday.

'Oh I don't know if I can decide,' she smiled as she checked her watch. 'I'll let you know, maybe once the jetlag has eased up a bit,' she smiled as she stood and threw her rubbish in the bin.

I followed her out and we went back to work. We had a team meeting in the afternoon and finished off Barb's cake. I sat back and watched people squabbling over accounts. It was always a fight for the best ones. I never fought and no one fought for my chicken men and it was just fine by me so I got to sit back and watch the show and enjoy my cake.

I flittered away the rest of the afternoon with some filing and planning, making some notes from my call with Robbo of Chicken Delight fame and promised him the perfect chicken man for his opening. And then the day was over.

'You can't stay here all night, Jaz,' Meg joked from the other side of the partition.

I looked up to see her smiling face. 'Delia won't even notice if I sleep here, I'll just find a corner and stay out of the way of the cleaners,' I told her.

'Delia will notice. Go home, Jaz,' Delia said as she passed.

I groaned and packed up my desk, turned off my computer and took as much time as I could but Meg was not giving up on me, she waited and smiled, knowing exactly what I was doing but being too good of a friend to call me on it.

Meg held my hand as we pushed through the throng of media at the end of the day. I didn't know how they'd found me so fast. Meg suspected Clary, she knew people she could call, she'd have known there was money to be made and connections to be cemented for future favours but would she really go through with it? Maybe. It didn't matter now. Pointing fingers wouldn't change anything. They were here now and after waiting all day to see me, they scrambled forward screaming their questions in my face like I wasn't even a real human being with feelings and personal space.

'Jaz, where have you been?'

'Have you been in rehab?'

'Jaz, where's your bodyguard? What happened to him? Did he leave when you had no money?

'Jaz, did your father cut you off?'

'Jaz, did you get invited to CeeCee Miles' wedding?'

I ignored them all, answered none, didn't even comment on the fact CeeCee couldn't invite me to her wedding because she didn't know where I was. Meg looked frazzled by the noise and the chaos as she helped me into a taxi but I couldn't even make sure she was okay, I had to leave to let the frenzy die down. They wouldn't ease up on their demands, on the pushing and the shoving to let me look after my friend, so I could only watch her frightened face out of the window as I drove away.

I hated to waste the money on a taxi and the driver's time when I lived so close but there was no way I could have walked without the journos following me and right now, my sanctuary was all I had left. I was holding on to it for as long as I could. So I wasted valuable, hard earned dollars to pay someone to drive me home the long way, around the city and through some back streets to my Victorian apartment building nestled above the shops and cafes of bustling Rundle Street. Inside, I locked the doors, closed the curtains, put a frozen dinner in the microwave and decided the only course of action was to hide from the world on my sofa until I had to do it all again in the morning.

Jay called while I was watching telly hoping someone else's life, even a fictional one, would make me forget mine. I almost didn't answer his call, I didn't want to tell him it was happening all over again and there was nothing I could do to stop them but I knew that if I didn't, it would cause more issues than it was worth.

'So, how bad was it?' he asked after the usual pleasantries.

'It was fine,' I lied, glad he couldn't see me. I hated lying to Jay. I never did it. One, because I didn't want to or need to and two, he always knew when I did. But he couldn't see me and I didn't want him interrupting his life for me, not over this. If he knew how bad it really was, he'd come and get me and drag me back to the beach where he could keep an eye on me before the sun was up. And really, it hadn't been that bad, it was only for five minutes. I'd been trapped inside the building for the whole day but I'd kept myself busy and distracted and it had turned out okay.

'Really? It was fine? Why don't I believe you?' he asked dubiously.

'There were a few journos but they didn't harass me too much. I didn't give them the chance. Meg went out for me at lunch and I caught a taxi home after work so they didn't bother me much at all. Have they posted anything online yet? No, don't tell me, I don't want to know,' I groaned.

'You sound more frazzled than you're letting on.'

'No, no, its fine. I just didn't think I'd ever have to go through this again. That we'd have to go through it again. But I'm fine, I promise, just tired.'

'Okay. For now. How's Delia taking it?' he asked.

'She'll get over it, hopefully they'll go away soon. Like you said, when they see there's no story to be had, they'll give up. Who's going to pay them to stand there all day photographing me doing nothing or buying a sandwich?' I told him before finally moving him onto the topic of his day, eliciting conversation about the locals, who came into the pub today and who had news, talking about the week's menu, stuff we both knew was nothing but a ploy to avoid what neither of us had the heart to discuss. That he was desperately resisting the urge to come and get me, protect me and I was resisting the urge to ask him to.

I could tell he'd seen something online. I knew he was worried about me, that he wanted me to go to him but until he said the words, I was happy to avoid all discussion because I wasn't leaving. I wasn't giving in to them and I didn't want to fight with Jay about it. I refused to give them that much power.

I hung up feeling exhausted. I was emotionally wrung out.

How had I survived their invasion into my business all my life? I guess I hadn't really. I had to do better this time. I would. I was stronger. I wasn't a frightened child anymore. I wouldn't let them break me. But I had to take care of myself, give my brain a chance to catch up and process so I turned off the telly and went to bed.

Tuesday was no different, they were back and obnoxious and desperate but I'd gotten in ahead of the journos and walked to work at 7.30 in the morning while they were still in their hotels eating eggs and bacon. I sat on the floor in front of the office for fifteen minutes before Delia arrived, mobile phone glued to her ear, coffee in hand, weighted down like a donkey with her laptop bag, her handbag, a bag with files and who knows what else as she struggled to make sense of the keys in her hand.

I smiled, took the keys from her and unlocked the door while she zipped past me and entered the alarm code. Queen Clary probably had her own set of keys and a code, but not me. I had a swipe card to get through the doors downstairs and up the lift before 9am, but that was it. I was way too far down the food chain for anything more than that, but I'd never before been the first one in, so it didn't really matter.

I left Delia to sort herself out and scurried to my desk before I copped the twenty questions on why I was in the office so early. I checked my messages, there were a few from eager wannabe chicken men for me to call later and schedule an audition, one from Shannon on reception telling me there had been a delivery after I'd left the day before and she was putting it in the kitchen and that was all. A nice easy start. Voicemails tended to terrify me and fill me with an insane sense of urgency. I much preferred email but with the type of talent I dealt with, some were old school as though by calling me and showing their enthusiasm, they'd have a better shot but usually it just irritated me that I had to call them back.

I loaded up my computer and all my programs, leaving them to do their thing while I went to get a much needed coffee from the kitchen. To make sure I beat the journos, I hadn't wasted time stopping at Joe's on the way in so had to make do with the instant coffee Delia supplied staff. There was a fancy machine in a little alcove off reception, which Shannon used to brew lovely things for visiting clients, and herself, a perk of not being able to leave reception, but the rest of us were stuck with Moccona. At least it wasn't International Roast, I suppose.

I weaved my way through the desks and into the kitchen. While the kettle boiled, I looked around for the delivery Shannon had put in there. There were no boxes, not that I was even expecting any. I wasn't one for deliveries or the one who received fancy thankyou deliveries from clients. There was just a massive bunch of bright flowers in the middle of the lunch table, no doubt for Queen Clary. I didn't dare touch them and went about making my coffee, figuring someone had just moved my box and Shannon would find it later.

'They're gorgeous, aren't they?' Shannon called from the doorway as she came in to make her own coffee, no longer being so stand offish, it seemed she'd made her judgements and chosen her route.

'Sure?' I agreed pouring hot water onto my freeze-dried beans.

'So, who are they from?' she asked.

'Oh I'm not touching them. Clary would kill me.'

'Jaz, they're not for Clary, they're yours?'

'The flowers are mine? Really? You sure they're not Clary's?'

She giggled. 'No, Jaz, they're for you. Go see who they're from, I'm dying to know.'

'Well, who would send me flowers?' I mumbled, putting my cup down and crossing the floor.

The vase contained a mix of gerberas and roses and a bunch of other gorgeous blooms I couldn't name in pinks and yellows, purple and blues. They'd have cost a small fortune. I pulled the card out, expecting them to be from Jay, even though it wasn't the sort of thing Jay ever did, but who else would send me flowers?

'My *sweet, my love, as perfect as the finest spring blooms, welcome back.*'

I froze, my heart stopping, my breath caught in my chest.

'Jaz? Are you okay?' Shannon called, coming to read the card over my shoulder where I'd stood frozen. 'Awe,' she cooed. 'That's sweet. From Jay?' she asked.

I shook my head.

'What's the matter?'

'Nothing,' I said, composing myself, remembering where I was and how much trouble I was already in by having journos camping out downstairs waiting to catch me messing up. Shannon certainly didn't need to see me crumbling. I didn't need to freak her or anyone else out. I could handle this. I could. 'Nothing, just a surprise, that's all,' I told her. 'I'm allergic though, do you want them?'

'Really?' she asked, her eyes wide with hope and excitement. Shannon was nineteen, gorgeous but a little pudgy and although cheery and sociable with us, add in some strangers and a bar and she hid in the corner. She didn't get flowers.

'Really,' I said, forcing a bright Harrington smile.

'Okay, thanks,' she smiled, quickly scooping the vase up and disappearing out to reception.

I rested my hand on the table and waited for my breath and heart to return to normal. 'Please, please, not again,' I whispered to the universe. Weird people had tried this sort of stuff too often in the old days. I'd been mostly drunk though so Jay fielded them but occasionally they snuck through, a creepy message on my phone, a creepy guy hitting on me at a party, some creepier than others. But there was one, he left notes in my school locker, sent flowers to the house, and always managed to give me the heebie-jeebies. I heard voices coming down the hallway, composed myself, grabbed my coffee and went to hide behind my computer. I couldn't believe it was happening all over again. I was not a Harrington anymore. Why couldn't everyone get that through their stupid heads and leave me alone?

To distract myself I started returning phone calls to those who had left messages for the Chicken Man job. The first was a guy named Malcolm. His bio said he was six foot two, ninety eight kilos and ran marathons in his spare time. I was willing to wage a week's pay that the bio was at least a decade out of date. But I called him anyway, because that was my job. I got his sappy, fake cheer voicemail, gave him the date and time for the audition and moved onto the next one on the list.

Kevin Dale, five foot eleven and a half, ninety two kilos, brown hair, brown eyes, likes hiking, windsurfing and camping. I rolled my eyes, didn't they all. In reality most were overweight, had lost whatever love they'd once had for the outdoors and spent most of their day consuming their body weights in junk food, smoking pot to block out the misery their lives had become and playing video games and watching Dr Phil.

Kevin Dale answered, his voice distracted as though I'd interrupted something.

'Mr Dale, it's Jasmine Harrington from Delia Edwards Talent returning your call regarding the chicken job.

'Oh. Um. Yes. Great. Of course,' he stumbled.

Great, it was never a good sign if they couldn't speak without tripping over their own tongues. I had to ignore it, though. This was a character gig, dancing, shaking people's hands and posing for photos, no speaking required so his inability to do so although inconvenient and annoying for me, was of no relevance here as was usually the case with the jobs I landed.

'Yes, well, we'd love for you to come in for the audition,' I told him as Clary walked past mimicking a falling crown and I seethed with jealousy at all the beautiful and coherent people she dealt with. The types of people I'd once partied with, I reminded myself as I gave Kevin Dale the audition details even though he only just made the height requirement for the suit.

'Well,' he stumbled and I imagined the bespectacled ruddy

face from his photograph smiling like a fool. 'Well, thank you. I'd love to come,' he said as though I'd invited him on a date.

I explained the audition process to him to be sure he understood what we were really talking about and that there'd be no drinks or dinner involved.

'Lovely, yes. Thank you,' he said. 'It's been very lovely speaking with you, Miss Harrington.'

'Okay, we'll see you then, bye,' I said, hanging up the phone groaning. There'd been too much emphasis on the Harrington part. Usually they didn't put two and two together. After all, what would THE Jasmine Harrington be doing working here, hiring chicken men and the sort? But usually I wasn't front page news.

I'd had enough creepy for one day, there was only so much a person could take but I had to return the rest of the calls. I made more coffee, ignoring the place where the flowers had been and got on with it. The only advantage was it made the time fly by and I could hear Meg on the other side of the partition humming so every time my adrenalin and panic levels started to rise, I focussed on her humming.

At five Meg stuck her head over the partition. 'You done?' she asked.

I was, but I couldn't face going downstairs just yet. 'Soon,' I told her.

'You want me to wait and go down with you?' she offered.

'No, no, you go. I'll be fine,' I lied but feeling bad for everything she'd already done for me. She'd become my personal assistant, getting my lunch, shielding me from the daily news and gossip. I didn't want to know what they were saying. No good would come from knowing. And after the night before, seeing her frightened face as the taxi drove away, I didn't want to put her through that again. They were always worse when I was there, she'd be better off leaving on her own.

'You sure?' she asked doubtfully. She knew me better than anyone else here. She was the only person I considered a friend. Not just a work friend, but someone I'd have dinner with on a Saturday night if I was in the city.

'Yeah, yeah. I can handle them,' I said, waving my hand towards outside as though they were no big deal. Truth was I just didn't want us photographed together again, especially if the freaks were coming out of the shadows. The last thing Meg needed was people thinking we were friends. The journos and the sickos all thought the friends were an easy target for intel and access. That's why people like me only had friends like me, people who knew how to cope with the journos and the sickos. People who had their own status and didn't need their fifteen minutes on the evening news or a need to sell their half-baked stories to the women's mags. In my old world, friends were chosen as much for their breeding, experience and skill set as for their likeability. You just couldn't risk befriending any old person, they just didn't get the world we lived in. I hadn't missed any of my old friends when I'd run. Maybe Alyssa, the daughter of a one-time rock star who laughed at the institution of fame from a similar perspective to me. But in the real tear away months leading up to my captivity, even she'd run for the hills. You knew you were in a bad way when rock stars ban their kids from seeing you.

Indi had stood by me though, her rock star father barely

knew what day it was though but she knew how to work the journos and she was right there beside me when they shoved their cameras in my face and she knew how to deal with it.

I'd do anything to protect Meg and our friendship from those unrelenting vultures. I knew Meg would never intentionally say something she shouldn't. She'd do her best to protect me and my secrets. But I also knew the lengths they'd go to for a story, even just a glimmer of a story. She didn't need to go through that. Her friendship was one of the few I had, so I farewelled her and pretended to work.

Work couldn't keep my attention though and instead I was resisting the urge to google myself, to see what inaccurate gems were popping up online. They'd already made error after error in the article I'd read in Sunday's paper. For starters, I'd never done drugs. Well, maybe once at a cast party with my ex tv brother, but I hadn't liked the way it had felt. I liked the way alcohol filled my veins, the way it numbed and soothed like an old friend, there was nothing like it. I shook my head. What was I doing? I hadn't thought about that in a long time.

I knew how detrimental it was to one's health to go down the google path, so I was still just staring blankly at my computer screen when Delia started turning off the lights. I'd made it through the day, just.

I felt her standing next to my desk, watching me blankly stare at the computer screen. 'Come on, Jaz, it's time to call it a day. I'll get you a taxi,' she said, surprising me with her kindness. We rode down in the lift in silence and then she stoically helped me through the media throng and waved down a passing taxi.

Once I was home with the door closed, blocking out the noise of the world I flopped on the couch, grateful to have made it through another day. I had to speak to Jay but I couldn't lie to him again. I'd had such a tough day and now that I was safe, that message kept playing in my head and I knew as soon as I spoke to Jay, he'd know something was wrong. To avoid having to lie to him, I sent him a text message simply saying today was worse but that I was fine, tired and going to bed.

After my frozen dinner, that's what I did and I tossed and turned half the night wondering about the flowers, who they were from, was it the same guy as before? Weirdos were plentiful in my old world but there'd been that one weirdo that stood out, one that was particularly creepy. He'd send me gifts and declarations of love, promises of our bright future. He got past security too many times to think he was a stranger but I'd kept my inner circle tight so I could never figure out who it was. Jay swept most of it away before I saw it, but I saw enough. But I trusted Jay, I believed in him to keep me safe and the continual flow of alcohol mixing with my blood and flowing through my veins kept me carefree. But I didn't have the luxury of numbness anymore and I remembered snippets of what I'd blocked, ignored, trusted to someone else and now my heart pounded and my mind raced as I tried to remember, to think, to plan, to figure what the hell I was supposed to do. Could it even be him? Why? Surely not. Surely he'd moved on by now. But how the hell I was going to stop whoever it was before they interrupted my life and Jay's life and the lives of everyone else around me.

Wednesday, Robert, the security guy that Delia paid to attend the fancy events she hosted for fancy clients was waiting in front of the building. 'Miss Harrington,' he nodded, his fingers tipping an imaginary hat in an old school gentlemanly way.

The crowd of people had increased. People shouted my name, journos, curious passersby, fans, why I still had any was a mystery. Why anyone still cared at all was a mystery. They wanted to know where I'd been. They wanted to know what had happened between my father and me.

'Have you spoken to your father?' they shouted

'Where have you been?'

'Why did you disappear?'

'Is it true Cam Taylor sexually assaulted you at a Christmas party? Is that why you disappeared? Did you have his baby?'

They pushed and shoved to get their answers until I felt like a ping pong ball jostling between them. I had to push my way through the bodies and the noise and resist the urge to fall to the ground in a heap and beg them to shut up. People in my life had stopped caring I was a Harrington, former child star, former 'it' girl, long ago, why hadn't the rest of the country? Why were they still waiting for a drunken headline? It was eight in the morning, did they really think this was when they'd get one? That I'd be stumbling along drunk as a skunk so they could all proclaim there she is and we could all go back to before and coexist while I stumbled through life and they documented it for bored housewives? It wasn't me, it was no longer my life, it wasn't happening but it didn't mean there wasn't still a fragile girl underneath barely holding her shit together. Or is that what they hoped, that they could break that girl to get their payday? Or did they really believe I was going to produce Cam Taylor's love child, born of an assault in the middle of a party? Wouldn't that cause an uproar with his lovely doctor wife and their two point five children? Seems the media doesn't want any of us moving on.

I pushed a woman with a microphone aside, I couldn't stand it, it was too much and I just needed to get inside. As she stumbled they all surged forward in a frenzy with their cameras as Robert finally made his way through to me, draped his arm across my shoulders and herded me into the lobby and pulling the door closed firmly once I was in, making the entrance again secure.

You needed a swipe pass or someone to buzz you in once that door closed before 9am so I watched them watching me from the safety of my glass bowl. They kept trying to shout their questions but their voices were too muffled for me to hear what they were. I breathed a sigh of relief as I turned away and waited for the lift to come down and get me.

I could feel all their eyes watching me while I waited. The longer I waited, the more tempting the stairs became but I refused to let them win so stood there being boring Jaz Harrington, hopefully disappointing them all to no end. They'd got out of bed at the crack of dawn for nothing. I gave them no scowls, no fingers in the air or shouted obscenities. I just stood there and stared at my distorted reflection in the metal doors, waiting for them to open.

I avoided looking at the flowers on Shannon's desk as I passed through reception, bee-lining for the kitchen and a much needed jug of coffee. A weekly gossip magazine was on the lunch table and on the front cover again, was my wide-eyed rabbit face and the question, *'What's happened to Jaz Harrington?'* Because apparently me being a normal, boring, functioning human was a cause for alarm and front page bloody news.

I groaned. I got a life you wankers, I wanted to scream. But I knew there was no point. There was never any point in trying to get the story right. They printed what sold magazines and Jaz Harrington leading a boring, ordinary life didn't sell magazines. Jaz Harrington off the rails and puking in the gutter is what sold magazines. It was disgusting.

The words they wrote, the salacious intensity with which the readers ate it up no matter the truth, no matter the context or how comments were misconstrued, were reworked to suit someone else's agenda without actually lying. Well maybe not the puking in the gutter, there was only one way to interpret that, but the other stuff they sensationalised, blew out of proportion as though I wasn't really a person with feelings, a family, a mother, a grandma.

It was cruel how they could print whatever they wanted with no regard to the cost of human life. They'd watched and laughed and shared my entire downfall with the world without any thought to my welfare, to the fact that I was a child who needed help and care. They never asked if I was okay, never helped, just sniggered behind their cameras counting their money. They'd documented it all to fill their fat bank accounts and line their pockets for their boozy lunches and visits to the strip clubs. I always assumed that's what they did in their free time because good honourable, kind people didn't do what they did to me. They never helped me, they never held out their hand to the lost, broken girl in the gutter, they photographed it for the masses and whispered behind their hands about how much of a tragic waste I was.

They struggled to hide their grins when I procured more alcohol, even though I was underage and already intoxicated. They saw the dollar signs never the humanity. What kind of people did that make them? My father might not have known how to help, but at least he tried, in his own twisted, controlling way, at least there was that which made the people who stood by celebrating my fall worse than my father and I didn't think anyone could be worse than him.

I sat at my desk sipping coffee, ready to go over the brief for Robbo's Chicken Delights. My phone light was flashing so I took a deep breath and checked my messages first. There was just one today. 'Didn't you like my flowers?' he asked.

I almost dropped my coffee cup, catching myself just in time. I couldn't fall. Not here. Not with Delia so close. Her eyes and ears were as keen as a hawk's. I couldn't afford to let her see there was any more wrong than a few nosey journos.

I took a deep breath. Played the message again. My jaw tight as I concentrated. Did I know the voice? Recognise anything? Something twitched in the pit of my stomach? Fear? Recognition? Anger? My heart pounded in my ears. Sweat dripped from my pits. But I didn't recognise him. Something said I should. I wanted to. I desperately wanted to. I could make it all go away if I could remember. But I didn't. People moved around me. A curious eye thrown my way by a passing colleague. I needed it to stop. To go away. I panicked. I deleted the message. There. It's gone. It doesn't exist. I wiped my sweaty palms on my pants, concentrated on my breathing like the doctors had told me to.

But he'd been here. In the office. Steps away from my desk. Shannon had seen him. Spoken to him. What if something had happened to her? She didn't know how to protect herself. She didn't know about shitty people. What if she'd waved him through? Or if I'd passed him in the hallway going to the bathroom? It was too much. I was a danger to everyone. To Shannon. To Meg. Even to Clary. I had to warn Delia. I had to tell Jay. But I couldn't make myself move. I couldn't reach for the phone. I couldn't make it real. Oblivion had always been my coping mechanism. It was harder to find without something to numb my brain. Ignorance was a poor cousin to oblivion. Denial. Perhaps I was just going mad? Perhaps I'd been mad all along?

I had to phone Jay. I knew I did but I also knew that as soon as I told Jay what was happening, he'd be whisking me away to the beach. He'd make it real. He'd keep me prisoner under his watchful eye. No more job, no more apartment, no more independence, it'd be all gone. Everything I'd worked for would be gone and there'd be no point arguing because he'd be right. I just had to take solace in the fact no one knew where I lived. Only Jay. Even Meg only knew the building, not the apartment. We'd rented the apartment under Jay's sister's married name, so it would take a bit of searching to find it and connect it all together. It would give me time to fix it, if I could just take a minute to breathe, maybe I could remember.

The hum of people starting their day built around me. I felt as though I were in another plane of existence, but slowly my breathing returned to normal. I sipped my coffee, reminding myself he didn't know where I lived and now the fans had begun to hover outside with the journos, Delia had changed the doors so instead of unlocking at 9am, they'd be locked all day and every visitor would have to be buzzed in. And there was Robert. He was no Jay, no Michael or Moe but he'd keep us safe.

Yesterday was one thing; today was another. This guy wasn't getting in again. I didn't have to worry, Shannon would be safe now, everyone would be safe. People would forget me again. The soapie fans, the Instagram followers, were just in search of some nostalgia. They'd return to their lives soon enough. The crazies would find a Kardashian to follow and I'd be free. It would all blow over. I had to be patient. I'd just surprised everyone. Like coming back from the dead. But they'd move on. There'd be someone new in a day. Maybe two. A news story to take my place. A new tragic actress doing something outrageous. Something. There was always something.

By the time Meg walked in and flopped into her chair with that post-holiday exasperation at having to do anything other than whatever she pleased, I was tidying up a calendar for one of our Easter Bunnies and ready to get back to Robbo's Chicken Delights, to start making the final calls and setting up the calendar of appearances Robbo had emailed me for the Chicken Man. I could do this. It was going to be okay.

'Time to get you into a taxi,' Meg insisted as the clock hit five.

'Fine,' I groaned as I started logging off my computer. 'So, we on for Friday night drinks? You can tell me more about this tour of Europe and the handsome man that drew the lucky straw, hey? I'm dying for all the juicy details,' I told her as we made our way through the office. She'd told me some of the polite snippets but we'd had no privacy for all the good stuff that happens on a European tour with a bunch of inebriated twenty somethings. She teased me with a silly grin whenever I mentioned her trip so I knew there was something to tell. I was dying to hear her secrets.

'Oh I can't. Sorry, but when I saw all the hoo-ha out there, I assumed Friday night drinks would be off for this week, so I told the folks I'd drive up to the farm for the weekend. You and me next Friday, though. I'm in like Flynn,' she smiled.

'You'll have forgotten all the good bits by then,' I sulked.

'Huh! Hell no and by then they'll practically be oozing to be told, it's not like I can tell my parents about what Olly did to me as we sailed down the Seine.'

'Are you kidding? What did he do?'

She smirked like the proverbial cat that got the cream and then blushed beetroot.

'Ooooh, it really must be good,' I teased.

'Oh, it was good,' she laughed as Clary stomped past throwing us one of her famous scowls.

With nothing else to delay us, we left. Meg and the security guard pushed me through the screaming journos again and hustled me into a passing taxi, which ferried me the long way to home.

Chapter 6

I put the key in my front door and as I did I heard the chatter of the television and froze. *'He doesn't know where you live,'* I reminded myself, quietly opening the door anyway to find Jay sitting on my couch and I exhaled.

'You scared the crap out of me,' I scolded him, half-heartedly, squeezing the shakes out of my hands.

'Sorry,' he said, getting up to kiss me hello.

'Where's your car?' I asked. Usually he parked directly in front of the building when he visited, which wasn't very often.

'There was a delivery truck there earlier, I had to park down the street,' he said going into the kitchen. 'I've made dinner though,' he smiled.

'Hmmmm. You or did Greg send it with you?' I asked, knowing it was usually Greg, the pub's head chef that sent me food when Jay came to visit, usually enough portioned containers to fill my freezer.

'Same thing, isn't it?' he laughed. 'You alright?' he asked when I didn't participate in the usual subsequent banter.

'Oh, yeah, just a long day,' I told him.

'I drove past on my way. There were more than a few Jaz. Is it bad?' he asked.

'Pretty bad,' I smiled tightly. 'But it's better now,' I said, wrapping my arms around him and sinking into his chest.

'Well how about we eat and I make sure you forget all about nosey, pushy journos?' he suggested, raising his eyebrows comically.

'Sounds good to me,' I smiled, kissing him, letting his mouth consume me, revelling in the toe curling feelings swirling through my body and erasing all thoughts of creepy voicemails and bad-mannered journos.

'First you eat,' he said, finishing the kiss and giving me that look. No matter our libidos, my health always came first with him. After all we'd been through, all he'd seen me go through, he'd become fanatical about it. I could fight him on it, tell him to back off, settle down, whatever, but he'd scooped me out of the gutter too many times for me to argue over something so trivial so I sat at my little round dining table and waited for him to serve up the hearty Irish Stew that Greg had sent over.

Big rounds of crusty homemade bread accompanied the stew and I wolfed it down. It was good. I was hungry after all. I'd gotten through the day on nothing but a sandwich and too much coffee. He'd kill me if he knew but I didn't want to be wandering around buying fruit and salad from all over the city.

'So what's Delia saying about everything?' Jay asked.

I shrugged. 'Not much yet but I'm sure she's working up to it.'

He nodded. 'Christian called the pub, asking if you were okay. He offered his security for you.'

'He still has Sam? Surely he doesn't need him anymore?'

'I think it's more for Ainsley and Henry. Or maybe habit or just for his peace of mind.'

'I suppose. You told him no though, right?'

'I considered it,' he said.

I glared at him.

'But yes, I told him no. You have me anytime you need and I could kick Sam's ass,' he grinned.

I laughed because he could. Well he could have back in his security days. It'd been a long time since he'd needed to kick anyone's ass. Drunk surfers in need of an uber didn't count.

I mopped up the last of the gravy and hoped that would be the end of the chit chat of the day. I didn't know how long I could avoid telling Jay about the flowers and the voicemail. Was it even worth saying anything? Was I just making a big mountain out of nothing? I used to get weird crap like this all the time. When Tom was on trial for murder and my family was falling apart, people screamed death threats and abuse at us all the time but we all survived. I had a beer bottle thrown at me while leaving school one day, that's when I got Jay. This crazy person crap wasn't new. I was just out of practice. I once had an enviable Instagram following, a burgeoning career as a child actress, whether I wanted it or not. I appeared in the glossies on a weekly basis. Having a deranged man thinking he was in love with me was just a part of the game. There'd been more than one back in the day, but once Jay came along so much was filtered and taken care of so I could go on my merry way but I knew they were there, they approached me in clubs and cafes, somehow found my phone number and sent me texts and gifts to one of the houses.

I'd become desensitised during my hiatus from the limelight. That's all. I was making more out of this than there was. So the note and the voice sounded familiar. Even if it was the same guy who was unrelenting back in the day, he'd never proven to be anything more than annoying. There was no point getting Jay all worked up over nothing. So when Jay's arms snaked around my waist at the sink as I rinsed our plates, I didn't protest. As his hand made its way down my body and between my legs, I gave in and let him do magical, beautiful things.

I walked into work the next day with a smile stretched across my face. A night in bed with Jay would do that to the coldest heart. I'd no idea where he learnt to do what he did but it was a question best left unasked. I'd decided a long time ago that because of what he'd put up with from me, all the things he'd forgiven me for in the name of love, I had no right to ask but geez, I was grateful he knew what he knew because it never failed to eradicate any other thoughts and make me soar on the clouds.

I thought I'd left early enough to beat the journos. Jay had left as the sun came up to get back to the pub for some deliveries so I'd left not long after thinking for sure they wouldn't be there yet and I'd avoid the throng and wait inside for Delia to arrive. But I'd thought wrong. There were hordes of them, clearly the price had risen for pictures of the troubled Jaz Harrington doing something other than waiting for a lift and they all stood around swilling coffee, laughing, waiting for their chance to get rich.

Delia crossed the street as I approached. 'Jaz, this is ridiculous,' she exclaimed as we met in the middle of the road and the journos went wild. They were like animals. Poor Robert couldn't even force his way through.

'I'm sorry Delia, they just won't stop. I've done nothing to encourage them, nothing at all, I promise,' I cried exasperated.

'I know,' she said sympathetically as Clary began screaming abuse at the people as she tried to get through the throng who didn't care, didn't care who she was or what she wanted and I'm not sure which one annoyed her the most.

'This is ridiculous,' Clary shouted at me. 'Why do they even still care? You do nothing. You're not interesting. You go nowhere and still they think there's a story. Or what exactly is it you get up to when you leave here? That tiara of yours get left on the kitchen table while you go out and do who the hell knows what?'

'Oh fuck off, Clary,' I spat, finally losing my composure.

'There it is,' she smirked triumphantly. 'Looks like the great Jaz Harrington has finally fallen,' she laughed, pushing her way through the throng and going inside with a smirk on her beautiful face.

'Perhaps it'll be best if you just go home and stay put until they go away? If they keep this up, someone's going to get hurt,' Delia groaned.

'I can't do that,' I said, my heart sinking.

'Of course you can,' she said, waving off my protests. 'None of us can take much more of this, it's ridiculous.'

'What about Robbo's? I've got auditions for chicken men today,' I said, thinking for sure she'd let me stay for those, the client was far more important than me and my pathetic drama.

'Robbos will manage. Shannon can cancel your auditions. Just go,' she pleaded as the journos continued screaming their questions, shoving microphones and cameras in our faces. 'I'll call you when they've given up this shit and it's safe to come back,' she added as she began telling the journos to get out of her way and shove their microphones in less sunny places.

'Fine,' I conceded, flagging a taxi. 'Delia?' I called. 'I'm sorry,' I said pathetically before getting in. I couldn't see her through the camera flashes, I just had to hope she heard me, knew I was sorry, that I was still grateful to have a job, that she'd taken a chance on me and that she cared.

I didn't have the heart to call Jay and tell him. So I just turned on daytime television, opened a bag of crinkle cut chips and camped on the couch. Delia was probably right. If I just stayed here until they were gone, until they gave up, everything would be okay. They'd have to give up if I wasn't there to provoke, surely? They all saw Delia send me home, after all. They'd know I wasn't coming back until they were gone.

I fell asleep watching Ita dole out wise advice on a morning program, wondering what wisdom she'd have for me. We'd been at a party together once, a fundraiser I think but I'd not spoken to her. She'd been too put together for me. I didn't know what to do with people like that. Next I knew I was rubbing my eyes as I woke to a vacuum commercial, groggy and disorientated. I got up to make a coffee, splash my face with water, stretch the kinks out of my body.

How long could they hold my life hostage? I wondered. How long could they keep it up? Would their editors let them keep going when there was clearly no story to be found? Surely no more than a day or two? Surely I was no longer that interesting? I was exhausted. They were exhausting.

I hated to think what they were saying about me to keep the expense accounts flowing, what lies they were saying, what lies my family and my clients were reading. How had everything gotten so out of control so quickly? I'd done bloody nothing, given them nothing, yet still they'd taken my life from me. Still I was stuck inside these four walls until the world gave me permission to leave.

I paced from the kitchen to the living room and back again. I turned on the kettle but forgot to make tea. I put bread in the toaster but forgot to retrieve, butter and eat the toast. Then I saw an envelope sitting under the front of my door. Had it been there when I'd come home? Had I been so distracted I'd stepped on it? All my mail went to a post office box under Jay's sister's name. All my deliveries went to the pub. I stared at the envelope for a long time. Stared at it like it was a bomb. For the first time in a long time, I needed Dutch courage. I didn't like how that felt. I didn't like the person that made me. I didn't want to be that person, to go to that place again.

'Fuck it,' I mumbled, ripping the envelope open. I'm not going to be that girl who crumbles. He won't do that to me. They won't do that to me. I unfolded the lined paper inside and read the handwritten words.

Now it's just us. Now we can be together. Soon it will be just you and me. I've missed you. Just a little longer, my love and I'll take care of you the way you deserve.

I dropped the paper. It fluttered to the ground like a feather as I stood frozen. He'd found me. Found my home. How had he found me? He couldn't have followed me, I'd made the taxi go the long way, I'd checked out the window as he'd wound around the back streets, went all the way around the city and back again in peak hour traffic. How had anyone followed us?

With fear rippling through my body, I double checked the locks on the door, the locks on all the windows even though only Spiderman could come in through them. Everything was secure, there was no way in. I slid to the floor against the wall and watched the door anyway. I should leave. Get in the car and go to Jay's. Even if the weirdo found me there, even if the journos found me there, I'd be safe. But I couldn't force myself up off the floor. I couldn't force myself out the door and down the stairs to the car park and into my faded red bug for the long drive out to the beach. I wanted to. I had to, but I couldn't.

The phone roused me as an audience applauded something on the television. How the hell had I fallen asleep? What was I thinking? I looked around to make sure everything was in order. There were no more notes under the door. Everything was still secure so I scrambled to my bag, rummaging in it for my phone, and answered Jay's call.

'Are you okay?' he asked.

'Yeah, course,' I said as though I was.

'I've been calling for ages. I even called the office but your phone went to Shannon who said you were at home. I was just about to get in the car and drive into the city.'

'Oh, I'm sorry to have worried you but I'm fine,' I lied. 'I was just sleeping, that's all.'

'In the middle of the afternoon?' he asked.

'I don't know, I guess,' I said, not knowing what else to say.

'Are you sure you're okay? Do you need me to come in?'

'No, don't be silly. There were just a lot of journos there today. Delia thought it would be best if I just laid low and this daytime telly is mind numbing. Not to mention someone had me up late last night putting on quite a show,' I added, trying to insert a hint of humour.

He laughed but it must have satisfied him because he said, 'Well, alright, if you're sure. I'll call again later. Have you eaten?'

'Yes, of course,' I lied again.

'Alright, call me if you need,' he said.

'Thanks, I will, but I'm sure it'll all have blown over by the morning and I'll be back to work as usual.'

'Good. Well, I've gotta go, a busload of tourists have just rolled in for afternoon tea.'

'Have fun,' I said before hanging up.

I had to stop lying to Jay. I'd meant to tell him about the note but as soon as I heard his voice, I just didn't have the heart. I hadn't lied to him a single time since I'd left my old life, since before that even. I might have done a lot of shitty things, but I'd never lied to him, to everyone else, yes but never Jay. I didn't like it. It felt far shittier than anything else I'd ever done. But there was no point worrying him. He had a bunch of people in the pub to feed tea and cake and no doubt a front bar full of thirsty surfers at this time of day. Besides, other than shaken and, now he mentioned it, hungry, I was fine.

I put one of Greg's frozen meals in the microwave as the wind picked up outside. I'd heard there was a change blowing in but seriously, couldn't it have waited? I turned the sound up on a retro comedy while I ate to drown out the sound of the rattling windows, the distant rattling fence that hadn't been secured properly, all sounds that I usually didn't even notice. I was losing my mind. Jay had upgraded the security on the door and windows. The old Jaz Harrington was nothing but a distant memory by the time I'd moved in here. The paparazzi and curious strangers had given up trying to find me. I was no longer a story anyone wanted to read. Someone new had no doubt taken my place on the cover of their magazines. We'd been cautious, anyway, old habits die hard but there'd been no security concerns, until now.

Jay called again around dinner time, reminding me I needed to eat again. I took my dinner to bed, leaving the empty container on the bedside cupboard when I was done and went to sleep. This was all too much and I just wanted to sleep it away. Not that sleep came. I tossed and turned, jumping at every noise, but I must have slept at some point because I woke to the sun squeezing through the gap in the curtains.

I told myself the day before was just a one off, the journos would be gone today. The stupid note was just a joke. It couldn't possibly be real. Who would even care enough to want me? It was a miracle Jay wanted to be with me.

I noticed on the way to the bathroom the wind had gone. It

was a new day. I'd blown everything out of proportion. I was suddenly very glad I hadn't told Jay any of it. I didn't need to feel any more stupid than I did.

Wrapped in a robe, I went to make coffee, following my usual workday routine. I glanced at the note I'd left on the ground where it had fallen. A fresh envelope now sat beside it. I froze, my breath catching in my chest. My heart pounding, my hands shaking, every pore sweating like a fat man in the sun.

I couldn't catch my breath as I forced my leaden legs forward, one step, two. 'Come on, Jaz,' I said, trying to pep myself up. I took a deep, shuddering breath, bending to carefully pick up the envelope and open. It was on the same A4 faintly lined piece of paper as the other one. It read,

'I knocked but you were in the shower. Everything's almost in place. I can't wait for you to see what I have planned for us. We're going to be so happy. See you soon my love.'

My legs fixed to the spot, my brain numb, unable to move, think, breathe. I punched myself in the chest, a trick I'd learnt from one of my shrinks to bring me back to the present. I had to go. I had to leave. Delia and work would have to wait.

I threw on track pants and a hoodie, threw a change of clothes and the bare necessities in a duffle bag, looked out the front window to the busy street below. No one appeared out of place. I couldn't see anyone watching my building. There was just the usual hustle of people bustling past doing their thing so I made a run for it, figuratively anyway. It'd do no one any good to attract attention by actually running. I took the back lift that strangers didn't know existed. It was an old Victorian apartment building. The original building was a three floor walk up. Someone added the lift when they converted it to office space and it stayed when they converted it back. Leading to the back of the café below, people preferred the walk-up street entrance, no matter the stairs. It took me down into a vestibule at the back of the café. There was a door there leading to a back alley but I watched television and people in my situation shouldn't walk into back alleys alone so I took the café exit that would lead me to the bustling Rundle Street. Walking out of the foyer I saw into the kitchen, nodded to the stringy guy who was always manning the pizza oven and into the chatter filled room. I walked through the café into the street, a few steps down the street I then turned into the carpark next door where we got a permanent parking discount.

The car park was quiet, empty, echoey and full of shadows from the tall city buildings and the moving sun. They made horror movies like this and the stupid damsel always ended up chopped to bits. I had to put those thoughts out of my mind. I was no good to myself if I was on the floor in a panic. I could see my car from where I stepped out of the lift. It wasn't very far. I wondered for a minute if I should just turn around and go to the bus station but I couldn't bring myself to. I wanted my car. It was mine. I felt safe with my car and I'd get to Jay's a whole lot faster driving.

I stopped and listened. There wasn't a single sound to be heard other than my own jagged breath so this time I did run straight for my car. I ripped open the door, threw my things inside and roared out of there so fast I'd have run over anything or anyone if they hadn't been paying attention.

I paused at the exit to lock all the doors, looked out the

windscreen to the sun filled street and saw the gift he'd left for me under the windscreen wiper. A single red rose. I forced myself to keep breathing. He knew where I lived. He knew what car I drove. He was too close. It was too much. I left the rose on the windscreen while I drove to the service station. I'd stop and look at it where there were lots of people and security cameras. I could probably use a top up of petrol, too. I didn't want to risk running out between here and Jay's, that'd be all I needed to be stranded and alone on the side of the road.

As always, the petrol station was full of comings and goings. I pulled up to a pump, got out, removed the rose and the note attached which read, '*as sweet as a morning rose, as will be our life together.*'

I took a few deep breaths, threw the rose and the note in the bin, despite what Jay had always told me about keeping these things for forensics. I didn't want to be driving all the way to Jay's with that thing in my car. I topped up the petrol tank while casually looking over my shoulder, satisfied no one was watching me, I went inside, got a couple of bottles of overpriced water from the fridge, a coffee and a couple of chocolate bars that were on the counter at two for one and I was back on the road.

Chapter 7

I zipped through the peak hour traffic like a rally driver. I was usually patient, rarely in such a hurry to bother with zipping about but today I zipped, today I wanted to be out of the city, on the highway and away from crazy, love struck stalkers and stupid journos that made all this shit happen in the first place. I wanted to be at Jay's, on the balcony where it was safe, where no one could get to me, where Jay could protect me and Greg could feed me some pasta and chocolate cake.

I had a better than usual run through the traffic. I stopped at the traffic lights leading onto the freeway, finally getting to take some breaths, guzzle some water and scoff a chocolate bar. I looked into the car next me, my mouth full of chocolate and the middle-aged man inside winked and smiled. I thought for a second he looked a little familiar but I couldn't see through my tinting and his tinting well enough to know for sure, so I told myself it was my exhausted mind playing tricks on me. Thankfully the light turned green, my heart returned to a bearable beat and I took off, letting the guy with the wink show how clever he was and race ahead of me.

My paranoia was bordering on ridiculous. I was jumpy any time a car got too close to my back end or on either side, panicking at weirdo strangers winking, thinking, *'is he my stalker?'* As if he'd be my stalker. Then the sugar from the chocolate bar kicked in and I felt better, more relaxed, so by the time I exited the freeway and made it to the quiet empty roads that wound around to Jay's, I was feeling far more Zen. Or perhaps it was just the proximity of Jay and the promise of safety?

Once I got to the pub I was tired, exhausted, I just wanted to sleep. Jay would have been tending to the brunch crowd, mostly fellow morning surfers grabbing a quick bite for getting on with their days in the office or wherever they earnt their money. Sometimes we had people staying in the rooms upstairs but mostly it was just a bunch of mates eating toast and eggs and cereal before they re-joined the real world. I didn't want to see any of them. I didn't want to have to explain why I was there, discuss what was going on. My brain hurt and my heart ached at the thought of losing everything, so I walked up the two flights of stairs to Jay's apartment, crawled in between his still slightly warm sheets and slept.

I woke with my body sweating under the heat of the high sun. I must have slept for hours. I reached for Jay's bedside clock and saw it was almost lunch time, no wonder my stomach ached. I couldn't remain unseen for much longer, someone was bound to see my car in the car park soon enough and ask questions. I felt stronger for the sleep anyway so I went down the internal stairs hoping Greg had something stodgy on the menu.

I received the expected cautious and surprised greetings from the staff as I came into the bar but there was no Jay.

'Hey Jaz, what's up?' asked one of his young waitresses, Sarah, just out of school, surfing the days away between shifts until she decided what to do with her life.

I shrugged. 'Same old. Where's Jay?'

'He's just gone into a meeting. Said not to disturb him for anyone or anything. You want something to eat? Greg's got spag bol on the menu today, he must have known you were coming.'

'Nice, sure,' I said and made my way through to the dining room. Comfort food was my weakness. Growing up, Margot had never been allowed to add it to the menu unless my parents were out of town and we were all far too grateful when she snuck it to us to ever tell on her. But even the promise of Greg's famed pasta wasn't easing this ache, this hollow pit in my stomach. Jay would have fixed it. Seeing him would have eased the thumping in my chest but spaghetti would have to do it seemed.

The dining room overlooked the ocean. It was extra blue today under the beating sun. Summer was dragging on, it seemed to get longer and longer every year or maybe I was getting soft sitting inside with the air-conditioning all day? I watched the people out in the ocean, a couple of kids throwing a Frisbee, splashing into the gentle waves as they caught it, no doubt laughing. Laughing at the heat. Laughing at the world full of responsibility while they lived in their carefree bubbles. I moved away from the door that led to the wraparound balcony. It was a beautiful space to be but I wasn't in the mood for the sun or the people or the sounds. I couldn't bear to hear those boys in the ocean laughing, I couldn't feel their joy.

I sat by the window that looked over the green grass where people lounged quietly with books and checked my Facebook feed and emails hoping to touch base with Meg, to see what was happening, see if I could somehow get a grasp on things. It already felt like I was fast losing my grip on everything, on the things I loved, the job I'd worked so hard for, the friends I cherished, my freedom, my safety, my sanity. I was holding on by my fingernails but no amount of information seemed to help.

Meg had nothing new to tell me but said she was jealous of my nice sun filled break and Facebook was just Facebook so was left with myself, my thoughts. I looked around the dining room but it was almost empty, nothing to see, no one to distract me from myself. The dining room felt small with the beautiful T-Bar closed. I wondered why Jay was in a super secret meeting if he had a conference or private function going on in the T-Bar.

Sarah brought me my food so I put it out of my mind. While I ate, I watched the ocean, the seagulls diving for food, the paddle boarders coasting across the glass topped water before the afternoon waves came along. It was peaceful and perfect. There was no sign of Jay. He was still being undisturbed when I'd finished eating. There'd been nothing interesting on Facebook. Meg had no news for me. The journos were still outside, waiting, hoping, Clary gloating about what she'd joyfully termed as The Fall of Jaz as she nestled her crown back on her head, so I told Sarah to let Jay know I was upstairs. I tried watching telly, reading a book I'd left behind but I couldn't focus on anything. I was too distracted and I just wanted it all to go away. It was exhausting, the worry, the thinking, the hiding and lying so I went back to sleep.

The sun was still high when I woke which meant it was late afternoon. Jay hadn't woken me so it made me wonder what on earth he was up to. He'd have woken me for an explanation if nothing else. I didn't just show up on a Friday morning. I'd assured him things would be back to normal, that I'd be back at work. He'd want to know what was going on. His super Spidey senses would be on overdrive if he knew I was here, if he'd found me upstairs sleeping in the middle of the afternoon again.

The doors to the T-bar were still closed when I came back downstairs looking for a cup of tea.

'He's still locked away, hasn't come out all day. Greg took in some food and drink but I haven't seen him,' Sarah said, indicating the T-bar.

He was in there? Why? He had an office for meetings so why would he need to block off the whole T-bar? 'Who's he with?' I asked, hoping for some corporate style explanation.

She shrugged. 'A bunch of fancy people in suits down from the city I think. They choppered in, he panicked, shoved everyone in the T-bar, closed the doors and that was that. I'm sure he'll be finished soon. Can I get you something?'

'No, I'm good,' I told her. 'I'm just going to let him know I'm here,' I said, heading for the doors, ignoring Sarah's protesting.

Something wasn't right. I could feel it. I had too much going on for Jay to shut me out.

I pulled the door open and froze. 'What's going on?' I demanded as too many familiar faces turned to stare at me. Jay, Tom, Christian, Lydia, Michael and Moe all sat around a table looking exhausted and frustrated.

'Jaz! What are you doing here?' Jay asked, shocked.

'There was no change at work so I thought I'd get an early start on the weekend,' I lied, again.

'Why didn't you tell me?'

'You've been in here all day! Sarah said you weren't to be disturbed,' I said, refusing for it to be my fault.

'How long have you been here?' he asked.

'Since this morning. I had nothing to do so I figured I might as well do nothing here,' I said, only partly lying.

He took a deep, shaky breath. 'What have you been doing all day?'

I shrugged. 'Sleeping,' I told him.

He released an audible sigh of relief, his whole body seeming to exhale. I waited for him to chastise me like a child for sleeping in the middle of the day. According to Jay, it wasn't good for one's mental health.

'What's going on?' I demanded when he'd said nothing.

'Nothing,' Lydia interrupted. 'We had a meeting in the city yesterday so we hung out with Christian last night and thought we'd come check out this place and hunt for some waves and organise that catch up,' she said.

'Well that doesn't require all this cloak and dagger stuff,' I challenged.

'Of course not. We just didn't want nosey people calling the journos when they saw us all together. We didn't need a repeat of the wedding pictures, did we?' she smiled sweetly.

'Fair enough,' I said, not actually believing a word of it but accepting for the minute they weren't going to tell me anything. 'I'll just leave you to your organising and find tea and cake in the dining room,' I said, turning to leave, annoyed no one had called me, no one had invited me to this get together. My brothers and sister happy to hang out with Jay without me. Well fine.

'Tea and cake sounds perfect to me,' Lydia said, following me out. 'We've some catching up to do, anyway,' she said, hooking her arm through mine.

'Don't you go pitying me Lydia. You want to hang out with Jay without me, that's fine. But don't pity me like I'm some fragile child,' I spat as I led us to the dining room where Sarah was setting up for afternoon tea.

'I'm not pitying you and I wouldn't rather hang out with Jay than you. What kind of stupid thing is that to say? You're my sister, Jaz.'

'Yeah, well, no one invited me to this little shindig, did they? If you were all in the city meeting with Christian last night, someone could have invited me to dinner, you know. Apparently I'm not that hard to find,' I told her, getting madder by the moment.

'I'm sorry, okay, it was spur of the moment and if I'm honest, there was some business talk involved.'

'What on earth could you be discussing with Jay that was business related?' I asked, my hands on my hips.

'It doesn't matter. Can't we just forget it and have a cup of tea?'

'Fine,' I sulked, dropping into the chair. 'But I'm not forgetting about it,' I told her.

She smiled. 'I would expect nothing less from my sister.'

Sarah brought over my favourite tea and a tray of cakes. It was always just whatever Greg and his team decided to make. Today it was mini matchsticks. Puff pastry with fresh cream dusted in icing sugar and cockles, these half cake, half biscuit delights with jam and pink icing that Greg's grandma used to make, they were my favourite.

'This is a great place, you and Ainsley would get on like a house on fire, you know, she loves all this fancy tea too,' Lydia said as she apprehensively sniffed her tea before taking a sip. 'Jay said the T-bar was your baby?'

'Yep. My contribution.'

'So why don't you live here. You obviously love the place.'

'After the way we grew up, I needed some freedom. I needed to find out who I was on my own. Become a better person. Be someone Jay could be proud of, that he could love.'

'He does love you. And I could never imagine him not being proud of you. When he talks about the things you've done Jaz, the man glows,' she smiled.

I couldn't help smiling too.

'Speaking of the things you've done, Christian is pretty jealous of this place. If you don't look out he and Tom might fight for your design skills.'

I laughed. 'I couldn't do this professionally. It was just because I lived here and I knew the people and I thought it would be nice. If it didn't work, it didn't matter. Jay wouldn't have cared. It was just a coat of paint and a few boxes of tea to get started and it took off from there.'

'And martinis at sunset with Jazz on the deck?'

'Who doesn't love a cocktail at sunset and Jazz? Other than me,' I smiled.

'You really haven't touched a drop in all this time?'

'Nope, not a drop. I wouldn't do it to Jay.'

'You really love him?'

I smiled. 'I really love him, Lids. You know what it's like,' I waved her off.

'I don't know if I do.'

'What about Andrea?' I asked.

She shrugged. 'I love her, I guess. But not like you love Jay. Not like Tom and Alex or Christian and Ainsley. Not that all encompassing my soul would crumble without you kind of love. I'd be sad if Andrea left. But I'm pretty sure my soul would still be intact. Maybe it's a gay thing. Maybe we don't feel it the same way?' she questioned.

'Lydia, love is love. It doesn't matter who it's with. Emotions don't change, just where the bits go.'

She laughed and I laughed and after everything that had been happening, it felt good.

'What if I'm not gay anymore, Jaz?'

'What do you mean?'

She shrugged.

'No. Out with it,' I told her.

'I love Andrea like I said. But what if my body doesn't anymore?'

'That happens in all relationships, you know, that's not a gay thing.'

'But what about if my body fancies a man?'

'Does it?'

'I don't know. I think. Maybe. I don't know.'

'Lydia, you are allowed to love anyone you want. Just because you loved Andrea and that what's her name, doesn't mean that's all you're allowed. You are allowed to love a person despite their gender. You don't have to love them because of it. There are no rules when it comes to love. You just have to follow your heart. That's the only rule.'

She nodded thoughtfully.

'What does your heart say?'

I haven't decided yet.

'That's okay. Just be happy, okay?'

She smiled, held my hand. 'If I can have what all of you have some day, I'd be the luckiest bloody woman in the world.'

I smiled. I often felt like I was the luckiest woman in the world and I wanted that for Lydia. But I knew she had to find her own path. It wasn't easy to be one thing then another when society judged so harshly, when society told you to make a choice and stick to it. Life is never that simple whether it's a job or where you live or a person you love. You can always choose. It wasn't always easy but people got over it, people moved on, for the most part.

'So,' Lydia started as she sipped her tea. 'What's new?' she asked as though we had tea and caught up every day.

'What do you mean? What's new since you ran off to Europe with Tom or since I saw you last week?'

'Are you pissed at us for running?'

'No. Yes. Maybe. I don't know. He locked me in my room Lids and he was going to dump me in some facility on the other side of the world and I kind of felt I had no one but Jay and he couldn't get past security. I didn't have a choice but to run.'

'I'm sorry,' she said, her eyes filling with pain. 'We didn't know until we were coming home, we didn't check our emails. Probably for the same reason you don't check yours,' she challenged. 'Didn't Christian try to help?'

'He did what he could, but you know Dad, he doesn't listen to anyone and Christian was just one man against Dad and his army, he never had a chance. Dad had Christian running all over the place from one project to the next most of the time. Christian set up the meeting with Jay though. But he probably didn't expect me to run. Is he mad at me?'

'Oh Jaz, no way. He understands. We all do. I really am sorry I wasn't there for you,' she said, placing her hand on top of mine.

'I know. It's okay, really. You and Tom did what you had to to survive, the same as me, I get it. I'm just feeling a bit out of sorts with all the crap going on, it's dredged up a lot of old stuff.'

'Tell me, what's going on?' she asked, looking at me suspiciously over the rim of her pretty Royal Albert teacup.

'Same old, nothing new,' I told her, suddenly feeling the familiar Harrington ulterior motives. None of us had turned out like Dad but we had Harrington DNA. That DNA said Lydia was fishing for information but for what information I couldn't be sure. She couldn't possibly know anything that was going on other than I was being harassed by journos. I hadn't said anything to anyone about the calls and the flowers and the notes. It must be my imagination. I decided the old paranoia was back. It couldn't be anything else. All the media attention was just stirring up some old bad Harrington memories and already I was back to feeling suspicious of everyone. 'You know,' I added, waving it all off, 'same old, same old crap that comes with being a Harrington,' I smiled. 'I don't know how you stand it.'

'They don't bother me too much. I've never been very interesting and to be honest, the little extra attention I do get from the media at an event doesn't exactly hurt when you're trying to be a designer,' she winked.

I took the opening to turn the conversation around onto Lydia's designing career where there was far more to tell and I could try and not think about creepy stalkers. Her face lit up as she talked of her upcoming show at fashion week and I was so happy for her to finally have the life she'd always dreamed of.

'You should come,' she said suddenly. 'Come to my show. I'll make sure you get front row, treated like a queen,' she gushed.

'It's not really my scene anymore, Lids and I don't know if I can get off work.'

'Oh please, think about it? Bring a friend if you want. Or Jay, he can always hang out with Tom or something,' she added.

'I'll think about it,' I conceded reluctantly. I was far enough in the spotlight already I didn't need to go in any further and I certainly didn't need to be sitting front row at my sister's fashion show but for Lydia, I'd think about it.

As we finished the pot of tea, the others joined us. Jay kissed the top of my head, Tom and Lydia had one of their annoying silent conversations then Tom and Jay had one of theirs and I rolled my eyes in frustration.

'Well, if you're all just going to have your secret squirrel conversations I'm going back upstairs,' I grumbled, pushing out my chair.

Tom smiled.

'What?' I demanded.

'Nothing. I like this feisty sober Jaz.'

'Oh shut up,' I laughed, smacking him. But I realised the last time he'd seen me sober, I was twelve. I forgave his stupid grin.

'Hey, Jaz, seeing as you have some extra time, why don't we go do something this weekend?' Jay suggested.

'What? Now? I thought you were all busy planning some big family catch up? What's going on? What are you all really up to?' I quizzed.

They laughed thinking I was too stupid to spot how guilty they looked.

'You're so paranoid,' laughed Lydia.

Tom and Jay shared a guilty look. They knew something. But how? What?

'Well I know I have no plans for the weekend,' Christian said. 'We're all here anyway, why don't we get everyone else in and make a weekend of it?' he suggested.

Everyone began talking about what a great idea that was and messages were quickly tapped into smartphones.

'In that case,' Tom said, slapping Jay on the back, 'I'm going to steal one of your boards and hit the water.' He grinned like a little boy just given the freedom to fly.

They all buzzed about as though I couldn't see their nervous energy. Fools.

'Hey Jaz, why don't I help you make up some beds?' offered Michael as everyone else wandered down to the beach.

'Ahuh, sure,' I conceded and led him upstairs to make up the beds before Ainsley, Henry, Alex and Andrea arrived for the weekend.

The rest of the night was loud. There's no other way to describe it. We sat around a large round table in the middle of the closed T-bar, Jay casually resting a hand on my knee while telling stories of our life, Christian trying to get Henry to eat while he insisted on singing which made Tom laugh and made Henry show off more. Ainsley was continually trying to wipe green goop off Christian's polo shirt and suppressing a smirk. I couldn't remember the last time I'd felt so content.

It was loud, it was crazy but it was family and it was perfect. Michael and Moe sat at another table with Sam, Christian's driver come security guy and a couple of other guys I didn't know who had arrived with the girls. More bodyguards, who knew? I didn't care to ask but knowing they were all sitting there made me feel safe enough to laugh along with my family.

'So what do you actually do, Jaz?' Lydia asked after I told a story of snotty Clary lording her superiority over the entire office.

'Talent management. But because I'm a Harrington and will always be a Harrington, Clary gets the fancy models and actors, you know, people I might've been friends with once or even worked with and I get the bloody chicken men. Any kind of gig that requires some poor, middle-aged slob, or wanna be movie star, dressing up as some kind of animal and dancing around for a couple of hours.'

'Why? Like you said, you're a Harrington,' Christian said, as though settling for chicken men was an insult to the family name.

'Christian, Christian, Christian, the real world, you beautiful man, is not a kind place to the likes of us. No, no, we spoiled little rich kids, no matter our education or breeding, no matter where we did work experience in the school holidays, or in fact if we were a rising child star of Australian television, in the real world, people like us are expected to pay our dues, bow down to the folk who had to earn their way, bust their guts as I've been told because apparently sitting through boring conversations with politicians and studying university business degrees at sixteen, is just spoiled rich kid speak for doing nothing. Add to the fact the bloody media loved nothing more than plastering my face across every magazine in the country puking my guts into a gutter or passed out in my bodyguard's arms, people think I did nothing more than drink.'

'Well...' laughed Jay.

'Shut up, you know how great a multi-tasker I was,' I smiled.

He laughed. 'You bloody were.'

'But that's all anyone sees, drunk rich kid who must have sat by the pool like in one of those American reality shows on the telly. The idea I had a brain as well, was just too much for anyone to believe so to pay my eternal dues, I manage the chicken men, the dancing dogs, the Easter Bunnies, leprechauns for St Patricks day, had a request for a horse once for a Melbourne Cup thing.'

'And this Clary gets models and actors and invited to fancy shindigs and you get invited to the opening of a chicken shop?' Lydia asked.

'Yep, that's about right. But you know what? They pay me and it's my money and I do as I please and it's bloody beautiful,' I smiled. 'Speaking of freedom. How did he get you back into the family business?' I asked Tom.

He shrugged. 'I like it. It's a bit like the army, coordinating and planning and executing a design. And Dad promised to give me free reign on my projects. I told him if he interfered or undermined me just once, I was out.'

'And what did that mean for you?' I asked Christian.

Christian and Tom shared a look before Tom turned with an apologetic look on his face and Alex squeezed his hand.

'What?'

'I got reallocated to that project in Adelaide, Tom got my international portfolio, a resort in Vegas I'd spent a year or so working on and he became Dad's next in charge.'

'He booted you out just like that? Took away your projects? The man has no bloody shame. What did you say, Tom?'

'I didn't know. Not at first. I tried giving them back as soon as I found out. But Christian was too mad to listen to anything I had to say, wouldn't even take my calls. Then he met Ainsley, Dad had his heart thing and tried breaking Christian and Ainsley up, which as you can imagine, didn't go down to well.'

'He did not?'

Christian nodded. 'So I quit, ran away and married Ainsley in Vegas and nearly gave the old boy another heart attack,' he laughed as Ainsley swatted him for his poor taste in humour.

'Well good for you,' I told him, tapping my glass to his.

'So now I have to snap up all the good properties before he does,' Tom laughed.

'There's something to be said for being a trust fund rich kid,' Christian joked to me. 'Those fools you work for should remember that. You could dip into your trust fund anytime you want and bring them to their knees.'

I laughed. 'If I dipped in to my trust fund, it wouldn't be to go up against Delia and Clary. The job is just a job. It's a pay cheque. I enjoy the work fine enough, I have some friends there, it's satisfying but I wouldn't put my trust fund into it.'

'What would you put your trust fund into?' Lydia asked.

I shrugged. 'Don't know. I've never actually thought about it.'

'Never?'

'I never thought we'd be here. I walked away from everything, including my trust fund and even still, I'm glad you're all here and everything but still, there's no way I'm letting him back into my life. You all might be able to forgive and forget or move on or whatever but not me. I don't want him in my life and I don't want his money. Now, tell me, why the hell aren't you two on your honeymoon, sitting on a beach and having monkey sex?' I asked Tom and Alex.

Tom almost spat out his beer, coughed a little as it came out his nose. 'My little sister is never to ask me about my monkey sex again. Let's just get that out there,' he grinned. 'We went to Hawaii for a few days but that was enough. We don't really like to go too far, we're perfectly happy in our house on our own beach.'

I got the sense he'd been away from home enough in his life and he wasn't in a hurry to go too far for too long again. Alex seemed to share the sentiment. They made a good couple, a good pair and they really seemed to adore each other.

They finished off the evening with some of the states best fortified wine while I had a cup of peppermint tea.

'I'd prefer the tea too I think,' Ainsley told Sarah as she served us.

'Told you you two would get along great,' laughed Lydia.

I smiled, it was nice to think I had something in common with my sister in law. 'I'll have to come and compare tea selections some time,' I told Ainsley.

'I'd really like that,' she smiled. She was a warm and kind woman. Both my brothers had chosen well. It was a comfort to know they had people in their lives making them happy, supporting them and loving them.

'That was a good night, wasn't it?' asked Jay as he threw his shirt onto the floor beside his jeans and climbed into bed.

'It was, yeah. But don't you think them showing up like this is a bit suspicious?'

'Suspicious? Why?'

'I don't know, but it's kind of sudden and with everything else going on I guess I just don't know what to think.'

'What everything else?' he asked, looking sideways at me.

'Just everything, the photographers and stuff at work, you know,' I said waving him off like I had done to Lydia earlier. Now wasn't the time. I didn't want to involve my brothers, my sister, their loved ones, Henry. It had been so long since I'd seen them. Surely I deserved just a minute of happiness before my world came crashing down. I suspected Jay knew more than he was telling me anyway but if not, I'd tell him everything after they were gone. Until then we were all safe here.

He shrugged. 'I don't think there's anything to read into, just enjoy it.'

'You're right,' I smiled as he snaked a hand around my hip and down my thigh, leaving goose bumps in his wake as he pulled me to him and made me forget all about stalkers and families showing up out of the blue with questionable motives. I knew he was distracting me with his body but I knew a storm was coming and this was still borrowed time, so I let him have his way with me and enjoyed every delicious moment of his mouth on my skin, the feel of him beneath my hands, the perfect completeness of him inside of me. I wasn't letting anything or anyone take that away from me.

Chapter 8

The breakfast room was quiet when I came down in the morning. Jay was taking care of a few pub things and only Lydia and Moe were sitting at a table together by the wall drinking orange juice. They sat as though blending into the dimly lit edges of the room and I wondered how much of that was habit from spending years in Europe hiding from moving shadows? There was so much about my sister I'd missed, that I was still to learn. The realisation stabbed at my gut. Had the sacrifice been worth it?

'Morning,' I called as I came in, stopping at the breakfast counter to get a glass of juice and order coffee and eggs from Sarah as she passed, her hair still damp from surfing, a grin on her face. We saw a lot of those grins here from people living their bliss. Even if it was just for a little while between the realities of life.

'Morning,' Lydia greeted as I reached the table.

Moe nodded and left to stand on the balcony, watching the water and green space in front of the pub like a sentinel. Out of habit? Or for some other reason? My Harrington senses were definitely piqued.

'What's going on?' I asked.

Lydia started to wave me off but then seemed to change her mind mid action. 'You're okay now, right?'

'What do you mean? I'm fine,' I said, as Sarah brought me my coffee and eggs.

'You know, with the drinking and stuff. Jay says you're fine but are you? Are you as fine as he says?'

'Lydia, I haven't had a drink since before I left. Not a drop since that weekend that started all this,' I told her, remembering Jay carrying me near comatose out of some club I could no longer remember the name of. The next morning he'd told me he loved me, made love to me, changed my life. That night I didn't know what to make of everything I was feeling, got rip roaring drunk, nearly slept with some politician's kid that was always hanging around and hitting on me and Jay carried me out of the party while I cried a river of tears, begging for his forgiveness. He'd begged me to love myself enough to want better. He'd understood. He'd seen through my bullshit and my fear and it had changed everything. I hadn't had so much as a sip since. I hadn't even thought about it in years. 'Lydia, I'm good, I promise. What the hell is going on?'

'We're not just here for a visit.'

'No shit.'

She smiled. 'I missed you, you know.'

'I missed you too. Now spill.'

'Since you've come back out of hiding,' she began.

'I didn't come out of anywhere. I went to my brother's wedding then happily crept back into my hole.'

'Yes, well,' she smiled. 'Whatever you want to call it, it's attracted some attention.'

'No shit. The journos in front of my office kind of gave it away.'

'Not just the journos. Back in the day, there was a guy.'

'I know of the guy,' I told her wondering just how stupid everyone had actually thought I was.

'You do?'

'Well not who he was but that he was there. Jay didn't intercept everything. The guy somehow got my mobile number, left things on or in my locker at school. Once he left flowers in my room.'

'He was in the fucking house?' she shouted.

'Shhh' I told her, looking around and realising my brothers were leaning in the doorway, the security team were at perfect intervals along the veranda. 'It wasn't when I was home,' I consoled her. 'Mum and Dad had had a party. Indi and I had gone out afterwards. I'd spent the night at Jay's, too drunk to come home. I came home the next day and the flowers were on my pillow. I thought they'd been delivered, that Margot had put them there until I got the text message asking if I'd liked his gift.'

'Did you tell Jay?'

'Are you kidding? No! He would have lost his shit. I did what I did, went on a bender and didn't come home for three days,' I smiled. 'What does this have to do with anything?' I asked. I knew why I had been thinking about him, but why was he on Lydia's mind.

'He's back,' she said quietly.

I waited a moment. Took a deep breath. There was no longer anywhere to hide. 'I know.'

'You know?'

'I know,' I confirmed. 'How do you know?'

'He's sent message to Tom and Christian's office, to Mum at the country house.'

'Shit. Does Jay know?' I asked, my heart pounding.

'He does now. We told him yesterday.'

'That's what the secret meeting was?'

She nodded. 'We wanted to make sure you were okay before we said anything. I promise, it's the only reason we went to Jay first. He wanted to call you straight away, get you back here where he could keep an eye on you. We were worried you wouldn't take it well and thought you were safe enough at work with all the journos around.'

'Those vultures would be no help in a crisis, they'd just sit back and photograph it.'

'Which is why no one would try to get to you while they were around.'

I grunted. I didn't want to verbally agree that they were useful for anything.

I looked up then to find Jay leaning against the bar, arms crossed, his expression a mix of emotions, anger, frustration, fear, concern. Our eyes locked and I couldn't look away. Why hadn't he told me? Why was it Lydia?

'We need the room,' he demanded in that commanding voice of his.

My brothers reluctantly left us but Lydia stayed where she was.

'Lydia,' Jay ground out.

I stood to meet him. Lydia looked from Jay to me, considering, then finally she gave in.

'Are you okay?' he asked when we were alone.

'NO! No, I'm not okay, Jay. Why didn't you tell me what was going on last night? Why was it Lydia?' I was suddenly angry it was her and not him. He was my person, my lifeline, the one who was supposed to have my back no matter what.

'I was trying to fix it, make it go away so you didn't have to worry. You're not surprised though, about what's happening, are you?' he asked.

I shook my head.

'You know and you said nothing either,' he challenged.

'I was hoping it would go away,' I admitted sheepishly.

'And it didn't?'

'No.'

'That's why you're here?'

'He knows where I live,' I confessed.

'What the fuck, Jaz?'

'I got out as soon as I knew. I drove straight here, I promise. Messages and flowers at work are one thing. Those journos gave where I worked away but I'm not an idiot, Jay, as soon as he came to my home, I left.'

'He was there?' he asked, the words struggling to get out through his anger.

'He pushed a note under the door promising we'd be together soon. He left a flower on my windscreen.'

'Give them to me. Tom can do something with them.'

'I don't have them. The note is on the floor where I dropped it. The flower I threw in the bin at the servo when I got petrol.'

'Jaz, what were you thinking?'

'That I didn't want to drive all the way here with it in the bloody car, Jay.'

'And the note?'

'I wasn't thinking. I dropped it, threw some stuff in a bag and left. Getting to you was all that I was thinking.'

'Good, good,' he said, wrapping me in his arms, pulling me tight against his chest where I could feel his heart pounding.

'It's going to be okay. I've got you,' he insisted, although I wasn't sure who he was convincing. 'As long as you're here with me, I can protect you. Tom and Christian, Michael and Moe, they can figure the rest out. I'm going to make sure you're okay.'

'I'm always okay when I'm with you,' I admitted with a smile in an attempt to lighten the mood, lighten his heavy heart. 'But I have to tell you, he scared me bloody witless. Knowing he'd been as close as my front door...'

'Your hands are shaking,' he commented, holding them tight in his hands. He edged me against the wall, his mouth close to my ear. 'I will protect you Jaz. I will protect you with my life,' he promised.

'That's what I'm afraid of.'

Tom cleared his throat from the doorway.

'What?' Jay asked, barely looking at him.

'Michael needs to speak to Jaz.'

'Well why isn't he interrupting me?'

Tom smirked, an expression that said no other fool had the balls.

Jay grunted, then led me to the chair I'd not long vacated before dragging over one for himself leaving the chair Lydia had vacated for Michael. Jay wasn't kidding when he said he wouldn't leave me. Despite my worry for him, that he'd go too far, put himself in harm's way for me, my whole body seemed to exhale with relief having him there, knowing he'd let nothing happen to me.

Suddenly I couldn't breathe. Suddenly it was too much. I had to tell them everything but as soon as I did, I lost everything. I wasn't ready to lose everything I'd worked so hard for.

'What's the matter?' Jay asked, his voice heavy with concern.

'Nothing. Jay. I can't do it again. I only survived last time because I was too drunk to notice. I can't,' I said, bending, gripping my knees trying to catch my breath.

'I'm right here. We're going to do this together. You're going to be okay. I promise,' he assured me, giving me strength.

Sarah brought in coffee and I spent the next 30 minutes telling Michael everything, doing my best not to look at Jay because even though I knew how angry he'd be with me for not having told him, I couldn't stand to see the fear and disappointment in his face.

'Why didn't you tell me,' he begged after Michael had gone to see what he could do with all the information I'd given him.

'Because of this. I didn't want you to be disappointed in me.'

'Jaz, I could never be disappointed in you. This isn't your fault. I'm disappointed you didn't trust me, that you didn't believe enough in us.'

'I was afraid. Afraid of losing it all. Afraid of what you would do. You're everything to me Jay, I couldn't stand for you to be hurt, to put yourself in danger for me.'

'Then how do you think I feel knowing you've been in danger all bloody week, that anything could have happened to you and I wouldn't have been there? The thought of it guts me, Jaz.' He pulled my mouth to his as though reminding himself that I was okay. 'You're my girl, Jaz. You're my world.' He reminded me, branding me with his mouth, his possessive hands.

'It's going to be okay. I'm going to make sure it's okay. You can stay here until it's over.'

'I can't stay here Jay. If I stay here, I lose everything and they win. I'm not letting anyone take my life away again. You of all people should understand that.'

'It's a week, Jaz, not an indefinite stay in a facility in Italy. It's not the same thing.'

'I'll lose my job. Jay, I won't get another one. I'll be completely dependent on you and I won't.'

'Hey,' he soothed, wrapping me in his arms. 'You will always be your own person, free to do as you please no matter what happens. You know that. I'd never take that from you.'

'It wouldn't be the same. I have a job and a pay cheque every month, people who take me seriously.'

'That doesn't have to change. You can get a local job, nothing is ever over. We both know that. We've both risen from the ashes of our lives before, we can do it again.'

He was right. He'd nearly drunk himself to death after Dad had banished him from the country house. I'd have been no different if I hadn't been denied my freedom and been locked in my room. I'd cried for days, couldn't leave my bed, I was a shell of a human. If it weren't for Christian, I don't think either of us would have recovered. But we did. We came together and we took on the world and we won. We could do it again.

'I'll go back Monday and sort out things with Delia and my apartment and come back until it's over and we'll take it from there,' I agreed.

'Good. I'm coming with you though,' he insisted.

'Don't be silly. You have that conference coming in. I'll be fine.'

He held me tight. 'Someone will come with you. You're not going into the city alone.'

'You mean I'm not going anywhere alone?' I asked suspiciously.

He smirked.

He didn't say anything else. Just held me too tight until Lydia knocked on the open door.

'You guys okay?' she asked.

I wiped a tear from my face. 'We're good.'

Jay kissed my head and nodded at Tom who appeared behind Lydia. 'We're fine,' he agreed. 'Aren't we?' he asked, tipping my face to his because he always saw the truth in my eyes.

I smiled, kissed him. 'We're always fine,' I confirmed, my hand on his face. I loved this man more than my own life. I'd give him anything, including everything I'd worked so hard for because breaking him would destroy me and I knew if I didn't do this, there was a chance it could all go very bad.

Eventually, unable to keep his nose out of things he was good at, Jay left me in the company of my sister, my sisters in law, their security people and Moe. We went outside to the grass where a few local crafts people had set up stalls of their wares. It was only steps from the pub and with so much security to keep us company we were perfectly safe. It was nice to be outside, to breathe some fresh air and get some perspective, to leave behind the hubbub of anxiety and investigation for the blue skies and community of a marketplace, even if it was a teeny tiny market. I knew the stall owners and a lot of the people gathering in groups to browse or drink coffee and it already lightened my heavy heart.

'Where's Andrea?' I asked as we walked across the grass towards the stalls.

'She's gone up for a rest.'

'Is she alright?'

'Yeah, yeah, just sleepy.'

I nodded. It was a restful place. People tended to find they slept so well they did a bit extra. Jay never cared about their mental health. It was just me he wouldn't let sleep the day away. With my history of addiction, he always worried about the mental and emotional ailments that could accompany addiction, but I'd let the causes go the day I walked away from my old life.

'To be honest,' Lydia whispered. 'I think she's having second thoughts about moving here. She's been sleeping a lot. Not wanting to go out as much.'

'Oh no, I'm so sorry. Are you sure she's just not under the weather?'

Lydia shrugged. 'I get it, I was away from home for a long time and it was hard, really hard.'

'And there's all that thinking you've been doing. You should talk to her about it,' Alex told her, squeezing her hand. 'You two have been through too much to not have a conversation.'

'I know. I will. Later. After,' she waved her hand in the air.

I wandered, preoccupied with everything that had been happening while the girls laughed and chatted, indulged and shopped up a storm.

'So, did Dad pop a vein after we left the wedding?' I asked, trying to bring myself back into this precious moment.

'Almost,' laughed Ainsley from in front of us, beside Alex, enjoying her time out without little Henry.

'He swore bloody murder for a while, threatened all sorts of torture to 'that, that paedophile,' as he calls Jay.'

'He does not,' I asked horrified. 'I was seventeen when I left with Jay. There was no impropriety.'

'We all know that,' exclaimed Lydia. 'He just doesn't know how to justify any of it,' she exclaimed.

'He could take responsibility for being an arse, that's what he could do.'

'Don't we all know it. But you know Dad, he can be a stupid, stubborn old bastard,' Lydia said.

'I know,' I conceded.

'Anyway,' she continued. 'As his head was about to explode,

little Henry tugs on his jacket and says, "Poppy, why you cross?" And his scared little eyes were big and his mouth pouty and Dad just turned to water, scooped Henry into his arms and disappeared for an hour. Henry says they went to Poppy's office and played Lego and built a tower for the beautiful princess then Henry had chocolate milk, Poppy had his Poppy juice, scotch of course, and then they went back to the party.'

'He's gone soft in his old age. But he still sees locking women away as a solution to his troubles. I guess some things never change.'

'Not women Jaz, the Princess,' added Ainsley. 'Henry was very specific. He said Auntie Jaz is a beautiful princess Poppy wants to protect from the whole world so they can't break her.'

'Great, so Henry thinks Jay's going to break me?'

'Nope. Henry says Poppy forgot Jay used to be an army man like Uncle Tom so he'll look after Auntie Jaz. No one can get past the army men.'

'Really?' I asked, my heart filling with love for my little nephew.

'Really. But then he said that when he grows up he wants to be a brave army man like Uncle Tom, Johnno and Auntie Jaz's Jay,' Lydia added.

'Christian's furious,' Ainsley smiled. 'He's one big ball of mush that man, when it comes to Henry. He'd wrap that boy in cotton wool until he was a hundred if he could. But, unlike your dad, he nods and smiles and tells Henry he can be anything he wants to and then buys him doctor kits and science sets. Not because he wouldn't be proud as punch to have his son serve but he'd be terrified of losing him. Like I said, he's become a big sissy,' she laughed.

We laughed too because imagining Christian as a big mushy sissy was hard.

'Oh you're here? I'm so glad you're okay,' cried my friend Kelly as we reached her jewellery stall.

'I'm okay, Kel,' I assured her.

'I've been so worried. I came into the pub the other day with Sime and was bugging the hell out of Jay to see if you were okay but you know Jay, just kept saying, she's fine, and that was it. It drove me mad.'

'You have my number, Kel.'

'I know. But there was so much going on for you and I didn't want to bother you with my silly questions. I just wanted to know you were okay.'

'Well you're too sweet but you'd never be a bother,' I assured her as Lydia handed over a pile of jewellery to buy.

'I like these friends of yours, Jaz,' winked Kelly, as she handed Lydia a bag bursting with her purchases.

'That's actually my sister, Lydia,' I smiled.

'As in Lydia Harrington?' Kelly asked quietly, slowly connecting the dots and the face from the magazines.

I smiled proudly at Lydia. I hadn't allowed myself much familial pride and it felt good. 'The very one,' I added.

'Make sure you pop your card in the bag so I can tag you on Instagram when I wear something,' Lydia added with a smile as she took the bag from Kelly who began fumbling, trying to refund Lydia's payment, telling her she could just have them.

Lydia of course refused and apologised for not being able to immediately Instagram any of the items, explaining she didn't want to curse me and Jay with a media circus.

Kelly was a friend with internet access. She understood. And somewhere in the back of her subconscious, she also understood that there was a chance Lydia could wear one of her pieces at an important event and for the first time in a long time, if ever, I saw how being a Harrington could be used for good. Someone as talented and sweet as Kelly should be successful. Once upon a time I had taken all the free stuff as though I were entitled to it without a thought for who was providing it. I never knew who they were, what they stood for or even if they needed my free publicity. I knew Kelly, I knew how hard she worked, her good heart, the quality of her pieces, the locally sourced materials she used, how she desperately wanted to make a living doing something she loved. I bought a bold statement necklace I knew would catch people's attention and planned to wear it next time I went to the office if the vultures were still around. They'd been using me all my life, maybe it was time I used them for the good of people like Kelly?

Halfway through the stalls, we came to Diggle wines, a local winery and a favourite in the pub.

'Hey, Geoff, I greeted.

'Hey yourself. Beautiful day, isn't it,' he smiled as he looked to the sky. Geoff was a hippie, he loved making his wine, he grew everything organically, used the most natural processes he could manage and loved cooking in an open fire in his back yard. He was a beautiful soul to be around and threw a damn good party.

'You doin' okay with all the stuff going on in the city?' he asked kindly.

'I'm okay. Thanks for asking.'

'Your friends wanna taste? He asked, knowing, as most of the locals did, that I didn't drink. A reason he'd been playing around with a non-alcoholic sparkling grape juice that I got to taste regularly and was coming along beautifully.

'I'm sure they do,' I said, as I lined them all up like sheep.

'Not for me,' smiled Ainsley as she stepped to the side. 'I'll buy a bottle for Christian, though, he loves finding new wines to enjoy and stock in the hotel bars.

'Why aren't you having any?' asked Lydia, clearly surprised.

'No reason,' Ainsley smiled.

'First no fortified after dinner and now no free wine tasting? What is going on?' Lydia asked, squinting at poor Ainsley in that Harrington way that made people squirm and divulge their deepest secrets.

'Fine, fine, but you can't say anything to Christian,' she caved. 'You're all going to have to add to your Christmas list this year. Henry's going to be a big brother,' she grinned.

'You're not?' Lydia asked, excitement bursting out of her.

'I am indeed,' Ainsley smirked. 'Now don't go telling him you knew. You have to be surprised.'

'Oh, we can be surprised,' smiled Alex, leaning in to hug Ainsley. 'Congratulations.'

'Yes, congratulations.' I said hugging her.

'Thank you,' she breamed.

'He'll go mental if he finds out you told us first,' Lydia laughed, hugging Ainsley.

'Oh, I know. That is why you can't tell him you knew. But I thought this was a good girls' moment and I wanted to share it with you.'

'Well it is great news and I'm glad you did,' I said. 'It's been a long time since I felt a part of my family and you just made that happen.'

Ainsley smiled, squeezing my hand.

'How far along are you?' asked Lydia.

'About eight weeks I'm guessing, so it's still really early days. But I couldn't imagine when we'd all be together like this again.'

'Isn't that sad?' Lydia said. 'We must make sure we get together more, regardless of distance and the boys' schedules.'

'Absolutely,' we all agreed before Lydia started insisting we all had to attend her fashion show together and make a weekend of it.

'We should probably think about heading back,' Moe thankfully interrupted.

'Why do I get the feeling this has something to do with my news?' Ainsley asked as she looked at the final few stalls we were still to visit.

He waved her off but she just grinned and we all followed Moe back to the pub. We could see Jay on the balcony in deep discussion with a lady called Marianna who came in regularly for cocktails on a Sunday. I also knew she was some sort of ex police officer, investigator or something like that, she always changed the subject too quick for me to actually figure out what she did. But seeing her reminded me how serious this situation was, how much danger I could be in. I didn't want the others to get too caught up in everything so when Alex asked who she was, I just shrugged.

'Oh, maybe Jay is planning a proposal or something,' Ainsley suggested.

Lydia rolled her eyes.

I laughed out loud. 'Oh Ainsley, you're so sweet. Jay knows better than to propose to me again,' I laughed.

'Again?' asked Lydia curiously. 'How many times has the poor guy asked?'

'Well, officially, none. There's been none of that bended knee hoo-ha. But he's mentioned it. One day I'll marry you Jaz and I tell him not to be ridiculous.'

'Why would you do that?' asked Lydia.

'Oh come on Lydia. It's me. He doesn't really want to marry me,' I laughed as Henry raced toward us screaming *Mummy, Mummy* and launching into a babble of surfing stories. 'I think we have another Harrington hooked on the waves,' I smiled as Henry reached us, grinning from ear to ear.

'You can't really think that, Jaz?' Lydia whispered in my ear.

'It's fine Lydia, don't make a big thing about it,' I told her as Christian and Tom met us.

We followed Tom and Christian into the T-bar. The bar remained closed off for us to prevent prying eyes so while everyone settled in, I went to organise a round of drinks. It was stretching past lunch time and it had been a long morning. Everyone could use a little something to chill out and regain their focus. I needed them to keep going so I could get my life back and I knew for regular people, that sometimes a beer or a glass of wine could do that and help them to restart.

Sarah automatically included a bottle of sparkling apple juice for me but for the first time in a long time, I found myself staring at the full supply of liquor on the wall behind her.

'You okay, Jaz?' she asked.

I mentally shook my head clear. 'Yeah, yeah, sure, I just need the bathroom,' I mumbled wandering off and leaving her to distribute the drinks.

I sat on the toilet with my head between my legs. What was happening to me? For the first time in a long time, I was afraid, truly afraid. Seeing Marianna had brought it all back up. I had to get myself together though, plaster on a smile and make believe everything was okay, that I hadn't just ogled a wall full of liquor like it was gold dust. I hadn't had a drink in years. I was a terrible drunk and by the time Jay bought this place I was clean and okay with my sobriety. I shook the shakes out of my arms. Now my sobriety seemed to be on shaky ground and nothing frightened me more than Jaz, The Princess of Party, sticking her head up out of her hole.

Chapter 9

Sunday morning I woke exhausted. I'd been through the emotional wringer with apologies and confrontations and forgiveness. We'd pulled so many things out of the dark corners of my mind where I'd shoved them, forgotten them as best as I could, but we'd talked through them all as a family, apologised to each other for coping the only way we knew how. We'd talked about the creepy bloke who was proclaiming his love for me, talked about protection and strategies and tried figuring out who it might be based on the information I could recall from before and what I had now. I'd eaten my weight in chicken wings and sticky beef ribs as compensation for the emotional torment but the worries only waited for me to close my eyes and plagued my dreams.

The demons still clung as I woke and I needed some air, some space to think and to process it all. The sun was already up, the sky outside my window bright blue and perfectly cloudless. Jay was communing with the ocean so I thought a walk on the beach would be perfect.

I threw on loose cotton pants and a t-shirt. I had no need for shoes, washed my face and put my hair in a ponytail and left. As I descended the outside stairs, I found Christian on the balcony below ours fussing with Henry.

'Good morning,' I smiled as he tried shushing Henry.

'Morning,' he grumbled.

'You guys are up early.'

'Yeah, someone's ready to play but his mama needs some sleep,' he smiled. They'd told us officially about the new baby the night before and those of us who knew were suitably surprised and happy for them. 'Where are you off to?' he asked, his eyes narrowing in suspicion.

'Just a walk. It's a beautiful morning and like little Henry here, I could use some air. Why don't I take him with me?' I offered.

Christian hesitated. 'Ah do you think that's a good idea?' he asked. 'He's a handful when he wants to be,' he added quickly.

'Why wouldn't it be?' I asked, 'I'm safe here, Jay's out on the water, no one even knows I'm here,' I protested.

'Morning,' called Michael coming out of his room, pulling on a t-shirt.

'Sorry, didn't mean to wake you,' I said as he joined us.

'Nah, it's all good. Early riser. Habit,' he said. 'What are you up to?' he asked.

'Just going for a walk. Offering to take Henry off Christian's hands for a bit.'

I sensed more than saw something transpiring between Christian and Michael.

'Great idea,' Michael said. 'Was just thinking the same thing, it's a gorgeous morning. Where's Jay, anyway?' he asked.

'Where he always is on a Sunday morning,' I smiled, pointing to the ocean where Jay bobbed with a couple of locals.

'Right. Why don't we go watch Uncle Jay surf, hey?' Michael said to Henry.

Henry clapped his hands and Christian looked relieved.

Was it just me he was worried about? He didn't want his crazy sister alone with his precious son? Or was he worried that by being with me Henry was in harm's way? So that had been taken from me too, a little bonding time with my nephew gone because wherever Jaz went, trouble followed and no one wanted their toddler mixed up with that. But I couldn't dwell on it for too long because little Henry was reaching for my hand and telling me to hurry up.

I took his tiny soft, hand in mine. It was so small and squishy and vulnerable. I looked down at him and our eyes met, waves of love and protectiveness, joy and happiness sweeping through my body. No wonder Christian didn't like to let him out of his sight. Then Henry smiled at me, my heart melted, maybe even stopped for just a second and the world was a perfect bubble worth more than anything I had to give.

He tugged on my arm, pulling me out of my head and we followed Michael down the stairs and I felt like I was 15 again and not allowed to take a walk without protection. I knew Michael was working and not taking in some leisure time. I knew the difference. But for Henry's sake, I didn't make a big deal out of it. I would never forgive myself if anything happened to Henry so I was happy to have Michael along for the walk. After walking a little way along the sand, we all sat and Henry and I started building sandcastles while Michael looked everywhere but at us.

'Wave to Daddy,' I said after looking back to the pub and seeing Christian watching us.

Henry stood, covered in damp morning sand and waved heartily. I couldn't help but laugh, it was beautiful how much they loved each other and suddenly, for the first time, I wondered if I wanted that. If I wanted to give life to a tiny human that was part me and part Jay that could bring that much joy into our lives.

'Look,' Michael called to Henry. 'Here comes Uncle Jay.'

Henry watched, his eyes wide with delight and wonder as Jay caught a wave, sweeping his board over the face of it, gliding across the white tips. Henry clapped his little hands together as Jay rode a wave to shore. Henry was jumping and dancing on his pudgy sand covered legs calling to Jay.

'Hey, little Buddy,' Jay cried, swooping Henry into the air. 'What did you think?'

Henry grinned, gave Jay a thumbs up and started babbling on and begging for a turn at a hundred words a second and Jay just laughed with as much wide-eyed wonder as Henry had just watched him with and I knew in that instant somehow, someday, I had to be better. I had to be whole enough, be the person Jay deserved to give him children because I'd never, in all our years, seen him come alive the way he did with Henry and just as quickly, my heart sank because I didn't know if I'd ever be enough, ever be good enough to do it without making a mess of it. What if I ruined my children or worse, cursed them with my addictions? How could I ever give Jay children when there was even the slightest chance that would happen and what if Jay couldn't live without them?

We passed the day with food and laughter, stories of mystical places and fabulous adventures. Ainsley told me all about her café and Henry, and the story of his namesake, the broken-hearted Bauble Bandit and before we knew it, Greg was feeding us a Sunday roast and we were preparing our goodbyes.

'I won't be far behind you all,' I said.

'Really?' asked Jay. 'Why don't you just give it a couple more days before you head back in and sort things out?'

'I want to get it over with. I don't want it hanging over my head day after day while I sit here and wait. I'll just check my emails, rearrange some accounts with Delia, sort stuff out and I'll be back by lunchtime. It's better if I drive in tonight and then I can get in to see Delia before the media throng is out of bed and then drive back here mid morning. It just makes sense.'

'Well why don't I come back with you?' suggested Jay.

'Jay, you have that conference thing coming in tomorrow?' I said, reminding him of the local business having their team building day at the pub.

'I have people who can manage that, you know,' he mumbled.

'I'll come with you then,' Michael insisted. 'Tom and Alex won't need me for a couple of days.'

'Really, you all don't have to go out of your way for me. I'll be fine. The door will be locked. I won't leave. I'll watch tv, go to work first thing in the morning and speak to Delia and be back here by morning tea. Seriously, it seems silly.

'Jaz, it's no trouble,' Michael said, raising his eyebrows.

'Just take him,' Tom said. 'Stop being an obstinate cow,' he grinned.

I grinned back. There was something special about your brother calling you an obstinate cow. There was no malice, all love but he was calling me on my bullshit in a way only someone who'd known me all my life could. 'Fine,' I groaned. There was no good reason for me to refuse Michael anyway. To refuse any extra protection. I just hated having people rearranging their lives for me.

So everyone left, hugs were exchanged, Henry threw his little body into mine for a hug, Michael went up to his room to pack and Jay and I were left alone with a pot of tea on the verandah overlooking the ocean.

'When are you leaving?' he asked.

I shrugged. 'An hour, two, I dunno.'

'Well, instead of sitting down here overthinking things, why don't we go upstairs and I leave you with a little something to think about? Something to remind you why the hell you have to take care of yourself?' he suggested, raising his eyebrows and smirking.

He was pretty hard to resist and I was never very good at it, so I groaned, 'Fiiine,' and let him lead me up to his bed and have his way with me, his freshly grown two-day growth, leaving reminders of him all over my body, all the way back to the city.

I was a little worried about what I'd find at my place when I returned, notes under the door, weird gifts in my parking space.

I was a little relieved to have Michael yabbering on beside me about how happy he was to not have to travel Europe like a gypsy anymore. But there was nothing waiting for me, no notes or gifts, just emptiness and quiet.

I defrosted a couple of Greg's prepacked meals in the microwave. We watched a Big Bang Theory marathon and laughed and that was it, nothing sinister, nothing untoward, nothing suspicious, which made everything far more suspicious.

I said good night, went to bed and checked in on Facebook. I'd been so busy with my family over the weekend, I hadn't bothered since Friday. A new friend request, from someone with a picture of an 18th century French gentleman, a white wig of curls as their profile picture. His name was Georges Barb and instantly, the hairs on my neck stood up. He'd been in my apartment. The painting above my bed was The Secret Kiss by Georges Barbier with an 18th century white-wigged Frenchman kissing a beautiful woman in a garden. It was a gift from Jay. No one but Jay and the fat old bloke who manages the building and does my quarterly inspections had ever seen that picture.

I instantly wanted to walk out and crawl into bed with Michael but I didn't. I lay in my bed, frozen, staring at the window as though waiting to be invaded. I knew if he'd been in my apartment and in my room, he'd have rifled through my things and maybe even taken something but right then, in the quiet dark of night, I couldn't look. I could only lie there and pray to a God I'd long stopped believing in.

I couldn't stop shaking. I had to tell Michael so I turned on the light and left the safety of my bed.

I stood in the doorway of the spare room feeling creepy watching Michael sleep. He looked so peaceful, something he rarely looked while awake. He was always watchful, curious, you could tell his brain was always running on fast speed. It seemed I didn't have the heart to break his peace and I turned to leave.

'Jaz?' he whispered.

I turned back to find him sitting up, bare chested.

'What is it?'

'He was here. In my room,' I whispered. The tears I was holding in began rolling down my face and I hated myself. I hated the creep for bringing me to this.

Michael was out of bed in a flash. 'Stay here,' he demanded.

'He's gone. It was while we were at Jay's.'

He stopped. 'Are you sure?'

I nodded.

'How do you know he was here?'

'He knows the picture that hangs above my bed,' I said, telling him of the Facebook request.

'Shit,' he said, rubbing his hand through his hair.

Michael went to make me tea, no doubt in the hope of calming my shaking hands. Before the kettle had boiled, Jay's face flashed on the phone screen.

'Are you okay?' he asked.

I nodded.

'Jaz?'

'Yes,' I confirmed. 'I'm okay.'

'I'm on my way. I'll be quick as I can. Just let Michael deal with the police.'

'Police?' I questioned to Jay as I looked to Michael.

Michael nodded.

'Of course he called them Jaz. He'd be fired if he didn't,' Jay added.

I nodded again.

'Jaz?'

'I'm fine. Don't hurry. Drive safe.'

I sat on the couch, looking out the window to the lights of Rundle Street. The sky above told me night was fading, Monday morning was rising. It was quiet though. None of the weekend revellers wandered the streets, they'd all returned to their lives, were sleeping, preparing for jobs and whatever else they did. I wrapped my hands around the warm mug of tea for comfort while Michael paced the kitchen nearby, his phone to his ear as he updated all and sundry on the new events. I imagined as he finished each call those people then waking other important people and demanding attention, action, something. I wondered as the light across the street for a camping store flickered in the wind how regular people managed these situations. Not everyone had the resources of my family.

A knock at the door interrupted my thinking and had Michael ending his phone call abruptly. He answered the door and let in the two uniformed officers and a plain clothes one. I didn't catch their names or their titles but I think I managed a polite smile. It didn't matter the situation, some things were so ingrained they happened without you even trying.

Thankfully Michael did most of the talking and I nodded occasionally in confirmation while the female uniform frantically scribbled in her notebook. I wondered why her? Why not the other uniform, the man? Was it even a conscious decision? Was it an expectation? Something she had to overcome every day like the judgement and bias I'd had to overcome every day for so long when I was trying to just be me?

'Jaz?' Michael asked.

'What? Sorry,' I apologised.

'Its okay, Miss Harrington,' the plain clothes said. 'Is there anything familiar about him, anything you can think of from before or now that seems the least bit familiar?'

I looked to Michael. How did I explain to this nice man, this respectable, hard working policeman that I was once a drunk who took vodka to school in my water bottle and that therefore my recollections of most days were hazy at best. People never saw the broken girl forced to live a life of other people's expectations, a girl so lost and alone all she needed was someone to see her, to love her for her, not for her money, not because of what she could give them, just because. No, they saw the indulged, entitled rich kid who should have been more grateful for the advantages and opportunities bestowed upon her. They never understood I never got to choose any of it. It was chosen for me. My father decided I'd be an actress and I'd had to quit dancing and forgo all the things my friends did. The directors and public decided I should be a star just because they liked the emotional journey of my character. My father decided I should take university level business classes in the school holidays. The media decided which parts of my life they'd splash across their magazines with outrageous, misleading headlines. The media decided who I was dating, when I lost my virginity, that I'd run away to have Cam Taylor's love child after being groped at a party. Men decided when I was drunk enough to be sexually useful. My friends decided which parties to invite me to and when my presence was of no advantage. Clubs decided when I was allowed in and how to use my being there. It was all decided for me. I never got a say. So I began self-medicating with vodka at thirteen, eventually needing more and more. But no one saw the desperation, the pleading for help, the broken girl desperate to choose, to love, to be loved. They decided who and what I was, they saw what they chose to see.

Michael told them something, explained away my life, my lack of knowing as best he could and I sipped my tepid tea.

As the questions finished Christian arrived, wrapping his arms around me. I wanted to cry, was sure I was going to, but I was numb. I felt his arms around me but nothing felt connected. He made me fresh tea and sat on the couch, my head on his shoulder, his comforting arm around me. Time passed, more police arrived, things were done that didn't happen for regular people and had Christian's name stamped all over them. Then just as they were finishing and pink touched the sky Jay arrived.

I was bawling in his arms. I blame it on the lack of sleep, the stress, the invasion of my privacy as the police had rifled through everything, I refused to blame it on him, the freak, the stalker who had come into my home.

The police left. Christian ensured I was okay, then he too

left. Michael had a shower and began his day of protection and Jay suggested I get some sleep.

'I can't. Not in there. Not now,' I begged, shaking my head.

'Then let's go to a hotel. You need some sleep.'

I couldn't even pack a change of clothes. Things had been moved, things were missing, he'd taken some things, the police had moved things, everything I owned had been violated. I'd have to go to Target in the morning for fresh underwear and a change of clothes. There was no way I was putting on anything that freak might have touched. 'Christian has already asked Ainsley to do it in the morning for you,' Michael instructed. He was in work mode now. His voice had lost all emotion, all friendliness. It wasn't offensive. I knew the drill. I appreciated that he cared.

I slept in a strange bed with Jay beside me. It was a suite Michael had sorted, which was no doubt paid for by my father but I was too tired, too wrung out to ponder how I felt about it. The money was all controlled by Tom now anyway, I told myself as I drifted off, the numbness finally lifting so I could feel Jay, feel his arms, his breath, his warmth, the beat of his heart. He was home. He was safety. He was comfort and love. He was my everything.

I hadn't slept long but I felt revived for the sleep I had. I left Jay to rest and joined Michael in the sitting room.

'Ainsley brought you some clothes on her way to the café. She said she'll run into Target as soon as they open but she thought you might like to change into something clean.'

'I do. She's a lovely woman. Christian's a lucky man.'

Michael smiled.

I showered and put on the clothes Ainsley had left me, some cotton pants with an elastic waistband and a t-shirt with Wanderlust written across it.

Jay was still sleeping when I came out and I didn't want to wake him. I begged Michael not to wake him but I needed to see Delia before the media masses arrived so he agreed to walk over to the office with me and we left Jay a note.

'I'll just be fifteen minutes, maybe thirty,' I told Michael. 'Why don't you go get some coffee and I'll message you when I'm done? You can get me a double shot latte while you're there,' I smiled.

He reluctantly agreed but refused to leave until I was safely ensconced inside the secure building.

Delia wasn't in yet so I sat on the floor in front of our office and waited, closing my eyes for a few more minutes of sleep, feeling comforted and safe knowing that no one could get through the doors downstairs without a swipe card.

The next thing I knew, Delia was poking my thigh with her pointy patent leather shoe. 'What are you doing here? Didn't I tell you to wait for my call?' spat Delia.

I took some things out of her hands so she could open the door. 'I know. I needed to check in, give you an update, check my emails and sort out some stuff before I go back to Jay's. I'm going to be there for a while. There's some other things going on that need to be sorted out and I wanted to make sure my work was covered.'

'You could have done it on the phone,' she grumbled.

'I care about my job Delia, about my clients. I wanted to see you and talk to you in person. It's important to me.'

She shrugged but I caught the tiny twitch of a smile at the corner of her mouth. She was a hard woman to impress so when you did, it was satisfying and she always appreciated people who were as passionate about her company and all that she had built as she was. She'd worked hard to build the company, her name and her brand and I admired her for that. I wanted her to know I cared too. That it was important to me too. That I appreciated the faith she'd had in me when no one else had taken the time to see beyond the image given by the media. Maybe it was because Delia had been a model from the age of five until she'd aged out of the industry. Maybe it helped her understand me a little better than others could, who knows, she'd never say and that was fine.

I made us both a coffee, put Delia's on her desk and ignored her suspicious raised eyebrows and went to my desk. I sorted through the papers on my desk working out what to do with each of the campaigns in progress. I could have gone through the envelopes on my desk but I had other things to do. I printed calendars, shared email conversations with the necessary people, making notes on where everything was at, what needed doing, any nuances people needed to keep in mind when dealing with the clients and the relevant talent. I had most of it in order when Meg arrived asking, 'You're back?'

'You can see me can't you, so I must be,' I grumbled.

'Oooh and you brought a little ray of sunshine with you,' she smirked.

'Sorry,' I conceded. 'I didn't sleep well.'

'I hope you're not worrying about those journos, or Delia. She's secretly glad for all the publicity, you know,' she whispered.

'They weren't there when I came in. Have they gone?'

'Nope. They're holding on, sure you'll appear sooner or later and look, here you are,' she grinned and we both knew my presence was only going to reignite their enthusiasm.

'Have you seen what they're saying?' I asked. I had been too afraid to look, but I suddenly needed to know, needed the full picture of what was happening. I couldn't stick my head in the sand any longer. Not with everything else that was happening. But I didn't want to read the articles, the highlights would be enough and I knew Jay wasn't going to tell me what they were.

'They're wondering if the party girl got fired. Speculating over why, those sorts of things. They really do have good imaginations, don't they?'

I smiled.

'Oh and they keep and asking whatever happened to the bodyguard you ran away with,' she chuckled. 'They're not all that good if the story's not smushed in their faces, are they?'

'Investigative journalism is definitely not their thing. They get paid for the pictures and that's all they care about. The more curious the picture, the more outrageous, the more they can interpret from it with their creative headlines, the more money they get. It's all about the money. Imagine living with no humanity in your heart,' I pondered out loud.

'A sad state indeed,' she agreed. 'My favourite though, is that online gossip site, you know the bright blue one, can't think of its name, anyway, they dead-set think you had Cam Taylor's baby in secret and are mad at your folks for making you give it away. They think that's why there's no Jay, he found out and dumped you.'

'Are you serious? Cam assaulted me, but with his mouth and only his mouth. Jay threw him and his hard-on, still in his jeans by the way, to the floor. That was when my father figured out Jay and I were sleeping together. There was a whole scene. It was awful. But I have never been anywhere near Cam Taylor's nude penis, that's ridiculous,' I laughed.

'Never?' she asked.

'No, never,' I defended. 'I slept with a lot men, forgot a lot of them most of the time too, but Cam Taylor and Lincoln Cummins were always off limits. It went both ways, they were like brothers. But Cam, after Linc left, he just, he was mad and drunk and he didn't know what to do with any of it,' I defended, although I didn't know why I'd defend Cam after what he did, but what I'd said was true, he was like a brother until that night when everything went to hell. 'Delia's really not angry?' I asked changing the subject.

'No, seriously. Her face and the company name are all over the internet. She's loving it. She's got so much new business coming in, she's not sure what to do with it all,' she grinned.

I was glad Delia wasn't too upset and what they were writing wasn't the worst they'd ever written about me. I sipped my cold coffee and checked for any new emails, making sure I'd sorted everything I needed to. There wasn't much to see though. Shannon had been taking care of any enquiries and keeping clients and talent updated on schedules and events and upcoming jobs, liaising with venues and doing a great job of it.

Delia would surely promote her as soon as a position became available. The way things were going, that was likely to be mine.

I said hi to a few people, gossiped about weekends and boys in the kitchen while making more coffee and eating the cake Barb from accounts had brought in. Leftovers from a party she always said and we all played along ignoring the fact we knew her husband disappeared for days.

With the sugar surging through my veins and a fresh cup of coffee, I cleared the last few messages from my voicemail, returned the only call that needed returning and started flicking through my physical mail. I didn't get much and suspected most of it would end up in the recycling bin. Usually, I wouldn't even check it for days at a time but I wanted everything sorted and clean before I left. A shiny white envelope caught my eye, it was like those fancy invitations that came in for Clary and I thought, finally, my luck was changing and I was going to be invited somewhere interesting. It wasn't just Clary who got all the good invites, even Meg got invited places as a Key Account Manager, just not me. But then, knowing my luck it *was* just an invite to Robbo's Chickens grand opening.

As soon as I opened the invitation I could see it was not for Robbo's, there were two entwined rings at the top, it was a wedding invitation. I didn't know anyone getting married so I quickly read down, and the swirly calligraphy read: *we request your pleasure in attending the wedding of Georges Barbier to Miss Jasmine Harrington.*

I dropped the invitation, gasped so loud that Meg stood up

to see if I was okay. I waved her off, shoved the invitation into my bag and called out I was done. I had to go. I could see Delia poking her head up as I rushed past and out the door. I didn't even wait for the lift and ran down the stairs.

I just had to get out. I needed air, I needed to be somewhere else, to think, to digest, to something, I wasn't even sure what.

The journos started scrambling as soon as they saw me and I pushed through, knocking them aside and ran down the street. I couldn't go home after it had been violated. I couldn't be at work. I didn't know what to do so I went down the steps to The Fox and Hound pub, our office local. They'd serve me coffee or soft drink and let me hide in a booth for a while, it was still early in the day, they wouldn't mind. I'd be safe in a corner and I could compose myself, think straight just for a minute then I'd be able to speak a word and a sentence and call Jay and let him know where I was and that I was okay.

I stood at the bar waiting to be served wondering where the annoying blonde was. Meg and I made fun of the way she flirted with all the men and the teeny tiny shorts she wore but she wasn't there and while I waited for the chatty part-time footballer to finish with his customer down the other end of the bar, I looked at the wall of liquor behind the bar.

'Hey! What can I get you?' he asked with a familiar smile.

But before I mumbled the words vodka neat I looked to the other side of the dimly lit room and there he was as though I'd asked and he appeared. Sitting at a table in the dark corner getting cosy with the missing blonde barmaid. He was looking at her in that way, smiling that way and flirting his arse off and she was loving every second. I could survive a lot of things, the journos, the lies, the crazies, invitations to my own wedding to a guy I don't know, but I couldn't survive losing Jay. He was my everything. Tears welled in my eyes as he leant in with that look of lust and whispered something in her ear, an avalanche building behind my eyes.

It can't be, I thought. No, no, it can't, he wouldn't. But as the barmaid placed her plastic nailed hand on his arm, as she giggled like a twelve year old, he giggled too and his head turned just enough for me to clearly see his face. Jay. Flirting with her as though they were old friends, as though they did this all the time, right down the street from where I worked, ten minutes from my home.

I watched for another minute, watched him whisper things in her ear, watched her giggle and shake her head while giving him the eyes. I couldn't move. What had happened to my life? All of a sudden, in the blink of an eye, I had nothing. Everything, all the years of hard work, everything I'd sacrificed, everything we had sacrificed, was for nothing. It'd all been ripped away and I watched from across the room as the love of my life, hooked his finger into the chain around her neck, played with the bauble on the end and then whispered some more in her ear while her perfect little Arianna Grande face wrinkled as she laughed.

A couple of guys in business suits came in, stood beside me, blocking my view as they waited to be served. I didn't know where to go, what to do, I couldn't breathe, I could hardly see. I couldn't go home, what if he was planning to take her there after their rendezvous? Then I saw Michael come in from the back, from the bathrooms heading for Jay and it was too much to realise everyone knew how he spent his time.

I stumbled off the stool and headed for the door.

A couple of journos had followed and waited and took their chance to photograph me leaving the bar. A few followed me as I walked across the city.

Michael called but I couldn't answer my phone, I didn't know what to say. Fear filled every cell of my body. Jay called. I answered but I couldn't speak. I was barely holding on to a sob that would quickly translate into an avalanche and I refused to cry with a camera in my face. It was all their bloody fault anyway. Before I knew it I was screaming incoherently at them while the shutters clicked. I shoved one out of the way and I ran. I ran until they gave up, until they had enough money shots to last them a while. Then I slowed to a walk and before I knew what I was doing, I was standing in front of Ainsley's café.

I stood staring at the pretty painted window until Sam came out. 'What are you doing, Jaz? You okay?'

I nodded and went to leave.

'Hey, why don't you come in for a cuppa?' he asked, catching my elbow.

I didn't know what to do, so I nodded and followed him inside.

'Jaz, hey!' cried Ainsley. 'Are you okay?' she asked as she took in my face, which must have looked less composed than I thought. 'Jo, you good? We're going to go upstairs,' she said to the brunette behind the counter who waved us off as though the café wasn't a bustling busy place.

I got halfway up the stairs and stopped. I couldn't drag Ainsley into this, she had a child, was growing a baby. I had to go so I mumbled an apology and left with Ainsley and Sam calling after me. Sam would be on the phone to Michael, to Jay and Tom and Christian and everyone else. I felt like a wild animal and I just wanted to break free and be left alone. I couldn't breathe. I couldn't think. It was too much. I just needed a quiet place to think, get my head together, make sense of everything that was happening, find some perspective.

I waved down a taxi and made him drive me home. It was the only place I knew. I couldn't go inside. But I hadn't taken a key to the hotel either. Jay had probably checked us out when he'd left anyway.

Rundle Street was busy so the driver dropped me a few doors down from my building on the corner in front of the Austral pub. I looked across the road to Cibo's thinking a coffee was just what I needed, but then the door to the Austral opened and the smell of beer wafted out and my decision was made. I walked through the doors of the Austral. Without Jay I might as well go back to Dad's prison or that facility on the other side of the planet. It didn't matter where I went now. Nothing was ever going to be the same. I wasn't going to be the same. Everything that mattered was over and I didn't care if it was here or there or in a ditch under a bridge. I didn't want to exist without Jay.

It was dark inside, the kind of place you could get lost in for hours or days. I ordered a double vodka neat and a bottle of sparkling wine, whatever they had, I didn't care. My hands shook as I waited for the hipster serving me to bring me my drinks. I paid him with cash, I didn't need someone to see where I was by using my card because I knew once Sam called Michael he'd have someone checking something by now. But maybe it was never about creepy stalkers for them? Maybe this whole time, this whole weekend was about Jay trying to offload me with minimal damage. He knew my family would catch me.

I sat at a table staring at my drinks. It had to happen sooner or later. I'd even told Lydia over the weekend Jay didn't really want to marry me, it was just something he said in the moment, he didn't really mean it. He couldn't. I was too messed up to marry. I'd told her I was sure if he spent enough time with me, he'd see it. Clearly he'd spent enough time, saw enough. This was just too much Harrington, the last straw, the camel back breaking straw. He was done. He wanted an easier life, a wife who could give him children without the risk of fucking them up. A wife who went to work each day and came home to him every night and made him breakfast and ironed his shirts and whatever the hell else regular women did for their men.

All the secret conversations, all the silent, unspoken words between him and Tom hadn't been about my protection at all. Even Michael coming back to the city was about getting me out of the way so Jay could move on.

The worst thing was, I didn't blame him. He was right. He deserved all of those things. Things I didn't even know how to give him because growing up a Harrington you learn a lot of things but making breakfast and doing housework and whatever else regular people do, wasn't one of them. I'd lived a life of privilege. I had a housekeeper tending to my every need.

I knew how to bake cookies because of that housekeeper's kindness but a roast or folding socks, those were things Harrington children didn't learn but Jay deserved a wife who could match socks and do the washing and know how often to use a vacuum.

I threw the double shot of vodka into my mouth. The burn took my breath but I closed my eyes and savoured the feel of it as it slowly seeped into my veins, as the numbing began to move through my body. Suddenly I remembered all the heavenly feelings and why I liked this so much. How had I so easily forgotten? Love, because I'd loved Jay. He'd become my addiction and I chose him over vodka. I loved him more than vodka and I wanted to be the person he deserved. I'd tried. I'd really tried and until Tom's wedding, I'd been doing a great job. I'd thought so. I'd thought we had a great thing going. He'd made me believe it just yesterday in bed. How can someone do those beautiful things to another person if they don't love them? Was it so good because it was goodbye? Then I imagined him doing those things to that woman, her touching him, calling his name as he did lovely, delicious things to her body.

I poured the sparkling into the glass and shakily raised the glass to my lips, sipping, savouring the sweet bubbles fizzing on my tongue.

I worked my way through the bottle as the bar around me filled with lunch patrons. It was easy to be lost among them. I watched for the bar staff to change and got another vodka. I was already unsteady on my feet but I didn't care. I no longer cared if I drank myself into oblivion, literal oblivion where nothing existed, not my lying family, not my cheating boyfriend.

The barmaid eventually dropped a bowl of wedges I didn't order on the table and went back to the bar. I ate them even though they weren't mine.

When the bottle of sparkling was empty I looked to the bar, the staff were the same so I knew there was no way they were serving me again. I went to the bathroom thinking after that I'd just go somewhere else. I was a great faker. It was an acquired skill of an alcoholic.

I'm not sure how long I was in the bathroom. I woke with vomit pooling between my feet. I left a scrawled note of apology for the poor person who had to clean up my mess, rinsed my shoes in the sink then left via a side door.

Chapter 10

I stood on the little side street outside of the pub not sure where to go. I could go back to Ainsley's? But the hustle and bustle on Rundle Street told me the business day was over. Ainsley's café would be closed. I could call Christian? I pulled out my phone but it was flat. I couldn't remember when I'd last charged it. The morning before, maybe at Jay's. Jay. My Jay. I'd never be there again, at the pub, in his bed, overlooking the ocean. It was over, our beautiful, perfect life was over.

I walked across town, wandering aimlessly like the drunk I was until I found a bottle shop and went in and bought a bottle of vodka. It had always been my drink of choice. I used to put it in my water bottle and take it to school. That's how much I liked it. And like a good little black dress, vodka went with everything, my morning orange juice, lemonade, ice cubes. It wasn't so great in coffee, I remembered with a smile, but there were other things that were. Baileys had replaced my milk by the time I was fifteen. I smiled at the memory. I could barely remember that person, that life. It all seemed so far away now.

Everything seemed so far away. I didn't even know who I was now. I was pathetic to be so lost without a man, that I was defined by a man but it wasn't any man, it was Jay. He was the love of my life, the only thing, only person who'd ever meant anything to me. The only person who'd ever believed in me, seen me when no one else had bothered to look. None of it mattered without him. The job, Delia, being safe, protecting myself from creepy stalkers, none of it mattered.

I spread my arms wide, 'Come and get me fucker,' I called to the man who so desperately wanted to marry me, he was prepared to break into my house and send me an invitation to my own wedding. The creepy fool could have me if I didn't die at the bottom of this bottle, I laughed as I took another swig.

I went to walk to the parklands but got as far as the alleyway behind the deserted factory one street over. They were clearly preparing it for renovations but they'd packed up for the day and for now it was as good a place as any to die so I sat against the wall and waited, drank and waited some more.

'Hey girl, what are you doing here?' asked a grey-haired woman carrying bags of possessions.

I shrugged.

'Oh honey, it can't be that bad,' she soothed.

'I'm sorry, is this your spot?' I asked. I supposed there were rules and hierarchy on the streets, just like at the office and amongst the fancy folk of my past, yet another hierarchy I didn't understand or belong in. I was Jasmine bloody Harrington and I didn't belong anywhere.

'It's okay, I can share,' she said. 'Can you?' she asked, indicating the bottle of vodka in my hands.

I shrugged, handed it to her and curled up on the cement and closed my eyes.

'That's it sweetie, sleep it off. I'll look out for you,' she said.

'Please don't take my money,' I begged. 'I worked really hard for my money,' I tried to say as sleep claimed me.

I woke as car doors slammed and voices carried from the front of the building. The lady was gone but she'd left me a bag of McDonalds with a note apologising for using my money but promising she only took enough to buy breakfast. I checked my purse and she was right, it was all there except for the $10 note the bottle shop had given me in change.

I picked myself up as I heard the workmen coming through the building and disappeared down the side alley. I wound my way over to the parklands and sat under a tree to eat my McMuffin and hash browns. The woman had left me a little vodka so I added it to the orange juice she'd bought me and just like that the old Jaz was back.

I slept a little longer under the tree. I was still in my work clothes from the day before so no one would be booting me out like a homeless person anytime soon. When I woke, I wound my way back to Rundle Street, went into the Exeter on the other side of the street from the day before's haunt and found an equally dark corner in which to drown my sorrows.

I liked these bars that had hidden dark corners. I hadn't needed them last time I was drinking, there was no one to stop me, no one to question me, until Jay. And just like that it all came flooding back. I had no one left, nowhere to go. I couldn't go home. I couldn't face him. I couldn't bear to have him look me in the eye and lie his arse off. God forbid he tell poor, fragile

Jaz the truth. No, he orchestrates my brothers and my sister to sort out how to cushion the blow, to protect me from the fallout. My showing up must have really thrown a spanner into things. Sped up his plan. I suppose that's something, that he cared enough to make sure I'd be okay.

Some guy, who looked as well kept as the homeless woman from the night before, sat at the table with me, put a bottle of vodka in the middle and two shot glasses beside it.

'You look like you could use a friend,' he said.

People like me always find people like me. Somehow we didn't even have to try. We were like moths to flames. I shrugged and he poured and we wiled away the afternoon grunting at each other about how fucked up life was until he invited me home.

I almost said yes. Jaz, The Princess of Party, would have said yes, but I wasn't ready to give that last piece of the reclaimed Jaz up yet. Jay was the last man to touch me, his two-day growth had left an impression in the most delicious of places in the most incredible ways and even though I knew I had to, he clearly didn't want me anymore, I wasn't ready to replace those memories yet, those feelings, the exquisitely beautiful feel of him. I dropped a fifty dollar note on the table to cover the vodka, Harrington's never left indebted, and I went out the side door, stumbled across the street and down the back alley that led to the back of my building. Perhaps I could go to the car park and sleep in my car? No, the creep knows my car as well as he knows where I work and where I live.

I sat on the kerb, lent against a dumpster and watched the windows of my apartment. The lights were off. Had Jay gone back to the pub already? Was Michael waiting for me? Was anyone? Was Jay in there with her? No one moved. I pulled out the leftover vodka the homeless woman had left me and drank from the bottle as I watched. There was no movement. He'd gone.

I took the back lift up to my apartment, there was no point hiding anymore. There was no one to hide from, no one but some crazy fool intent on marrying me and at this point if he wanted in on this, more power to him, I chuckled as the lift deposited me on my floor.

Inside my apartment, everything looked in order, from what I could see, not that I could see very well. I got as far as the hallway, only steps from my bedroom before my legs gave out, and I slept where I fell.

Chapter 11

I knew where I was before I opened my eyes. The smell of salt, the ocean, cooking bacon and Aussie man told me I was at Jay's. It had always been a second home. Especially in summer when I could step out onto the balcony with a mug of tea and look out at the ocean. Or watch Jay surf as I drank my morning coffee. But those days were over. Despite my pounding head, I hadn't forgotten. I was yesterday's news so I didn't know what the hell I was doing here on his couch.

How I got here was a mystery, well not so much a mystery but I didn't remember coming here. The last thing I remember was falling asleep in my hallway, my equilibrium claimed by vodka. If Michael had found me after all, he should have just shipped me over to Christian's. Maybe Christian didn't want me. No one wanted drunk Jaz around, especially not around their toddler or their pregnant wife.

Unable to return to sleep I lay on the sofa looking out the big sliding door windows that overlooked the ocean. If I stared at it long enough could I get lost in the water, I wondered? I knew I couldn't but I wished for it anyway.

'I know you're awake, Babe, why don't you sit up and I'll make you some tea,' Jay called from the kitchen.

I sat up, slowly, unwillingly, knowing it was easier than pretending he was wrong. He is a trained professional with sensitive hearing among his repertoire of now useless skills. 'Don't call me, Babe,' I spat, wrapping a blanket around my shoulders and crossing my legs on the couch.

'Here,' he half smiled, handing me the hot cup of tea. 'Why not?' he asked.

'Seriously? I saw you Jay. With her. That woman from the bar near my work. Flirting, having a drink together in the dark corner, getting all touchy feely. Did you take her back to my place when you were done? Did you fuck her in my bed?'

'What? Don't be ridiculous, Jaz. I didn't fuck anyone. You are the only woman I even think about fucking,' he dared to sound shocked and annoyed.

'You flirted your arse off, you wanted something from her,' I spat.

'Yeah. Information, Jaz. Information on your bloody stalker. I can't bloody believe, after everything we've been through, you'd think that little of me?'

I didn't speak. I didn't know what else to say. I was ashamed and he was right to be mad at me.

'Or do you really think that little of yourself?' He asked.

I wondered if he knew how much closer he was.

'Bloody hell Jaz. I don't know what else I can do to prove to you I love you. I gave up everything for you. You're it for me. How do you not know that?'

'I guess I just always thought you'd eventually see the dark in me, you'd see my father. If you looked long enough, hard enough. Sometimes I remember, when I'm going to sleep I think about that time, when we met and what I did and I can't stand myself Jay. I guess I thought one day you'd wake up and think what the hell am I doing?'

'Jesus, Jaz. Is that why you would never live here?'

I shrugged.

'How the hell am I supposed to deal with this stuff if you don't talk to me? I thought we were more than that? I never thought we were one of those couples?'

'I was afraid to say it. Afraid that if I said it you'd realise I was right.'

'Never. Never,' he insisted, his voice raspy as he pulled my head to his lips. 'I'd never speak to Lisa like that if I wasn't desperate to find the freak intent on marrying the love of my bloody life.'

'Marrying me? You know about the invitation?'

'You know?'

I nodded. 'I got one.'

'So did Tom, Christian and your bloody father. Even Delia got one. Called me after you'd left yesterday freaking out.'

'I'm sorry I left without calling you or Michael. I spun out. I saw the invitation and I just couldn't think. I couldn't breathe. My brain stopped working.'

'Come on,' he said, reaching for my hand, helping me up and leading me out through the doors that had been holding me back from the call of the blue ocean and we sat on the deck. The water was still at this time of day and the late afternoon sun was squeezing down to us the last of its warmth for the day. It was a clear sky so I would need more than a shawl if we sat out here for too long. But for now, the golden rays and my warm tea felt nice.

'So what's going on Jaz? After everything and I know the last couple of weeks have been off the charts but you were doing okay. I thought you were doing okay. Why did you drink?' he asked finally.

I shrugged, suddenly ashamed, feeling ridiculous. I didn't want to discuss it with him. I didn't want him to know. I couldn't look at his face, I couldn't bear the disappointment in his eyes.

'Babe, why? I can't help you if I don't know why.'

'You. Her. I thought I'd lost you. I can lose anything, Jay. I could lose anything else, all of it and I'd be okay. But losing you...' I couldn't even finish the sentence.

He held me to him, held me tight and when he spoke his voice was tight. 'You didn't lose me, Jaz,' he said kindly. 'You will never lose me, never and I'd never take another woman to bed. I couldn't. I love you. I love you more than anything. You're my girl, Jaz, that's all there is to it.'

'So what were you talking to her about? What information do you think that woman had for you because I doubt she knows much about weather patterns and surfing?'

He gave a slight chuckle, 'No, no she does not,' he shook his head as if thinking the idea she might was too funny to mention. 'But she does know people and I needed to find this stalker.'

I nodded. 'The man who thinks he's going to marry me? Fine,' I huffed. 'Did she? Know anything?'

'Some guy had been lurking at strange times. Lurkers aren't uncommon she said, but usually they're locals, faces she remembers but this guy she didn't know but all she could say was he was average this and average that.

'How mad is Michael?'

He smirked. 'I won't leave you alone with him for a while, let's just leave it at that.'

'I'm sorry.'

'He was worried sick. Then Sam called when you went to Ainsley's but you ran out too fast.'

'I didn't want to involve Ainsley. Not with the baby and everything. I didn't mean to go there. I was just walking and I was there and I didn't know where Christian worked or where they lived and it wouldn't be right with Henry and the baby anyway, so I left.'

'Where did you go?'

'Home. I didn't know what else to do but the road was busy and the taxi stopped at the Austral, on the corner and I was going to go to Cibos. I didn't know if you were taking her back to my place when you were done so I was just going to hang out there and then the door to the Austral opened and I smelt the stale beer and like a magnet, I went in. I just wanted to forget. I wanted that image of the two of you out of my head and being sober didn't matter any more, not without you, not without the life we'd built.'

'And so you drank?'

'I didn't plan it. I just wanted to forget. Nothing mattered without you, my job, my sobriety, none of it. That was all I could see, so yeah, I drank.'

'It was one of the only places we didn't look. I didn't think you'd go back.'

'My hand shook so badly I could barely lift the glass, then I puked over my shoes in the bathroom'

'Like old times then,' he joked.

'Shut up,' I laughed.

'Where did you go after that? They wouldn't have let you stay.'

I didn't want to go home in case you were there doing...' I shook the image out of my head and kept going. 'I wandered a while until I found a bottle shop and made a friend at the back of an old warehouse where I slept the night. She didn't steal my money and brought me breakfast. I put vodka in my orange juice, walked back to Rundle Street, drank shots with some sleaze at the Exeter, gave him fifty bucks for the vodka as an apology for not going home with him, then went to the alley out the back of my place and watched the window. You were gone. I thought you'd given up on me so I figured it didn't matter if the freak came in and found me. Nothing mattered.'

'I hate that he was in your house,' he said, and I could see the anger rising in him.

'I wasn't there Jay,' I reminded him.

'But you could have been, Jaz,' he reminded me. 'You kept it all from me for a bloody week, more. He could have been there any one of those nights and what would you have done?'

I shrugged like a child while he vented at me, trying not to cry because he was right and I didn't deserve to cry.

'Anything could have happened there and I wouldn't have known. Jaz I can't protect you if you don't tell me things,' he yelled as he ran his hand through his hair in frustration.

'You shouldn't have to protect me anymore Jay,' I defended. 'Everything is so fucked up. All I did was go to my brother's wedding. It's not fair,' I cried. Couldn't he see that it wasn't just my freedom I was protecting? It was him. I'd do anything to keep him safe and I knew that once he knew he'd do anything in his power to protect me, even give his own life. I couldn't let him give his life for mine. His was worth far more than mine. Couldn't he see that?

'I know, it's not fair, Babe, it's not. I can still call you Babe, can't I?' he asked with a smirk, all the anger seeming to have dissipated. He could do that. Be furious one moment and not the next. He didn't hold a grudge. He said his piece and he moved on. I guess he'd seen a lot, he knew what life meant, what mattered.

'Shut up,' I laughed, snuggling in to him.

'I can't believe you didn't trust me. That you didn't believe in us. You say I'm your everything Jaz. You are mine. You are my heart and my soul. You didn't believe in me, you didn't trust me and it hurts, Jaz. What have we been doing all these years if you don't bloody trust me? Everyone else, I get it. But I'm not everyone else Jaz and it could have gotten you bloody killed.'

He was mad. He radiated it. He vibrated with it and it sliced at me that I did that to him, that I made him think he wasn't enough. That he could think for a second he wasn't the one person in the world I did trust. The one person I loved more than my own life. Couldn't he see that?

'I could still feel where you'd been on my body the day before but watching you, it seemed so clear and I didn't blame you, you deserve better than me, Jay. You always have. You deserve someone who can look after you, who knows how to care for you the way you deserve.'

He held my face in front of his, kissed me hard and fast. 'You give me everything I need. You are everything I want. You are already more than I deserve. Don't ever think you're not,' he begged. 'You're my world, Jaz. I searched the fucking city for two days looking for you thinking that fucker had taken you, that he'd won, and I'd lost you,' he cried. 'I can't fucking lose you. I can't.'

He carried me to his bed and made love to me like they do in the movies, with kindness and sweetness so pure and beautiful and joyful that it filled my eyes with tears, good, happy, tears and then he wrapped me in his arms, holding me as though that alone would save us.

I blinked into the morning light, the remnants of my binge still clung like webs but were easing thanks to all the water and Panadol Jay had force-fed me. A smile took over my face when I realised Jay's arms and legs were still wrapped tight around me as though he were afraid I'd escape while he slept. It wasn't often I woke to find him still in bed so I enjoyed it when I did.

I carefully extricated myself, not wanting to wake him because he'd barely slept in the days I was gone. I went barefoot to the kitchen to make coffee, the warmth of the morning sun already overpowering the chill of the night. Looking through the glass doors out over the ocean while the kettle boiled I watched the waves crashing to the shore. He was missing a great morning for surfing. It was clear Jay's overprotective side had kicked into gear. With Jay's history what it was, I knew he wouldn't be letting me out of his sight again anytime soon. I had really scared him. It was a really shitty thing to do, especially with everything going on. I should never have disappeared like I did but I wasn't thinking. I was barely functioning after I'd seen him with the barmaid and lapsed into the only coping mechanism I knew other than Jay.

Then I couldn't see what was real and right. Drinking did that to me, it wiped me clean. Guilt began to twist in my stomach, not even eased by his casual kiss on the side of my head as he passed on his way to the cupboard. I hadn't even heard him get up.

He placed his mug on the cupboard beside mine and looked at me. 'You look good,' he smiled.

'I feel good,' I smiled back through the guilt that was trying to overpower me. 'I'm sorry Jay,'

'Hey, it's okay. It's a miracle it was the only setback you've had. It's been a tough few days. I get it.'

'It's the last one too, I promise. You don't have to worry about me Jay,'

'I know.'

'Then why does the surf look so lonely this morning?'

'It's not lonely. Look the boys are out there doing their thing,' he joked. 'Babe, the surf will keep. I just wanted to hang out with you this morning,'

'Well it was nice to have you wrapped around me when I woke up,' I told him.

'Then why did you leave me?' he asked, nuzzling my neck.

I giggled. 'I needed coffee. I really needed coffee.'

He laughed. 'I don't doubt it,' he said tapping my nose as we took our coffee out onto the deck to watch the morning take its place.

An old couple were walking their dog on the beach and raised their hand in a neighbourly wave. We snuggled on the love seat. It was always nice here, everything seemed to work at a different pace, time was in slow motion. Unfortunately the rest of the world wasn't, so as nice as it was sitting cocooned in Jay's arms in the morning air, I went to shower.

I had just turned the water on when Jay knocked on the door.

'Yeah?' I called to him.

'Babe? What ya doin?'

'Ah, showering?'

'Why?'

'I can't just sit here and do nothing, Jay.'

'That's exactly what you're going to do.'

'What like some bird in its gilded cage? I'm stuck up here in the tower, locked away from the world.'

'You're being dramatic. It's not like that and you know it. I'm not him, Jaz.'

'I know, I'm sorry,' I said, turning off the water and reaching for the towel he held out of my reach. 'What are you doing?'

'Enjoying the view,' he smirked as he stepped towards me with that predatory look in his eye.

He'd kicked his board shorts to the floor before he reached

me. His mouth locked on to mine, desperate, wild. He was claiming me, owning me.

'It seems I need to remind you that you're the only woman I want to fuck,' he declared as his hands began to do those incredible things that had me sighing, that left me putty in his hands.

His mouth never left mine as he edged me back into the bedroom, onto his bed. Then it began making its way down my body, licking, sucking, nipping until he made it between my legs and I lost all conscious thought.

'Remembering yet?' he asked as he drank a glass of water and watched me recovering with a grin on his face.

'Maybe,' I joked.

'Maybe?' he asked with a smirk before getting down to the business of really reminding me.

He made himself clear, very clear and I could feel the smug look on my face that matched the one I could see on his face. But it didn't change our reality.

'Seriously though, Jay, what are we going to do? I can't just sit here doing nothing. I'm not built that way. You're not built that way,' I said as we ate breakfast in bed feeling rather satisfied.

'You think I'm doing nothing? You forget how good a multi tasker I am, Jaz,' he smiled. 'I can appreciate my girl and have people finding out what's going on.'

'Are they? Finding anything?

'I have no idea what they've found in the last two hours, I was a little distracted but seeing as you're safe right here in my bed, I wasn't in a hurry to ask anyone questions.'

'Well now that your reminding has been taken care of can you see if our lives are going back to normal any time soon?'

'Oh I like it when you're bossy,' he said, claiming my mouth before stretching over to the bedside for his phone.

'Anything?' I asked impatiently.

'Not yet.'

A knock at the door interrupted further discussion, so Jay threw on clothes and went out to open it. I followed him after doing the same and he was talking to Sarah from the pub, telling her to manage whatever was going on because he wasn't going down.

'Jay, you can't not work as well.'

'I can do whatever the damn hell I like, Jaz, I own the place. Sarah can manage, can't you? She'll call in some help and it'll be fine.'

'Sure, it's no problem, Jaz, its fine. It's managed,' she smiled before sheepishly leaving us alone.

'I'm okay, Jay. I'll be okay.'

'Jaz, you just went on a booze-filled bender. Some creep who thinks he's marrying you broke into your apartment. You are not okay and I'm not leaving you here alone.'

'I'm not a child Jay.'

'And I'm not an idiot. I know you, Jaz. You'll sit here and you'll worry and you'll wallow and you'll do something stupid to try and fix it.'

'Someone needs to do something.'

'Plenty of people are doing plenty.'

'Fine,' I groaned like a child, flopping onto the couch. 'I'll just sit here then like a helpless bloody vegetable.'

'Sulky Jaz is just as hot as bossy Jaz, you know,' he grinned.

'You have a one-track mind,' I laughed.

'What the hell else are we supposed to do?' he laughed, clearly as frustrated by confinement as I was. We weren't the kind of people who sat around doing nothing. Especially not when the weather was beautiful and the waves were up. We worked, we played, we lived.

We whiled away the next 24 hours though as best we could with Netflix and sex and pizza. It was just like the old days when I'd sleep on Jay's couch after a night of too much partying, too drunk for him to send home. It really wasn't such a bad way to spend our time but then Jay really did have to go downstairs to check on some things and I was alone with my thoughts and nothing to do.

I was wracked with guilt and shame. So much shame. I'd worked so hard to be a good person, a functioning person, the person Jay could love and I'd slept in the gutter and puked on my shoes in a pub. Again. How could he look at me, love me?

He was right. He'd known exactly what my brain was going to do the minute he left me alone. I'd promised him I wouldn't so I had to distract myself. I messaged Meg to see what was happening at the office.

'Delia's going ahead with Chicken Men auditions for tomorrow,' she told me.

'What? Without me?'

'Robbo couldn't wait any longer, he needs a Chicken Man.'

'Who's doing it?' I asked, cringing at the thought of someone else doing my job. Sure, I might not get the fancy accounts, but they were mine. Robbo's was my account.

'Me,' she said with a sad face emoji.

That made me laugh. At least it wasn't someone else. At least it wasn't Clary. But of course it wouldn't be Clary, she'd die first.

'I'll try and come in and save you,' I told her.

'I was hoping you'd say that. But Delia will kill you.'

'She'll have to get in line, seems there's a queue,' I joked.

'????' she asked.

'Don't worry about it. Besides, you're giving me all the goss on Olly tomorrow night, I'm not missing that!' I told her. 'How many journos are still hanging on?'

'Actually, they seem to be giving up. Mostly gone. Weak as water they are,' she sent with a smiley face. 'I miss you. This place is sooooo dull without you.'

I missed her too. I didn't have a lot of friends, not in the city anyway. It was a result of my former life. I was too cautious about who I let in. I had friends out here though, at the beach, it was easier to see people's truths out here and I had Jay. Everyone was friends with Jay which meant they were friends with me by default. No ulterior motives in that.

Jay and I had been doing this thing we had for a while now, so I had built up a few things in his wardrobe, thankfully and threw on a pair of slimline black pants I forgot I owned and a pale pink t-shirt. I found a pair of low-heeled court shoes in the back of the closet. That'd do for a Friday.

'Where do you think you're going?' Jay asked. He was lying shirtless on the bed with his arms behind his head.

'Going to work. The coast is clear. No more journos and

Robbo needs his Chicken Man. Delia booked the auditions for today and if I don't do it, it goes to someone else. That's just the beginning. I lose one account and then they all start to fall. I've worked too hard, Jay.' I ran a brush through my hair swiped on some lip-gloss and went in search of my bag. Surely Jay brought it when he rescued me from the floor of my apartment. Then I remembered I had no car and was at Jay's mercy. No wonder he wasn't putting up much of a fight. I looked at him and he smiled.

'C'mon Jay, I have to go to work, just for a little bit, just for the auditions, I promise.'

'I'm coming with you.'

'You're not going to sit in my office are you?' This would be interesting, I thought. Jay hated the city. He especially hated the corporate wasteland of forgotten dreams, the city became during the week. His words, not mine. I love the city. I love the buzz. I love the anonymity it brought. Most of all I love being self-sufficient and being a number, sitting on a bus or walking across a crowded intersection with the hundreds of others on their way to their cubicles and offices drowned in artificial light and recycled air. It was heaven.

I wasn't sure what was scaring Jay the most. My meltdown or my stalker. It was clear by that look on his face, I had no choice though. If I was going in to work, Jay was coming too. It was like the old days. When he was just my bodyguard and I'd continually tried to get rid of him, upset him, freak him out hoping it'd be too much but he'd just give me that look that said do what you like, say what you like, you won't win, you won't beat me, I'm not leaving. I had no idea what he and

Tom actually did in the army, he didn't talk about it, it was one of the only banned subjects we had, but whatever it was, he'd developed a hard as nails skin and a no nonsense look that went with it. Many withered under it but back in the day I'd taken it as a challenge. I'd gotten weak.

'Fine, then,' I huffed, finally locating my bag at the end of the sofa and walking to the door as he threw on a t-shirt he'd found on the floor. I rolled my eyes and headed straight for the car.

After a long drive into the city with Jay controlling the music, he eventually parked the car and walked me to my favourite caffeine supplier, ordered me a giant latte, figuring if I had that much caffeine, I'd have no need to leave for more, then he walked me to the front door of the office.

'I'm going down the street to speak to Lisa. Now swear to me you won't leave the office until I come back for you at five, or you call me.'

I nodded, grumbling, 'Ahuh.'

'Promise me Jaz or I'm not leaving and I'll sit up in that office for the whole day. I don't care what Delia says.'

I knew he would too, stubborn bastard so I said, 'Fine, I swear, I promise, is there a grave I should declare it on?'

'Don't get smart,' he laughed. 'Now don't go nuts on me. I'm just going to talk to her, I'll leave and I'm going back to your place, alone, to catch up on some book work.'

'I'm fine Jay, go,' I insisted. He was like the parent of a five year old on the first day of school. 'Go,' I laughed, playfully pushing him.

'Fine, fine, I'm gone,' he said, strolling down the street

towards the pub after I'd scanned my pass and was safe inside the building.

Chapter 12

'What are you doing here?' asked Delia when I stuck my head in her office.

'Working. I heard you scheduled auditions.'

'Meg!' she screamed but Meg wasn't in yet, only Shannon and accounts were in.

'Don't blame her, it's not her fault. I asked, she told. She told me she had it under control but the journos are gone, so she doesn't need to do my job.'

Delia sighed. 'You know there's more going on than journos, surely?'

I nodded.

She slapped a copy of the newspaper from Tuesday with me coming out of the pub dazed and confused and then beside it, a copy of the wedding invitation.

'I'd heard you'd gotten one too?'

'Good, so you do know,' she sighed.

'I know. Jay knows. Everyone knows. The whole Harrington clan are looking into it.'

'That's it? They're looking into it? This guy means business, Jaz. He's serious. He keeps calling reception. We're not sure how many times he's done it or what Shannon might have said before she realised what was going on. He does it under different guises, changes his voice. It was a while before Shannon caught on. She thought he was just an eager chicken man. He might still be, we don't know. I'm not putting you in a room with a bunch of strange blokes when he could be one of them. That's why I didn't call you. That's why I gave it to Meg. She should have kept her mouth shut.'

'She didn't know what she was doing. Did she?'

'I don't think so.'

'Well I'm here now, I'll just help her.'

'Why can't you just go home?' she asked exasperated.

'Because Jay had an appointment. I'm not allowed to leave without him,' I said, feeling victorious for the first time since Tom's wedding.

'Fine,' she sighed. 'But you're never alone with them, do you hear me? I'm not going to be responsible for whatever happens to you. I'm not having that boyfriend of yours or for that matter, the whole bloody Harrington clan up my arse because you wouldn't listen.'

'Fine, I won't be alone. I won't do anything that gets you into trouble, I promise.'

'Good. Keep it that way,' she said answering her ringing phone and signalling the end of our conversation.

'You made it?' Meg asked with a smile as she dropped her bag on her desk.

'Yep.'

'How's Delia doing about it?'

'We have an understanding. Unfortunately you're not fully off the hook with the Chicken Men, she wants us in there together.'

'Really? Why?' she groaned as we walked to the kitchen for coffee.

'Who bloody knows,' I fibbed.

'Anything to do with that photo of you in the paper coming out of the pub?' she asked.

'Maybe. There was nothing in it though. I didn't have a drink in there,' I said. Which was true. I didn't, not in there and I was so incredibly grateful I'd lost the journos before I went into the Austral and stumbled my way around the city.

My desk phone jingled. I checked the caller ID to see it was just Shannon on reception. 'Hey Shannon, what's up?'

'Your Chicken Men are all here. I've set them up in the conference room. They're ready when you are.'

'Great, thanks Shannon,' I said hanging up, sculling the last of my coffee and throwing a handful of smarties in my mouth from the bowl I kept on my desk. 'You ready?' I asked Meg.

'Argh,' she groaned. 'Come on then, I cleared my calendar anyway so let's get this over with,' she said, dipping her hand into my smartie supply.

I took a deep breath before walking into the conference room. You never knew what you were going to get on a good day. Now I had to throw in a potential stalker so intent on marrying me, he'd invited my whole family, my boss and who knew who else? If only he'd put a location of the festivities on the invitation, we could have been done with it already but no, he had to go and stoke the hornet's nest instead.

What did wait for me when I opened the doors were fifteen thirty-something blokes who'd once wanted to be actors and like me, were just grateful for the call up to anything on offer. I ignored the oozing desperation, the looks that went from my head to my toes as the slow burning twinkles of recognition set in. The only way I was getting out with my sanity intact was to do it fast. The quickest way to do that was to start eliminating for the obvious reasons.

'Is this normal?' Meg asked as she looked the men over, clearly used to a much higher calibre of client.

'Yep.'

'Oh shit,' she whispered. 'How have you not thrown a tantrum yet?'

'I'm grateful, Meg, you know that.'

'Yes, but you've been doing this a while now, most of us had forgotten you were a rich party girl.'

'Until last week,' I grinned. 'Now I'm right back at the beginning.'

'Maybe, maybe not.'

'We both know it Meg. It's fine, really. At least I know no one is going to try and steal my clients from me. Unlike you. You get a good enough client willing to pay for the good talent and you'll have Clary blowing smoke up your arse and stabbing you in the back the minute it's turned.'

She laughed. 'Ain't that the truth. But I can deal with Clary, so can you.'

'I know, but I'm fine with things as they are. Now let's get this done.'

'I'm just here to keep you on track,' she said, finding a seat in the corner as far away from the talent as possible. 'You just holler if you need me,' she grinned.

I couldn't help smiling. I'd missed her. She was my friend and I really liked having her around. She didn't care about who I was, made fun of it but didn't care. It had no bearing on whether she liked me or not and that's why I liked her.

I put everything aside and got down to business. The sooner the auditions were done, the sooner we could get back to important things like gossiping about what I'd missed while in exile.

Four of the guys in front of me had clearly let themselves go since they'd last updated their profiles so I ignored the disappointment in their faces and sent them away. There was a couple that were clearly too tall, the chicken feet would be hanging somewhere around their calves and one who'd lied about his five eleven height altogether and would have gotten lost in the suit. I apologised for the error and moved on to the next in the elimination process.

'Okay guys, Robbo's Chickens needs to you to sign a contract guaranteeing you'll be available for all openings state-wide for the next twelve months, so you need to be sure you can commit.'

As always a couple of guys still waiting for their break into the big time apologised and left, not willing to make such a long commitment.

'The contract will require you to do both print, television

and in person appearances at all openings, you all good with that?'

One bloke snuck towards the door. I caught his eye and he whispered, 'Sorry, I just can't be on the telly dancing as a chicken.'

'I understand,' I smiled. The more that left, the easier this all got. Not many were left. There was a guy brooding in the corner with a watchful eye, perhaps biding his time until everyone was gone, a few blokes who looked to be familiar with each other having a laugh in the other corner and a couple of nervous looking first timers who looked a bit down on their luck. One of those would be my choice, they'd always show up. I would wager coffee on the three in the corner being Mr Mums from some Mr Mum's group that liked to make a few extra dollars to get them to the football on the weekends when they finally offloaded the kids to their hard working wives. I'd seen one of them a few times. I'd given him a clown job a while back. Coming in for an audition was probably a great excuse for the three of them to offload the kids to day care and get themselves a day off. None were in the running, they always thought they could commit but baulked as soon as they had to travel because they had responsibilities but I'd put them through their paces anyway.

'Okay fellas,' I said unzipping the bag containing the chicken suit. 'Here it is, who wants to go first?'

No one moved. They all looked around the room waiting for someone to volunteer. When no one did, I selected the Mr Mum I'd given work to before. 'You, I recognise, show them how it's done,' I said, handing him the suit and pointing to the door at the end of the conference room that held the tiniest change room known to man.

We used to send them down the hallway to the men's room but the last time we'd done that, the bloke disappeared without a trace, taking the suit with him. After that, Delia let us convert a small portion of the catering kitchen into the change room.

Contender number one eventually came out suited up. I straightened his suit and made him dance, 'show us what you've got, then,' I insisted. I had to see what each was willing to do. They had to be able to free form whatever it is chickens do at such events.

Contender number one was a little stiff, but gave it a shot despite Meg's sniggering in the background. Then one by one his mates did their auditions. They were even stiffer and returned to their places de-suited and red-faced. The two blokes who looked a bit hard up went next and as expected, gave it a good shot, dancing with gusto. It's the sort of thing you have to really want to do, really need to do. The brooder was last and he was just downright creepy. He sauntered up to me like a stripper, gave me a once over with his eyes as though he had x-ray vision, then smiled his creepy smile as he took the suit from me.

I cringed, took a step back and told him, 'thanks, you can get changed now.'

I walked out of the room needing air. The act itself wasn't too uncommon, men often thought that was the way to get the job but there was no way I could let such a person loose on children. This guy though, made my skin crawl.

'You alright?' Shannon asked from the reception desk on the other side of the glass doors.

'Yeah, just about to cut to the last two. Got a creepy one, needed some air?'

She scrunched her face before saying, 'You have Meg in there, right? You're a bit pale.'

'Yeah, Meg's in there. I'm not sure how much more weird I can cope with.'

'Understandable. Let Meg take on some of the load,' she said.

'Thanks Shannon.' I said, appreciating the conversation and the support. Sometimes that's all you need.

'No worries,' she smiled, glad for the compliment.

'You alright?' Meg mouthed when I came back in.

I nodded as the creepy guy came out of the change room and handed me back the costume on the hanger with that predatory look in his eye. I tried examining him. Did I recognise him? Was he the one who'd been turning my life upside down? But then he winked at Meg and I decided he was just a regular all round creep and made a note in his file on the tablet to never call him again.

The remaining Chicken Men had all resumed their previous positions and were patiently waiting, sipping on free coffee, expectant looks on their faces.

'So who's your pick?' Meg whispered.

'Those two, I reckon,' I nodded indiscreetly to the hard luck boys.

'Good choice, they'll show up every time they're needed,' she agreed.

'Okay, thanks everyone for coming in, we've narrowed it

down to the final two. You and you,' I said pointing to them, 'If you could stay and go over some particulars with us that'd be great. The rest of you, thanks again for coming in, maybe next time.'

The Mr Mums nodded with a couldn't care less look on their faces, sculled the rest of their coffee and sauntered out to make the most of whatever free time they had left. Creepy guy watched me intently for a minute before also leaving neither pleased nor disappointed.

Meg sat with me while I went through some particulars of the job and interviewed the two remaining guys one by one. 'The blonde one would be my pick,' she suggested, he's just a little more charismatic, a little freer.

'Yeah, mine too,' I agreed.

'Alright, Tony, job's yours. Sorry Pete, top of the list for the next one,' I said as consolation.

He smiled tightly, thanked Meg and me, congratulated Tony and left.

'Nice guy,' I whispered to Meg. 'I'll have to see if I can find him something.'

'Yeah, nice guy,' she agreed. 'Well, if I'm done here, you know where to find me,' she said.

'Thanks, I owe you.'

'No trouble at all,' she assured me.

I sorted out the paperwork with Tony and that was that, the day was done. I went back to my desk and tidied up.

'How's it looking out there?' I asked Meg, referring to the media swarm.

'Think they've actually be gotten bored with you,' she laughed.

'Thank God for that. About time,' I said.

'You still coming for Friday night drinks?' asked Meg hopefully.

It was only four o'clock. Jay wouldn't be back for another hour. I'd forgotten all about drinks and my promise to Meg. Sure, she'd understand. But as I saw Delia gathering her things though, I didn't have a choice.

'Jay on his way?' Delia asked.

'He'll meet us at the pub,' I said, not wanting to be anyone's burden. I couldn't stay here by myself. Surely I'd be safe if I walked the few doors down to the pub with the whole office? Certainly safer than sitting on the kerb by myself waiting for Jay.

'Well, you stay close,' Delia insisted as I sent Jay a quick message while we waited for the lift.

Chapter 13

Meg and I left the office with the others. It was like a mass exodus as we headed to the pub.

'Did you let Jay know?' Meg asked as we walked in the sunshine.

'Yeah,' I mumbled as his reply dinged.

We stopped on the footpath in front of the office as the others wandered off and I rolled my eyes at his insistence that I wait. I replied telling him I'd be waiting alone and it would be safer with the group and I'd see him at the pub in a little bit.

'He's mad with power,' I laughed with Meg as we hurried to catch up with the others who'd gotten a few steps ahead and were chatting and giggling like old hens while Delia talked incessantly on her phone behind us, as though herding us like cattle but trying not to show it. It was insulting if she didn't think I knew what she was doing. But Meg didn't seem to so I changed the subject. 'So, what'd I miss while I was gone?' I asked Meg and we were soon doing our own version of giggling hens.

'Barb brought in double chocolate cake.'

'Oh no, poor Barb,' I joked before the stab of guilt pierced my stomach. Poor Barb coped the best she could. We should praise her for trying. 'Tell me about the holiday, tell me something funny, I need funny,' I told her.

'Well,' she started as a door slammed near by. 'I accidentally flashed a nipple as I posed for one of those silly photos in Pisa in front of the tower,' she began with a laugh.

I laughed but before I could ask what happened next, how did her nipple come to be out, a hand wrapped around my mouth and something stabbed my neck. I was instantly dizzy. I fought it, tried kicking out, punching aimlessly at something because I could no longer see. But all I found was air, then arms wrapped around me and all I heard was Meg screaming bloody murder and Delia's heels clicking on the footpath in the distance before everything went black.

I woke dizzy and sticky, achy, my throat dry and sore as though I'd screamed all night long. The air was arid dry, sucking all the moisture out of my body through the pores of my skin. I tried to focus, to think, what the last thing I remembered was. I remembered a hand clasping around my nose and mouth. I remembered the sting in my neck and my eyes going blurry, my legs giving out and the sound of Meg screaming bloody murder. Meg! My heart pounded as I tried to move my leaden arms, tried to sit when my muscles refused to move. I sucked in air and waited for my head to stop spinning and looked around the room.

There was a lump a few feet from me on whatever it was

I was on, a mattress I think, not a good one, nothing from the posturepedic range, more a lump of foam. I recognised the orange satin shirt with the little crochet details in the arms as the same shirt Meg had worn when I'd last seen her at work. I remembered it because I'd commented I'd seen it on my sister's website. It was one of Lydia's and nothing I could ever afford on my salary. But Meg had treated herself to something nice while she'd been away and upgraded it from weekend wear to Friday wear because we were having drinks.

'Meg,' I whispered but there was no reply. I wiggled down the mattress until I reached her. She looked small, bunched up in the corner. Meg was not a small person. She was beautiful and buxom. It suited her full of life personality and she carried her curves with pride. Seeing her so small, my heart sank to my toes. I scrambled over on my heavy limbs, nudged her with my hand and sighed with relief to find she wasn't ice cold. That was something, right? I nudged her again, whispering her name and finally received a guttural groan for my efforts.

I waited for her to wake. Slowly, I could see each of her extremities start to move and then she rolled onto her back, groaning, revealing her newly acquired black and blue face.

'What happened?' she whispered, trying to sit up and wincing from the pain of moving.

'I don't really know, I was going to ask you the same thing,' I told her. 'Last thing I remember you were telling me about your nipple slip in Pisa then there was a hand wrapped around my face and something stung my neck. You were screaming and I heard Delia running.'

She stretched out her arm as though it ached and then

studied a mark inside her elbow that looked very much like a needle mark. She nodded. 'I remember a guy with a grey hoodie and sunglasses grabbing you. I screamed hoping someone would come. I saw Delia coming but I don't know if she made it in time. It happened so fast.' She stopped for a minute, thinking, her face scrunched in thought. 'He shoved you in the van. I wrestled with him trying to get to you but he punched me in the face, that's the last thing I remember. I think I heard Clary shouting for Jay but nothing else, I don't remember. No wonder I hurt so much,' she said, reaching up to touch her face. 'How bad is it?' she asked.

I shrugged.

'That bad huh?' she tried smiling, groaned and slumped back on the dirty mattress.

'I thought I heard voices down here,' a man chirpily called as he descended the stairs with a tray of food.

As he reached the bottom of the stairs and turned towards us, the light from a doorway above illuminated his face. 'You?' I asked in a whisper.

He smiled. 'I wasn't sure if you'd remember me, I was cut from the auditions so fast. Why was that by the way?' he asked.

'You were too short for the suit,' I told him.

'Ah, I knew it couldn't have been because you didn't like me, not after everything I'd done for you.'

What the hell was that supposed to mean? I looked at Meg and she was as blank faced.

'You don't remember me from anywhere else, though?' he asked innocently.

'Sorry, no. Should I?'

'My tongue has been in your mouth and the last time we met, my penis and your wet pussy were about to get well acquainted, so yeah, you should remember me. But we'd partied so much you can be forgiven a little memory lapse. I'm sure I'll come back to you, soon enough. Maybe we need get the anatomical parts of us back together to jog your memory?' he winked.

My mind went blank, not from not recognising him, there were plenty of people I didn't recognise from that time in my life, whether I slept with them or not. My mind went blank from fear, fear that this man was clearly hoping to rekindle something and that he was so calm about it as though it was inevitable, as though he hadn't kidnapped us off the street in broad fucking daylight.

'It was just meant to be the two of us though, so sorry to your friend here, but she was making so much noise I just had to throw her in and get outta there. With all those people hanging around all the time making a nuisance of themselves, I had to take whatever opportunity came along or we'd have been kept apart forever. How did your father not stop that man from stealing you? Everywhere we were, he swooped in and stole you from me. Well, he's out of luck this time, isn't he? You deserve more than a lowly security guard, more than he could ever give you. I can give you everything you deserve, anything you've ever dreamed of,' he grinned, clearly proud of himself.

He was utterly deluded. He thought Jay had kidnapped me and he was going to be my saviour? He was out of his mind, which made him all the more dangerous and unpredictable. I tried forcing a smile, hoping he'd go away, and Meg and I could get down to the business of finding a way out.

'Anyway,' he said. 'There'll be plenty of time for us to catch up. Eternity in fact. Now, first things first, you need to take your medicine,' he said holding a small paper cup of liquid out for me. When I didn't take it, he shouted, 'Drink it. You need it. You need to get back to your old self.'

'I don't drink that anymore. I don't drink.'

'That's the problem, isn't it? You need to get back to who you are, the girl we all loved and stop being this prissy fucking bitch.'

I still didn't take the cup so he squeezed my nostrils together so tight I thought he'd pull my nose off and poured the liquid down my throat. The vodka burned and I spluttered but it had gone down and there was nothing I could do to change it.

'Now, have some food,' he said, placing the tray on the floor in front of us. 'You'll need your strength,' he added, winking at me.

'Don't go worrying your pretty little head though, you won't have to stay down here for too long. Once we're married you can come upstairs and share my bed if you behave. Not sure what we'll do with your friend yet, but I'll figure that out soon enough. We will have a use for her if she can do as she's told. We'll have to wait and see.' He sank his hands in my hair and smiled down at me like I was dessert. 'You'll be back to your old self in no time, just you wait,' he grinned, giving a self-satisfied grunt before walking away, back up the stairs and locking the door above, leaving us in our muted light to eat the bowls of slop he'd brought us.

I slumped back against the wall, dumbfounded at what had just happened. My old life, my booze-fuelled promiscuity had come back to bite me and it wasn't just me paying the price, Meg had gotten caught up in it too. 'Why didn't he just throw you on the footpath and leave you there?' I asked not really expecting an answer.

'I saw his face,' Meg said, leaning forward, shovelling the slop into her mouth.

'What are you doing?' I demanded.

'I can't help it,' she growled. 'I'm fucking starving.'

'There could be anything in that food,' I told her remembering all the things Jay had told me. Part of protecting me had involved preparing me for situations just like this. He'd forced me to listen while eating pizza on his couch, too hungover to run my smart mouth or escape. He was smart that man of mine. I'd diluted so much of what he said with booze and passing time but I hoped that it was there somewhere in my memory bank.

'I know,' she said, shaking her head. 'But seriously, I just can't help it. It's like my insides are going to cave in if I don't eat.'

'But we ate cake together this afternoon, lots of cake so Barb didn't feel bad. We ate so much after the Chicken Men left, we groaned like fat old men in the lift.'

'I know. I remember. That double chocolate mousse cake was divine,' she groaned.

'Seriously?' I smiled.

She shrugged.

'Well, if you don't die in the next ten minutes, feel free to eat mine because there's no way I'm eating it.'

'Not even a bite? Aren't you hungry?'

'I'd starve first. Jay would kill me if I ate that. He's going to kill me as it is. I promised I wouldn't leave without him. After the other day...'

'What happened the other day?'

'Nothing.'

'Not nothing. If we're stuck down here you might as well come clean.'

'I had a relapse.'

'But you said you didn't have a drink at the Fox.'

'I didn't. I went into the Fox after I got an invitation to my wedding with that freak show up there. I was just going to hide in a corner and call Jay to come and get me. Then I saw Jay talking to the barmaid from the Fox, you know, the blonde with the little shorts and the bad makeup.'

She nodded, she knew the one.

'They were in a corner looking really cosy and I lost my shit. It'd been a tough week. Between that delusional fool upstairs and then Jay and the fucking barmaid, and I couldn't deal with losing him so I went on a bender. He didn't find me for two days. He was a mess. I promised I wouldn't do it again, that I'd be careful.'

'This isn't your fault. It was a busy bloody street. We were with fifteen other people. The guys got brass bloody balls.'

'Yeah, well, you tell that to Jay when you see him because I doubt he'll be speaking to me.'

'When's he coming to get us by the way?'

I shrugged. 'Depends on where we are. What time is it anyway?' I asked, trying to get my bearings on something.

'Don't know, your creepy stalker broke my watch punching

me in the face and throwing me into the back of his van and I can't see our handbags, so no phones.'

'Fucker,' I swore.

'Fucker,' she agreed, slumping against the wall next to me. 'Seriously though, Jaz, what are we going to do?'

'As soon as I can feel my toes, I'm going to get us out of here.'

'Can you do that?' she asked like a little girl who was no longer sure she believed in anything.

'I can try. I got you dragged into this, I'm going to get you out of it. Don't worry. We'll be okay. Even if I have to play along with that sick fuck upstairs, I'll make sure you're okay.'

'But will you be okay?'

'It doesn't matter.'

She tried protesting. 'Maybe we could take him. Once the headache passes, you and me could take him. He's not that big.'

'Yeah, but he's crazy. Crazy people are far stronger than regular people and if he keeps pouring vodka down my throat I'm not going to be able to fight off anyone.'

There wasn't much else to say and before long we sat staring into the darkness across the other side of the room lost in our own thoughts. I don't know what Meg was thinking about but all I could think about was Jay. It all happened too fast. How was he going to find me? I had to find a way out but how? It looked like we were in a basement. There were no windows to climb out of and the only door in was locked from the other side. Could I charm my way to the other side of that door? Would it be before or after he married me? I didn't care about the marrying part, it would get annulled as soon as I could get out or Jay found me, whatever came first, I was worried about the consummation of the marriage part. I couldn't do that to Jay. How could he be with me if that man had defiled me?

I couldn't dwell on things that hadn't happened yet. I had to focus. I had to come up with a plan, put a time frame together in my head. How long had we been driving for? How far could we have we gone? How long were we out for?

Delia had seen everything. She'd have something Jay could work with. Did she see enough? What was I even questioning her for? She's Delia. Delia would be able to recount every minute detail down the colour of his undie band when he bent over. And there was Clary shouting for Jay. Did that mean he'd been nearby? I only lived ten minutes from the office, he could have made it if he'd hurried. He'd have looked for the right things. It would give him something to work with at least. Something was better than nothing.

'Shit,' cried Meg, jumping from the mattress and racing across the room to vomit in the corner.

I followed her over and held her hair back. 'Are you okay?'

She hurled a final time and nodded, then stood up.

'I told you not to eat whatever that slop was,' I smirked.

'Shut up,' she said, shaking her head and walking back to the mattress. 'I don't think it's the slop, this keeps happening after breakfast. I must have a tummy bug. Good too, I hope I give it to him. But at least we have our timeline? We must have been out long enough for it to now be breakfast, right?'

'That's something. But that's twelve hours. We could be anywhere. He could get a long way from the city in twelve hours. We mightn't even still be in the state?' I shuddered at all the possibilities flashing through my mind. 'Just don't go giving me your wacky bug, I need to figure out how to get us out of here,' I said, trying not to let my growing fear show in my voice.

'You think you can do that?' she asked dubiously.

'I have to. We have to do something. We can't just sit here and wait to see what his plans are.'

'Evidently, it's to get you drunk, marry you and move you upstairs to his bed and me in the dirt under the roses unless I'm a good girl.'

'How does he think he's going to manage marrying an unwilling participant anyway?'

She shrugged. Held her finger up in the air then raced to her vomit corner and heaved.

When she returned and caught her breath, she said, 'I guess any psycho with enough motivation can make anything happen.'

'Great! You made me wait all that time just to tell me I'm screwed?'

'You're not screwed. You're going to find a way to get us out. Either that or that super-human boyfriend of yours will sniff out your trail and come swooping in to rescue his damsel and her very good friend,' she smirked before racing to visit her corner again.

When she returned, she groaned. 'It'll pass in a couple of hours, it's one stupid bug.'

'Exactly how many days has this been going on?'

She shrugged, 'Since I got home, I suppose. A week? Must have caught it on the plane. Those things are like one enormous petri dish.'

'That's the truth. But is it just in the mornings?'

'So far, I guess?' she answered, laying down for a rest.

'Honey, are you sure it's a tummy bug?'

'What else could it be?'

'I don't know, maybe a baby?'

'Don't be ridiculous,' she laughed.

'Is it?' I smirked.

'Noooooooooooooo,' she groaned. 'We used protection. I'm not stupid,' she scoffed.

'It doesn't always work.'

'But this time it had to. I don't even know his last name,' she laughed.

'Well maybe this time it didn't.'

'Fuck,' she said, going white as a sheet, making her purple bruises show up even more. 'What am I going to do?'

I shrugged. 'One catastrophe at a time, hey?'

She nodded.

'Get some sleep, you look like you need it,' I told her.

She nodded, tears spilling out of her eyes.

'Hey, come here,' I said, scooping her into my arms and letting her sob into my shoulder. 'Well, I guess we're finally alone, so now you can tell me about this Olly,' I said, trying to distract her and myself to be honest. 'Maybe finally finish your nipple slip in Pisa story.'

Meg burst into tears. 'It doesn't even matter anymore,' she cried. 'I don't know his last name. How to find him. I'm never going to see him again.'

'Hey, hey,' I soothed. 'You don't know what is around the corner. We never know what is in store for us. Sometimes we have to just roll with the punches. For example, I bet yesterday you'd never have guessed you'd be kidnapped off the street on the way to Friday night drinks and held captive in a basement while pregnant.'

She smirked, 'I don't think either of those things rated on my list of expectations.'

I smiled. 'Now I'd be worried if they did. But it does prove my point that you don't know what or who is around the corner and you have to live for now, in the moment. Cherish the good that comes your way even if it was only for a little while. A few weeks with Olly had to be better than never having met him at all, right?'

'He changed my life, and not just by possibly impregnating me,' she smirked. 'But he changed the way I look at the world, at myself and no, I would never give that up. Or the, oh my god, mind blowing sex. I tell you Jaz, that man knew things,' she said smiling wistfully.

'Tell me,' I asked, wanting to keep her distracted more than wanting to know the intimate details of her sex life. Cold had begun seeping through the stone walls. Meg and I huddled in the corner of the mattress for warmth, it was only going to get colder I predicted, until the sun fully rose.

She laughed. 'I know what you're doing, you know. And no, you do not need to know those details. How did you meet Jay?' Meg asked.

'What do you mean, he was my bodyguard, you know that,' I told her, wondering why she'd ask a question she already knew the answer to.

'No, I know that. Tell me about when you first met. Did sparks fly and birds sing?'

I laughed. 'No!' I replied emphatically. 'I was watching tv, sprawled out on the couch after school, so it was cartoons, Ninja turtles, if I remember correctly. Tom walked in with Jay, I didn't even look at them. Tom called my name twice before I turned to him, gave him the devil eyes and groaned, "What?" "This is Jay," he tells me. "He'll be your bodyguard, so don't go giving him grief,"' he ordered.

'I'd known Dad was organising someone after a beer bottle was thrown at me but I didn't want some nosey bossy bloke following me around and poking his nose in my business. So I rolled my eyes, turned my head back to the telly and drank from my litre carton of iced coffee. Tom watched me for a second and then grabbed the carton out of my hand. "What's this," he asked, smelling it. "What does it matter," I spat, reaching for the carton. "Are you kidding me Jaz, it's three fucking thirty in the afternoon," he screamed at me before storming into the kitchen to pour it down the sink. I ran after him, screaming bloody murder, pummelling his chest with my little girl fists, crying, "how could you? I hate you. What kind of brother are you anyway?" Then he just stood there taking it until I fell in a heap on the floor. Tom couldn't do anything. He looked out the window trying not to cry in front of his big tough army buddy while I cried hysterically on the floor until Jay wrapped his arms around me and held me so tight. It was the first time in years I didn't feel on the edge of breaking into pieces. I breathed him in and even now, that smell is what takes me home, to a place of love and safety. I knew right then something had changed. He says I was the most fragile, beautiful thing he'd ever seen. I told him he was a masochist who should have run for the hills. I still don't know why he didn't. The fool says he just wanted to wrap me in cotton wool and protect me.'

'That's the most romantic thing I've ever heard,' she smiled.

'Are you kidding me?' I asked, dumbfounded.

'Even still you can't see it?'

'I was a fifteen-year-old drunk and a brat to boot. How could anyone love me?' I asked.

'Because he saw past the pretence. He saw into your soul. They say it's in our rawest moments of weakness where we truly open the window to our souls.'

'My soul was black. There was nothing beautiful to see and I think I proved that in the years to come. I didn't even know how he could look at me most of the time. I'm only who I am now because of him, because of his goodness and faith and kindness. Without him, there is nothing. I am nothing. Without Jay, I'm a mess and the mere thought of losing him the other day sent me spiralling into the gutter. I don't deserve him. He deserves more than me but he doesn't want it. I'm not a good person, Meg. Deep down, the things he had to see, I'm an awful person. If he saw my soul, he would have seen the black.'

'No, you're not an awful person, Jaz. Your soul is not black. You are bright and beautiful. You're amazing and kind and thoughtful. Who baked me cookies when I got dumped a week before my birthday? Who organises the office toy drive every Christmas and the clothing collection for the women's shelter?'

I shrugged. I didn't do those things for kudos, I did them because they needed doing. Every child deserved a gift at Christmas. It was something Mum, Lydia and I had always done and I knew what it was like to have to run, to leave everything behind to be free and safe but to have nothing as the price.

'Is that why you won't live with him? Why you're not married, because you don't think you're good enough for him?'

I just shrugged. 'He hasn't asked me to marry him anyway, not properly, not officially.'

'What does not officially mean?'

'Sometimes he says, "*Someday Jaz, someday I'm going to marry you.*" But he's never actually asked me to.'

'Okay, I'm going to need some context,' she said.

'Sometimes he says it when I'm leaving to come back to the city so it sounds more a threat, like some day I'll marry you and you'll never be able to leave.'

'And other times?'

'Sometimes he says it while we're sitting on the balcony, drinking tea and watching the sunset.'

'Well that sounds very romantic.'

I shrugged.

'And what do you say on the balcony when he says this?' she asked sceptically.

I could feel myself blush. 'Um, I tell him don't be ridiculous. Why would you want to marry me?' As I said it I could see where Meg was going to go with it. I could also remember the feel of his arms around me and how they tightened when I said it. 'He's waiting till I'm not broken anymore,' I said sadly, as though suddenly realising the truth even though I knew it all along.

'No Jaz, he's waiting for you to forgive yourself, to love

yourself and to love him enough that nothing else matters. No matter how much it hurts him, he's giving you the space to do that.'

'But I already love him. I love him more than my own life. I'd give my life for him.'

'Does he know that?'

'How could he not?' Then it dawned on me that maybe he didn't. Maybe my selfish need for independence has clouded just how much I love him. 'Oh no,' I said as my stomach sank to my toes. 'Meg we have to get out of here. I can't die without him knowing how much I love him, that without him, my world is nothing,' I cried as I got up and began pawing at the walls for a way out.

'Jaz wait,' she said, steadying me as panic surged through my veins. 'He knows, he knows,' she said making me look her in the eye. 'He's just waiting for you to forgive yourself, do whatever you need to do to get there, to come to terms with your future.'

'Oh,' I said, taking a deep breath.

'Tell me another story,' she said. 'Tell me a funny one.'

I sat back down on the mattress, snuggled against my friend. 'A funny one? I don't know if I have funny ones. They all seem a little tragic in hindsight.'

'Come on, the great Jaz Harrington, The Princess of Party, has to have a funny story or a hundred.'

I laughed at her mocking of my old moniker used by my friends and then the press. 'One of my favourite memories was before everyone knew I was a drunk. My brothers and I used to rendezvous down by the creek and behave like trust-fund brats.

One time we were trying to create a love heart in the grass by putting a solution Christian had learnt about in science class into the dirt. It was supposed to turn the affected grass pink but we were all drinking bubbles and dancing like witches in a full moon ritual but with our clothes on and somehow the solution got poured into the creek and turned it blood red for days. We all feigned innocence while people searched for a body or who knows what and we high-tailed it out of the country house and back to the city as quick as we could. It was in the local papers, the mystery, but someone had to suspect it was us. They just didn't like pointing the finger.'

'You were all close once?'

'We were. Until Tom went into the army to escape Dad. Then he came back and Dad screwed him over and within weeks he was fighting a murder charge.'

'I remember that. What really happened?'

'Lincoln Cummins. He was way more fucked up than any of us. Liked wearing women's clothes. We thought it was just a thing he did for a laugh when he was wasted. There were always clothes lying around at the end of a party and he'd put them on and parade around and disappear. Turned out he liked more than wearing the clothes, he liked bribing and manipulating people, mostly vulnerable men, into fucking him while wearing them. Which made no sense because he was hot and could have had anyone he wanted, male or female.'

'Didn't he go to the States with that blonde heiress?'

'Yeah, she dumped him as soon as the police came knocking. He's doing time. I didn't pay attention to where, probably Queensland as that's where it happened. That was my world though. No one took responsibility, no one even pointed a finger at Linc because of how powerful his father was. Mine wasn't quite as high up on the societal ladder, which is saying something considering my father's friends and colleagues but there are hierarchies in every societal group and we fell a small rung below the Cummins' in ours. Anyway, Tom was supposed to be managing the project where the kid died so the blame came to him. But it was all Dad. Tom had tried to tell him that things weren't right but he wouldn't listen. It was all about what was best for his business, for his social status and having Linc on the project was good for Dad's business. So Dad sided with Linc, ignored Tom when he said something was wrong, then there was a collapse and a dead raped kid. There was no hiding from that. Tom of course was eventually cleared but not everyone was happy about that so Tom and Lydia left and I spiralled further into the abyss.'

'Until Jay saved you?'

I smiled. 'Until Jay. Then Dad found out, went nuts, ruined Christmas and eventually I ran before he dumped me in a facility in Italy.'

'He was really going to do that?'

'He thought my love for Jay was just an affliction. That a seventeen-year-old drunk couldn't know what love was. But he didn't know by then I was sober. Jay had made me go sober. Made me want to be better.'

'It sounds dark. That whole world.'

'People think it's all glitz and glamour. But it's not. It's more cutthroat than Clary, that's for sure. That poor girl would be eaten alive,' I laughed, imagining Clary up against the likes of Lydia's friends or even Indi. Indi would go to town. She'd become quite the society princess since I'd left. Gotten sober herself, married an important, respected news reporter. I missed her. Sometimes. But we weren't good for each other.

'What's the most outrageous thing you've done?'

'Wow, you're really going to town, aren't you?'

She smiled.

'Skinny dipping at the Prime Minister's Australia Day party,' I smiled.

'You did not?'

I nodded. 'I did. As did Indi and CeeCee and the PM's son, among others.'

'How much trouble did you get in?'

'We were fifteen then. It was just before Jay came along. Everyone thought we were bold and funny.'

'Are you kidding?'

I shook my head. 'It was a really fucked up world, I tell you.'

'It must be. My parents would have gone nuts.'

'My father eventually did.'

'Your father tried to lock you up for loving someone.'

'In his defence, he'd just come across a magazine cover of me being carried, comatose out of a club with an inset photo of some strange guy with his hand up my dress having a good grope.'

'What was Jay doing while some guy groped you?'

'Seething. Trying not to kill him. Caught me when I passed out.'

She shook her head and I wondered if she was regretting

asking the questions. 'Do you think this guy was someone you knew then?'

I shrugged. 'Could be. Seriously though, I drank from sunup to sunset, unless you were a regular in my circle, I couldn't say. I met a lot of people, even slept with a lot of people whose names I didn't even know. It wasn't a good life. I wasn't a good person.'

'Yet Jay saw the person beneath and loved you.'

'He's a crazy man,' I laughed.

I held Meg until she fell asleep but then I couldn't let her go. I needed to hold on to someone, to keep grounded and stop myself from drifting to places I didn't want to go. I had to focus; I had to think. How long would it be before something happened to Meg's baby? Before he poured enough vodka down my throat that I could no longer function? Before something awful happened to either of us. Not long I suspected.

I finally laid Meg on the mattress to rest while I scrunched myself in the corner, my knees pulled up to my chest as I tried desperately not to panic, tried to think of all the things Jay had taught me about survival and self-preservation. We hadn't needed to talk about those things in a while but surely it was all stored somewhere in my memory bank? I reached up to fiddle with my necklace, a nervous habit when I was concentrating and gasped. It was gone. It was one of the few things I owned that I truly cherished. I had no idea of its value but it was from Christian, our last Christmas together days before I ran. It was a silver infinity pendant with an onyx stone in the centre. 'To infinity and beyond,' I whispered to the night.

They would find us. They had to because I couldn't see any way out.

Chapter 14

As if I could sleep. Just like Jay couldn't sleep through a thunderstorm, I couldn't sleep in a locked room to which I didn't have a key. We all lived with our demons, we breathed and walked with them every day, we didn't fuss about them, we didn't make it a thing, we just found a way to co-exist with them. I could feel the panic deep in my belly trying to rise up. Jay quelled his thunderstorm-fuelled sleeplessness with old movies. We didn't speak of it, we just each did what we needed, the other understanding. But I had no Jay today, only the image of him. If I closed my eyes and if I concentrated hard enough, I could feel his arms around me, his breath on my neck, hear his soft whispers of comfort.

I startled at the sound of a door closing and chastised myself for stupidly losing concentration. It left me vulnerable but as I snuck a peek at my surroundings, all seemed to be in order. I looked towards the door and the basement stairs and found my captor struggling down the stairs behind a big pouf of white in a clear plastic dress bag. I took a moment to watch him. He was my height. His body didn't appear to get much TLC but he wasn't fat. He wasn't ugly but he wasn't handsome either. Too soft for my liking. He hoisted the bag to stop it dragging on the dusty cement steps. I knew what was in that bag but I tried not to think about it. What was in that bag made whatever he was planning serious, he had every intention of going through with this nonsense and my insides shook with the fear of it.

Meg was still asleep so I walked over to him, up the two steps to meet him, hoping not to wake her, hoping to rattle him a little. 'This,' I said, grabbing hold of the bag. 'This is never going to happen, you know that right?'

'Of course it's going to happen,' he said matter-of-factly. 'It's all set, dates, celebrant, everything. It's all in place. I was just bringing you your dress.'

He held the dress out to me and I swatted it to the floor. 'No one will marry us. I won't agree to it.'

'Ah, you say that like you have a choice. The celebrant is being paid rather handsomely to not listen to your ravings.'

'Ravings? Do not talk to me like I'm a crazy person.'

'But aren't you? And once you're back to your old self, then, oh then we can have some real fun,' he smirked, handing me a bottle of vodka.

'I am not drinking that. I drink that and I'm a danger to society, to you, to me, to everyone.'

'No, no, that's not how I remember it at all,' he said, his hand stroking the side of my face.

I tried swatting his hand away but he grabbed my hair, holding it tight in his fist. Then he held my face in his hand so tightly, I thought the bones in my jaw would crumble to dust.

My knees shook and my stomach revolted, cold fear freezing the blood in my veins as he brought his face towards mine, his hot breath smelling of curry. There was nowhere for me to go except tumbling backwards. Tears streamed down my face as I thought of Jay, my perfect, beautiful, Jay, who I'd already put through so much and now this man was going to ruin me, taint me forever and I couldn't even fight him without falling down the stairs. He poured vodka down my throat until I gagged. He stopped and I gasped for air but I only got in a lungful before he shoved his thick, slimy tongue into my mouth, blocking my airway and I began to dry heave.

He pulled away, his eyes filled with rage and hate, slapping my face so hard I fell backwards onto the filthy floor. My head rolled to the side and I saw Meg was not only awake but whimpering with such uncontrollable fear, her whole body shook, the smell of fresh urine filling the air and breaking my heart.

'You'd better find a way to get used to this, you little bitch, because that wannabe Rambo boyfriend of yours won't be saving you this time. This time tomorrow you'll be my wife and he'll have no claim anyway.'

He waited for me to react but I was a Harrington and now that I was out of his grasp I sat tall and quiet and stared ahead, an image of Jay holding me tight, holding me together, was all that was keeping me from falling apart.

He picked up the dress and threw it at me before walking out. 'You will get on board with this. You keep fighting me and it's your friend here who's going to pay the price. If that's what it takes to break you, don't think I won't do it,' he snarled as he left.

'There has to be a way out of here,' I whispered to Meg. 'We just have to find it,' I said, my fingertips scrambling against the exposed rock wall.

'This is it Jaz, a stone walled box with stairs leading to his lair, that's it,' she insisted, pulling me back from the wall before I ripped my fingertips to shreds

'No, no, there has to be another way, there's always another way.'

I looked around the room frantically, fear rippling through my body and keeping me going. My head was starting to get fuzzy from not seeing daylight, from what he'd drugged us with, the vodka he'd poured down my throat, who knew. I had to find a solution before I was forced to marry him, before I couldn't think straight anymore. I had to do it for Meg.

I was staring at the wall opposite covered in dark shadows, hoping something would come to me, an idea, a way out, Jay materialising through the wall. But there was nothing. Meg was right.

Meg slept, snuggled up to my side. I couldn't sleep. I wouldn't be that vulnerable again. I thought of Jay and how he'd been threatening to marry me for years, begging me to move to the beach with him. I'd laughed every time, playfully swatting him then kissing him. Sometimes I ripped his clothes from his body, had my way with him and asked isn't this enough? He'd laugh, pin me to the bed and in his deep throaty post orgasm voice whisper, '*for now*,' before making me pay with pleasure for my refusal.

Now all I could think was what a fool I'd been, how perfect it'd have been to marry him and wake beside him every day. Did I really need my independence and a job in the city more than I needed Jay? No. I needed nothing more than I needed Jay. Besides, I knew he'd never trap me, I'd still have my independence anyway I wanted it with him. I'd just always been too afraid that he'd get tired of me, someday, somehow, finally see the truth, that he was too good for me. That he deserved better. But that wasn't Jay. He loved me. He'd give me anything, he just wanted me, he just wanted to wake up beside me and I'd never told him how much I dreamt of that but how afraid I was of giving in to it. But I knew better than to fear him. To fear the emotion with him. I trusted him with my life. I could trust him with my heart and my freedom. Typical of me to realise the truth, all the possibilities when it was too late.

The dark eventually grew shapes as my eyes grew weary.

'Tell me another story,' begged Meg. 'Tell me about your and Jay's first date. Did he take you somewhere lovely?'

I laughed. 'Our first date was technically pizza and an Outlander marathon on his couch and it came right after a big fight that resulted in him telling me he loved me, me yelling at him for being so stupid, having beautiful relations on his bedroom floor followed by me trying to ruin it with another guy at a party.'

'What? Tell me the rest?'

'No, that's it, Meg. That's who this guy is. He'd been hanging around for ages but I never bothered to learn his name. I didn't care who he was. I don't even know how he found his way in. I was at Indi's; she was having a party. It was supposed to just be the two of us. Jay was really mad when we walked in and found the living room full of people snorting and fucking.'

'What? Just out in the open for everyone to see?'

I laughed. 'Everything we ever did was out in the open for everyone to see. But anyway, I danced, I drank and Jay had filled me with feelings I didn't know what to do with. The only way I knew how to deal with it all was to erase all memory of that morning, so I got rip roaring drunk and when this guy, that pig up there, hit on me. I let him but I couldn't go through with it and ended up crying in a foetal position until Jay came and scooped me up while whatshisname, oh God, what is his name, shouted obscenities at me. I think it was something dull, something boring and ordinary. Kevin Dale is what was on his call card but that doesn't sound right. The Kevin yes, maybe, oh I can't bloody remember. His father was a politician, I think, not an important one though, one of those no one ever cared about. That would be how he got into our circle. I knew that life would be the end of me. I knew it.'

'It's not the end Jaz. We'll get out of this. Finish your date story,' she begged. 'After that awful bit with whatshisname.'

'Jay took me home to get myself together, then the next day after I had behaved like a brat all morning, he eventually took me out of the house. We went to his place and camped on the couch. We couldn't actually go on a real date because if it ended up in a magazine my father would... well, we all know what happened when my father found out. So I guess our first real date was a month after we left and we went down Rundle

Street for noodles. Not very romantic but trust me, he's a man you can forgive,' I laughed.

'Oh, I don't doubt that for a second,' she smiled.

'What about Olly, tell me about him?'

'Oh, he wasn't very tall, just a little taller than me and neater than me in that his clothes were never wrinkled and his hair was always neat but he was funny and sweet and kind. He was a doctor, one of those that work in poor countries but we never really talk about it. We just had fun and enjoyed where we were and enjoyed each other. I didn't think I could attract a man as handsome as him. I'm a little curvy, a little loud but he didn't mind. He thought I was funny and beautiful and sexy. For such a neat man, though, he really knew how to let loose when it counted,' she giggled.

'I like the sound of him.'

She shrugged. 'He left before the last day. Had an emergency of some sort. He left me a note at reception but someone spilt a drop of coffee that distorted his email address. I tried a couple of combinations with what I had left to work with but they all bounced back. So I just guess it wasn't meant to be.'

'Meant to be can come in many forms and be for many reasons.'

'That's very true and you were right earlier, I wouldn't trade any of it. He kissed me under the Eiffel Tower like in the movies. But he was a gentleman, he wasn't allowing any of the other shenanigans that go on under the Tower. Did you know people have sex there, right out in the open?'

'Maybe they're old friends of mine,' I joked.

She laughed and it felt good to share a joke. It chased away some of the fear, helped clear my head a little.

The evening chill returned with the night and Meg snuggled a little closer. She'd eaten a little bit of the bread that came down with dinner but was too worried about vomiting to eat anything else. The smell of last night's dinner was a little rancid as it was. We didn't need her adding to it. We'd been peeing in the other corner so if we didn't leave soon, we'd die from the smells alone.

As I stared into the shadows while Meg slept, the shapes returned, twisting and turning. It's funny what your eyes and mind can do to you. I prayed to those distorted images that Jay would be okay, that he wasn't losing his mind because after the other day, I didn't know how he'd be getting through. He was going to be so mad at me though for not waiting for him.

He was never going to let me out alone again. I could feel it. But I didn't care, it was a small price to pay to be free, to be with him. I'd give up my freedom, the one thing I treasured in the world almost as much as him. I'd give it up for him because he meant more. That's how much I loved him.

The silence was becoming deafening when I heard a soft whimpering. I looked down at Meg to make sure she was okay. She looked perfectly peaceful. The whimpering sounded again but it wasn't coming from Meg, it was coming from the other side of the room. I listened to make sure it wasn't my deprived brain playing tricks on me and made sure it was something. It sounded like a cat, stuck behind the opposite wall.

I nudged Meg awake and held a finger to my lips to shush her. I held her hand for strength as we walked across the room. The wall hidden in the shadows wasn't stone like the others. It was chipboard, a fake wall. I tapped on the wall as quietly as I could, careful not to wake up my future husband somewhere above in his bed.

'Did you hear that?' I asked Meg as the wall echoed under my knocking, feeling the mania of relief and adrenalin pumping in my veins.

She looked back blankly.

'It's hollow, Meg.'

The cat whimpered again and Meg's eyes widened with hope.

'There has to be a weak spot here somewhere,' I said, running my hands over the wall. 'There's always a weak spot in the work of home handymen and this definitely looks like he did it himself,' I muttered.

Standing on a discarded milk crate buried amongst piles of other useless crap, I was determined to find a way out. If he'd built the wall himself, I doubted he'd have done a very good job. He didn't strike me as the think-in-advance, attention-to-detail handyman kind of guy. He didn't appear too adept at much.

I stretched, reaching for the top of the wall. It was the most likely place for a weak point. He wasn't very tall maybe he couldn't reach all the way up.

I stretched my arms as high as I could, stood on my tip toes while Meg held the crate steady, desperately picking and pulling every rough-edged seam and join until I found it, the weak spot. Not nailed properly. He had either forgotten where he was up to, been distracted or too lazy to nail up that high.

Whatever the reason, it was loose and I pulled on the sheet of board, loosening the grip the short nails below had on it until it came apart just enough for me to see what was on the other side.

'What can you see?' Meg asked, hope filling her voice, raising its pitch.

'A window, a big window,' I said, feeling the smile cross my face. 'And a door. Well, at least I think it's a door. We have to get this cheap-arse sheeting down. The fool hasn't even used proper board or decent nails,' I smirked.

Meg and I climbed together on the milk crate, trying to keep our balance while also pulling on the board. Bit by bit the cheap nails too bent and gave way.

'I know it's not very wide, but do you think you can squeeze through the gap?' I asked Meg, reluctant to pull much more on the board in case it all came crashing down.

'I'll try,' she said doubtfully.

I pulled the board as wide as I could for her. We'd only pulled half of one side away from the studs so there wasn't much room to move and even though they were small and cheap, there were nails to be dodged and a feral cat waiting on the other side but Meg took a deep breath and squeezed herself through like a contortionist but with no foot hold on the other side fell to the floor with the cat and what appeared under the sliver of moonlight from the window, to be a litter of kittens.

The cat was annoyed but not as feral as expected. Perhaps it thought we were its saviours.

Meg pushed the board forward from her side, while I pulled on it as best I could from mine so I could squeeze through. I caught my sleeve on a nail, damn that I thought and pulled as hard as I could until it ripped free, taking a slice of skin with it but I didn't care about the missing skin as I fell to the ground on the other side.

'Now what?' asked Meg.

'I don't know,' I smiled. 'But, if that cat was able to get in, then there has to be a way out.'

It was hard to see with nothing but a bit of moonlight creeping in through the smeared, dirty windows, but our eyes had become adjusted to the dark, so it was enough to see the broken door.

There were no stairs to the door, it was about head high and only half open, but it would have been enough for the cat to sneak in through but too high for it to get out again with its babies.

I pulled on the broken part of the door, hoping I'd get lucky a second time. The wood was thick but it was rotten, either by weather or eaten away by termites. I didn't care which.

'What about them?' asked Meg pointing to the cat and its litter as I offered her a foothold to climb out.

'Really?' I asked.

'Well we can't just leave them here can we,' she said, suddenly all maternal. 'Besides, if it wasn't for them we'd still be sitting on that shit-stained mattress hoping for a way out.'

'Fine,' I groaned. But there was no way I was approaching a scared cat with a litter of babies. 'Off you go then,' I smiled at Meg.

She shook her head and carefully bent down toward the cat.

It had nested amongst some old newspapers and didn't look like it planned to move now it had the chance.

'You get one end and I'll get the other, hold it up to the door and she'll take it from there,' Meg insisted.

'Fine,' I groaned again as I bent down. I wanted it done so we could finish escaping before we were caught.

The cat hissed and I jumped back.

'It's alright. She's just scared,' insisted Meg.

'Well kitty, you get one chance to let us help you or we're leaving you behind. You got that?'

The cat cowered and hissed as we picked up the paper but didn't scratch and when we held the ungrateful beast to the window, she pushed all of her babies out, gave us a final death stare and she ran off into the night to terrorise the native wildlife with her babies in tow.

'Can we go now, please?' I begged her.

'Absolutely!'

Meg climbed into the foothold I made with my hands and I boosted her up and she pulled herself through the hole. 'Thank goodness for the gym,' she whispered with a smirk knowing full well how much I hated the gym and how often I'd refused to join her with an array of bullshit excuses.

'See if you can open the door,' I whispered back, ignoring her gym jibe.

I heard her fiddling about on the other side as she tried opening the door. Cursing as she caught a nail, she rattled the door some more, making far too much noise, and then voila, the door was open and she grinned with pride. I had no idea how I was going to pull myself out. I needed Jay to pull me out but he wasn't here, he was nowhere, so I had to rely on the adrenalin pumping through my body to give me the strength I needed. I reached up, gripping the edge, grateful it was brick and not timber even though it bit into my fingertips and after giving myself a bouncing start, I pulled, hauling my entire body weight until I was high enough to flip a leg over the edge and pull myself up enough to climb out. It was not the least bit glamorous but I did it.

'Are you okay?' Meg asked as I panted in the dirt, finally free.

I nodded. 'Where are we?'

'I don't know,' she said, looking around as though the answer was going to magically arrive before us. 'It looks like nothing but desert.'

'That's not helpful Meg.'

'I didn't create the environment, you know.'

'Sorry, I know. No wonder Jay hasn't found us, we really are literally in the middle of bloody nowhere,' I sighed looking around at nothing but pitch-black emptiness and the occasional rangy tree shadowed by the sliver of moon.

Chapter 15

'What do we do now?' Meg asked as we rubbed our arms as the cold desert air bit at our skin.

'What makes you think I know?'

'You're the one with all the self-preservation training from the Rambo boyfriend, aren't you?' she said nudging me, doing her best to lighten the situation.

I laughed because it worked, it always worked and it helped spring my brain into action. Meg was right, I had some semblance of training and it was my fault after all that she was here and after the pregnancy revelation I had to step up. There was more at stake than just our own survival. 'We get walking before that freak show inside wakes up, I suppose,' I told her. It wasn't a genius plan but it was the best I had.

'Walk? Where?'

'I don't know. That way I guess,' I said, pointing forwards figuring it was as good a direction as any other.

She shrugged and started forwards. 'I suppose we have to hurry before he realises we're gone.'

'That'd probably be a great idea,' I agreed. 'Don't suppose you can run in your condition?'

'What condition?' she asked.

'The pregnancy one.'

'Oh shit, I'd forgotten about that. But still, pregnant is only pregnant, if I even am,' she added as though we hadn't been tracking the time and days by her puking schedule. 'I can still run just as much as you and if it means I might get to live, I'm fine with the risk, I assure you,' she said, grabbing my hand and picking up the pace.

The cold air sliced my lungs and slapped my face, the warm rocks and the coarse red dirt ripped at my bare feet. My feet stung with every step but my survival instincts were kicking in, adrenalin taking over and the pain no longer mattered. All that mattered was getting Meg to safety and finding my way back to Jay.

I'd woken in the basement minus my court shoes, not that I could have worn them anyway. Running through the red desert in the middle of the night where hungry dingoes prowled, the brownies waited and who knows what else lurked about, was crazy enough, doing it in any sort of heels would have been madness. But I wondered, as a sharp edge of a rock sliced my skin, if it'd have been as mad as barefoot. It'd have slowed us down though and we needed as much speed and distance as we could get.

There were no other sounds as our bare feet hit the dirt, still holding its warmth from the day, only the panting of our breaths as we focussed on moving forward and keeping momentum. We had no way to know where we were headed.

There was nothing either way to signify a direction, no sign of life, no roos, no trees, nothing but two stupid women running through the black of night.

The moon was sinking before we finally spotted a scrubby outcrop of saltbush. It wasn't much but it was something and at the very least, a place to rest for just a minute, to catch our breaths and see if we could get our bearings. It'd all be for nothing if we were running in the wrong direction.

We took cover in the saltbush, panting as we sucked cold desert air into our desperate lungs.

'What I wouldn't give for some water,' Meg said as she fell into the dirt.

'Don't think about it. It makes it worse,' I told her as I willed myself to think of anything else which wasn't easy when your throat was dry as bone all the way down to your stomach where the dust was sucking you dry.

We looked around, trying to decide which way to go, to keep going straight or if we could see something else that would help us decide? I prayed with my heart and soul that where we wanted to be, where we needed to be wasn't a hundred kilometres in the other direction.

The saltbush beside me rustled. I grabbed Meg's hand. 'Come on, it's time to go before we have another predator to worry about.' Something glinted from behind a bush further down. Eyes? I wasn't waiting to find out. Where there were eyes, there were teeth and a hungry stomach. I followed my instincts and we ran into the open plains where the moonlight was clearer and there were no places for hungry animals to hide, to wait and ambush us. I'd seen how they did it in the docos. Sure that was Africa, but isn't a desert a desert and a hungry animal a hungry animal?

'Come on, we have to keep moving,' I said reluctantly. 'Can you keep going?'

'Yeah, I can keep going,' she said, as we did our best to dust ourselves off but I suspect we were only smearing the red dust and making it worse.

'What's that over there?' Meg asked, pointing into the far distance.

I squinted. There was a rose hue rising behind tiny dark shapes on the horizon. Meg was right. It was something. It looked like a teeny tiny town.

'It's a fair way off. We better hustle if we want to get there before he brings down our breakfast and fires up his van to come looking for us.'

Meg nodded and forced herself into a jog and I followed suit. My entire body screamed for relief but I ignored it, let the adrenalin and fear take over and eventually, gradually picked up the pace. Our eyes focussed on nothing but that little town taking form under the rising sun. Our only hope was to reach it before the sun finished rising and Kevin discovered our absence. I had to ignore my aching muscles and keep moving. I could collapse when we were safe.

Bit by bit as the sun crept out of hiding, we got closer and closer to the town. We were almost at the trees edging the street. We'd been running for what seemed like hours, when Meg grabbed my arm and pulled me into the bushes.

'Ow, what are you doing?' I demanded.

'Ssshh,' she whispered, putting her finger to her mouth.

Meg pointed down the street. Our kidnapper was climbing out of what looked to be a rusted, falling apart, four-wheel drive. Not quite the rusted van Meg had described but just as ready for the scrap heap.

'Shit,' I said. 'What's he doing there? Why wasn't he chasing us?'

'I don't know. Maybe that heap of junk can't hack the terrain we just ran over and he's thinking he'll just head us off on the main street.'

We watched him get out of the oversized vehicle and wrap his bum bag around his round waist. 'Is he whistling?' I asked as we watched him walk two doors down to the bakery, evident by being the only shop open in the dusk of morning and already displaying its A Frame sign advertising *'best pies for miles'*.

'That fucker,' Meg spat.

My stomach rumbled with the smell of fresh baked bread wafting on the air but I stayed still, frozen, waiting for him to come out.

Dawn had arrived when he came out, still whistling, carrying a giant wedding cake.

'You have to be kidding me?' I said exasperated. 'He's that deluded he even had a cake made?'

Meg was speechless and fair enough too. What was there to say? We watched him put the cake in the passenger seat then come back around to the driver's door, climb in and after the car spat out gusts of thick black smoke, he drove off down the street.

We waited until the dust showed he'd turned off the main

road as he headed back towards the house in the middle of the desert.

'We've got about an hour before he reaches the house to find safety,' I said.

'Do you think we'll have safety here? What do we say? Clearly the baker's his mate.'

'Shit, do you think?'

'Dunno. What about there, that looks like a hostel or something. We'll be less out of place there, won't we?'

I looked down at our dirty bare feet and red dust smudged clothes. We were going to be out of place anywhere we went but I didn't want to rain on our moment of victory. 'Good point,' I said, pulling her to her feet.

We ran along the tree line for as far as we could, until we were almost opposite the small, white-washed frontage of the hostel.

'Act natural,' I said, ignoring Meg's smirk at the suggestion.

Holding my head high and like a true Harrington, I walked across the street as though I did it every day and pulled open the hostel door like I owned it and walked in like I belonged.

The small reception area was crowded with men who all turned as we walked in, their jaws dropping as our jaws dropped and then Jay stepped forward and I ran, crashing into his rock-hard chest and holding on as though my life would end if I let go.

A little lady with short brown curls tugged on my arm and held out some water. 'Come, dear, sit. You need to sit,' she said, leading me to a chair beside Meg who was already sitting, sipping her water.

I guzzled the water like a man who'd been lost in the desert. I had been that man, I reminded myself as I tried not to make a spectacle of myself. 'What are you all doing here?' I asked, looking from Jay to Tom to Moe to Michael.

'We came looking for you,' Jay said squatting before me. 'Are you okay?' he asked, his hands scouring my face and arms for injuries.

'We're okay,' I confirmed. 'Mostly,' I shrugged. 'How did you find us?'

'Well clearly we didn't, this is as far as we got. I followed your necklace,'

'My necklace?' I asked, reaching for it and remembering it was gone.

'It was fitted with a tracker,' he said softly.

'Christian had me tracked?' I shouted. 'How could he?'

'Don't be mad at him. He was worried that either something would happen to you or you'd run, just like you did. Sam got it for him and he gave it to you that Christmas.'

'So they've known where I was the whole time?' I asked quietly, tears filling my eyes.

'No, no,' Michael insisted. 'I swear it Jaz, swear on my life. Sam and Christian were the only ones who knew about it and Christian refused to look. He gave it all over to Sam, told him to just make sure you were okay and then, with all the stuff happening when Tom returned, honestly they forgot all about it. It wasn't until we were almost out of options after you disappeared, we'd tried the GPS on your phone but it was off and we weren't able to turn it on remotely. Turns out your kidnapper had crushed the phone to dust. Sam had to hunt down the transmitter for the necklace in a box buried in the back of his parent's shed,' he assured me.

'We haven't been gone that long and it sounds like you all managed quite bit in that time?'

'We did achieve a lot, courtesy of the Harrington chopper,' he smirked. 'Sam's been liaising with us from his parent's place while the chopper went where he said.

I watched him for a sign of a lie but I didn't see one so nodded. 'So Dad knows?'

'We had to tell him, Jaz,' Jay smiled tightly. 'You and Meg were kidnapped off the street. This was bigger than you and me. I couldn't do it alone and I knew it would take too long involving the police and they'd just tell him anyway, so I phoned Tom and he took it from there.'

'None of it matters right now, anyway,' Tom said, pulling me into his arms. 'As long as you're okay. And you can tell us how to find that bastard.'

'I am okay. And thank you. For coming. For the chopper. Everything,' I said, hugging him back. 'And the fuckers name is Kevin. He goes by Kevin Dale now but it's not what his name was when I knew him before. I can't for the life of me remember his last name or his dad's name. But his dad was one of those boring, low level politicians that managed a portfolio no one actually cared about.'

Just as the local old copper and his fresh-faced deputy walked in, Meg and I told everyone what each of us remembered, what I knew of Kevin from before when he'd hung around trying to weasel his way in. We told them about the run from the house to here, guessed at how long we ran, the terrain, the house itself, the basement we'd climbed out of, what we remembered of our kidnapper, the fact he'd just been in the bakery to pick up a wedding cake, enough it seemed to have the coppers headed in the right direction.

'There's more comin' out but it'll take some time. It's a high profile case and big wigs wanna make sure we cover it right,' the policeman in charge insisted. 'But I don't wanna wait and I've been given the okay to use the Harrington security team as back up. But only we get to fire and arrest, you hear?' he said, waggling a finger at each of the guys. 'You're just back-up muscle in case things go pear-shaped.'

'Yeah, yeah, course,' agreed Michael. I might not have known Michael well over the last few years but I knew him well enough to know that that look on his face was purely to be polite. If he got within cooee of our kidnapper he'd shoot him before Jay or Tom got to him for everyone's benefit because no one could predict what those two would do in this situation.

As they headed out the door I got up to follow.

'Hell no, girly,' insisted the old copper.

'No way am I staying here waiting for you to return. If you're going to get him, then I'm coming. I want to see you take that bastard down. I want to make sure it's done so I can maybe sleep at night.'

The old copper sighed with exasperation. I suspected this whole ordeal was more than he was happy to have land in his lap and was no doubt messing with his routine.'

'Well if you're going, I'm coming too,' Meg whispered in my ear, grabbing hold of my elbow. 'I'm certainly not staying here by myself with only the little lady to protect me, not when you have your Rambo boyfriend and his entourage. I don't even know where we are or how to get home. I don't have the keys to chopper,' she rambled.

I smiled, hooked my arm through hers. 'Come on, then, let's go see the pros take him down. Fool won't know what hit him,' I said as we stepped out into the rising heat.

It was just the kind of desert heat that made Jay nervous, had him pacing the halls and the beach, grumpy and touchy as a bear. It's why he never strayed far from the ocean, Tom too, I suspected, and no doubt Johnno and their mates. Such heat never lasted long with the salt spray and ocean breezes to quell it but until they did, I usually steered clear and let him do what he needed to get through. He'd never wanted to talk about his time in the army so I never pushed him. I looked at him to see how he was doing and his eyes told me he was struggling to keep the memories locked away but he definitely had his don't ask face on.

We climbed in the back of a shiny black Volvo four-wheel-drive that had Christian's name all over it. 'So where'd the car come from if you were all choppered in?' I asked when I saw the black family helicopter on the other side of the main street where it had landed.

'They had one on a truck headed to Adelaide from WA, Christian did whatever it is Christian does to get what he wants. I suspect some people were paid well for the inconvenience,' Jay smiled.

'He couldn't have just got something else from nearby?'

'You know Christian, it wouldn't have crossed his mind to do anything other than phone the poor folk at Audi, BMW and

Volvo until he found something. He had it all sorted within minutes of Sam activating the tracker and getting a location,' Tom added.

We followed the police cruiser across the red dirt road, the dust swirling all around the car, making it hard to see.

'Here, have some water,' Jay insisted, handing us each bottles from a cooler at his feet.

'You should have some sugar too,' said Tom, coming up with some snickers bars.

Meg and I added the sustenance to our systems while we drove. I could hear Moe in the front passenger seat making calls, giving updates on the situation, I daresay to Christian and my father.

'You feeling okay?' I asked Meg, trying to distract myself from Moe's conversation up the front of the car.

'Mmmm,' she shrugged. 'Just hungry I think. And bloody tired.'

'Meg needs another Snickers, Tom, are there more?'

'Yeah, course,' he said, passing two more over.

I wasn't sure I was still hungry but I ate another anyway. The sugar mixed with the adrenalin made my head spin but it stopped spinning as soon as the car stopped.

'This it, love?' The old copper called through the window Michael had just wound down.

I couldn't see past the red dust caking the windows so I got out to have a proper look at the house. I looked over the dilapidated white-washed homestead that would have once been the pride of the district but now felt the shame of rejection. It looked different with the sun beating down on it, catching the gaps in the dirt on the windows and glinting just a little, but I saw the basement we'd climbed out of, the window we'd pushed open, the marks we'd made in the red dust, it was the same place we'd run from during the night. 'Yeah, this is it,' I told them.

The cars emptied in the blink of an eye.

'You two stay in the car,' Jay demanded.

'Jay,' I began to argue.

'No, Jaz. Not this time. No arguing. You get in that car and you stay there. In fact, I'd feel a whole lot better if you lock the doors and lay down on the seat just in case he comes past. I don't want him seeing you in there, either of you,' he added, the last holding his hand up to Meg just in case she dared argue with him. But I could see from the look on her face she wouldn't dare. He could be pretty scary when he fired up but I was so used to it. He didn't intimidate me anymore but I was smart enough to know when I wasn't going to win so I gave in, grunted and hmphd more for affect than anything else and followed Meg into the car and did as we'd been told. I watched them until they were swallowed by the old house and then I did what Jay asked and laid down.

'He's really bossy isn't he?' Meg smiled.

I smiled back with a little pride as I got comfortable.

I'd planned to look out the window again as soon as I heard them come out, because I was sure I'd hear them, that there'd be a kerfuffle but there were no sounds but our heavy shallow breaths. And then suddenly, the door was pulled open.

'Hey,' Jay said, resting his hand on my leg when I jumped up startled.

'Hey,' I whispered. 'Did you get him?'

He shook his head.

'What do you mean no?' I near shouted.

'I'm so sorry, Jaz,' he said, 'but he was gone. There's no sign of him other than a couple of empty tins of stew, some dirty bowls, a crushed wedding cake and a dress ripped to shreds. What the hell was going on in there?'

'Shit,' I spat, purposely ignoring his question. 'What the fuck do we do now?' I asked.

'It's okay. This isn't the end. We're going to find him. Well the police are going to find him. We're going home.'

'What? No! I'm not going until they find him.'

'It could take a while, Jaz. There'll be a lot of coppers involved. It's going higher up than these fellas. We'll just be in the way. Tom and Michael and Moe are coming back to the pub. Meg should come and stay too. We'll wait to hear something from there.'

What could I do? There was nothing we could do but I felt sick, my stomach twisted and somersaulted, threatening to heave out the peanuts and nougat. The only things I'd put into my stomach since before I'd been kidnapped off the street by this bastard and now I just had to go to the pub and sit on the beach as though everything was okay.

'How do they even know what he looks like?' I asked, childishly.

'They know who he is Jaz. They didn't know he was a kidnapper before now but they know who he is or at least what he looks like. They'll find him. We just have to let them do their jobs.'

'Fine,' I sulked as we all found seats and headed back to the main street where we were to climb in to the freshly fuelled Harrington chopper.

Chapter 16

I registered the looks on Tom and Jay's faces as they climbed aboard the helicopter and the rotors fired up, their bodies tensing. I put it into the same box as dry arid weather and thunderstorms. I suspected they were considering driving the fancy Audi SUV back to Adelaide but Meg had already curled into a corner and fallen asleep and Tom was looking at me with worry.

As I found a seat on the helicopter, I suddenly felt like I was stepping back in time, back to another person, a person I didn't particularly like, from a time in my life I'd rather pretend never happened.

Jay gripped my hand as the chopper's vibrations shook the blood in our veins and the memories in his head, whatever they may be, because he never spoke of them. Tom sat stiff and straight his mouth a tight thin line, his eyes seeing something other than the retreating red dirt of the outback. These were men of strength, men who had fought and survived and protected beyond war, but even they had demons that threatened to bring them to their knees. But in true displays of strength, it all happened on the inside and unless you were a part of their inner circle, of their most intimate of companions, you'd probably never even notice they suffered.

I sank into the corner, against the window and watched the ground sink further and further away, feeling as though I was leaving myself down there in the red dust, even though there was the last place I wanted to be.

Even though I'd protested about leaving, I couldn't wait to be done with the whole business and get back to whatever was left of my life, which was probably not much at this point. Delia would be having kittens with this new twist and I'd involved another staff member. I was officially a danger to the company. Not that I could have considered returning to work until they caught him. As it was, I was going to be lucky if Jay ever let me leave his side again.

Someone had roped off the grassed picnic area in front of the pub for the helicopter to land. There was a crowd of familiar faces waiting for us, Lydia, Andrea, Alex, Christian and Ainsley.

Once we were on the ground, the helicopter turned off and we all exited to stand on the grass in the sunshine. My family rushed forward, enveloping me in hugs.

'Are you okay?' fussed Lydia.

'I'm fine, I'm fine,' I assured her. 'Where'd Meg go?'

'Michael took her straight up the back stairs. Christian has a doctor up there waiting for her to make sure everything's okay,' Ainsley told me.

'You should get checked out when he's done with Meg,' Lydia said.

'I'm fine,' I said, waving her off.

'No you're not,' Jay interrupted. 'I saw your feet, Jaz, they must be killing you.'

I looked down at my feet. I'd completely forgotten we'd never recovered our shoes. Red dirt and blood caked my feet and suddenly the pain was excruciating. I guess that's how it works when you're focussed and fuelled by adrenalin, you don't notice things like your feet being ripped to shreds but as soon as the adrenalin's gone and some fool points out you're supposed to be in pain, your brain switches on and it's all over red rover.

'Come on,' Jay said, rolling his eyes and scooping me into his arms. He carried me up the back steps without even losing his breath. Up two flights until we reached our own apartment.

'Bet you never thought you'd have to do that again,' I joked about how many times he'd had to carry me home when I'd been drunk beyond repair.

He smirked but didn't say anything.

Two strangers stood in front of the entrance, a man as big as a tank and a woman who looked like an Amazonian warrior in black.

'You must be Bill and Al,' Jay said, introducing himself. 'This is Jaz. We good in there?' he asked.

'Yes sir. No one's been in since we secured it. Drew and Stevo are on the other door.'

'Thanks,' Jay said as Al opened the door for him.

Jay took me straight into the bedroom and laid me on the bed before disappearing into the bathroom.

'What are you doing?' I called.

'Getting something to clean your feet,' he said, almost laughing at my question as though he'd have been doing anything else.

'No, don't be ridiculous,' I said heading into the bathroom. 'I can shower by myself, fix my own feet,' I insisted.

'Come on, Babe, now's not the time to be stubborn.'

'I'm not being stubborn, Jay,' I said, tears overflowing. 'I need to do this. He is not going to break me. I'm a Harrington for crying out loud. I can clean my own fucking feet,' I sobbed as I walked in and turned on a tap.

'I'll be right here, then,' he said, his voice choked as he let himself sink to the floor and wait for me.

I hadn't expected to be so overcome but now we were here, now we were alone, the magnitude of the last three days hit me, everything that'd happened, could have happened, hit me. The power I'd lost, the possibilities and I couldn't deal with it. I needed to regain some control, even if it was just cleaning my own damn feet.

They were a mess too and as soon as the water hit the cuts they stung so badly I had to hold onto the cry that tried to escape my throat. Jay was struggling enough, he didn't need me crying out in pain too.

I watched the red dust run down the drain, waited for the stinging to stop then lathered up my loofah and scrubbed every inch of my body, washed my hair and scrubbed my body again. I brushed my teeth twice, gargled with mouthwash twice in the hope anything left behind in my mouth from that man would be dead. I'd come so close to losing everything that meant something. I'd come so close to losing Jay because how could he have touched me after that man?

Jay was waiting as I stepped out of the shower, helped me dry for which I was grateful because I'd suddenly lost all my strength.

'How are you doing?' he asked me once I was sitting on the bed as he inspected my feet.

'I'm fine,' I said exasperated, sick of telling everyone the same thing. 'How's Meg?' I asked.

'She's just fine,' he assured me. 'Now, let me look you over,' he insisted, scouring my naked body. 'Did he?'

'No,' I said knowing exactly what he meant. 'He kissed me once, but I just disinfected my mouth multiple times.'

Jay nodded as the doctor came in.

'Is Meg okay? The baby?' I asked.

'She's fine. Let me look at you,' he smiled, checking my feet, disinfecting them cut by cut and wrapping them before checking the other important functions that could have been impacted by being drugged, dehydrated and exhausted.

'How is she?' Jay asked when he came back in as the doctor was finishing up.

'Oh she's fine,' he smiled. 'Other than the cuts on her feet and a bit of dehydration, she's fine. Could use a good feed though I daresay and just stay off your feet, alright?' he said.

I nodded. He shook hands with Jay and left.

'So what do you feel like eating?' Jay asked.

'Nothing, I'm not really hungry,' I said.

'Well that's a clear sign you need something decent in your stomach. When was the last time you ate properly?' he asked.

Sheepishly I admitted, 'Lunch the day he grabbed us. I didn't eat anything he gave us. You told me not to if that ever happened.'

'That's three days ago Jaz, fuck,' he said, running his hand through his hair. 'I'll get Greg to whip you both up a green smoothie and send up some soup. You can have something heavier later.'

I nodded. There was no point arguing.

'I'm proud of you, though,' he smiled. 'Glad you listened to something.'

'Are you mad?'

'What?' he asked, surprised.

'I didn't wait for you,' I sobbed. 'On Friday, I didn't wait for you. Everyone was leaving. There were fifteen people. We were just going down the street. I thought we'd be okay. But they got ahead of us and I didn't notice and Meg and I were talking and I wasn't paying attention. I'm sorry, Jay,' I sobbed. 'I should have waited for you.'

'Hey,' he soothed, holding me to him. 'None of this is your fault. It's his. It's all on him. I'm just glad you're okay,' he insisted, holding my face in front of his. 'So bloody relieved you're okay,' he smiled, pulling my mouth to his. 'Okay, enough,' he said, his hand softly on the side of my face as though making sure I was real. 'I'm going to get you a smoothie and some soup and Greg will make you some pasta for later.'

I nodded. 'Can someone bring Meg up here? I don't want her down there all by herself.' We'd been through so much, we'd been terrified and were exhausted and being afraid and alone in that little guest room where there wasn't even a table to eat at was not where Meg should be

'Sure,' he said, going out to speak to one of the people guarding our doors.

'Jay,' I called before he left. He turned, his face worried and pained, aged since Friday. 'I love you.'

He beamed. 'I love you, too.'

Meg sat at our dining table fifteen minutes later. She slowly regained some colour as she sipped a cup of tea.

'I've got to go downstairs and check on some things, you two eat and do not leave this room, do you hear me?' Jay said when Al brought in the smoothies and vegetable soup Greg had sent up.

I saluted him, I had no words, I'd started stuffing soup-soaked bread in my mouth and was suddenly so hungry I was sure there wasn't enough food in my bowl.

Jay smiled, a proper smile, the first I'd seen since I'd walked into the hostel and left us to eat, promising Greg would send up some bolognaise as soon as it was ready.

Once our tummies were full we had to sleep. I insisted Meg stay and we fell asleep on the bed I shared with Jay. When I woke, it was Jay lying beside me reading a book with the first of the morning's light.

'Hey,' I said.

'Hey,' he replied, putting his book down. 'How are you feeling?'

'Better,' I smiled. 'Where's Meg?'

'Al took her back to her room and is sitting in there with her.'

'Good,' I smiled. 'How are you,' I asked.

He smiled at me, his eyes looking into mine as though it was the first time he'd ever really seen me, even though this was a regular occurrence and said, 'I'm much better now you're here and that you're okay.'

I put my hand on his lovely bicep in comfort.

'I was so worried, Jaz. It was like my heart was splitting open every minute, every second you were gone. I've never in my life felt that kind of fear. I'm not much of a man without you,' he said, gathering me into his arms and pulling me to his chest. 'So he didn't touch you? What did he want with you then?' he asked in a whisper as though afraid of the answer.

'To marry me. We were to consummate it all after the nuptials, which was the day we ran.'

'That explains the cake and ripped wedding dress,' Jay nodded, taking it in. 'I can't believe he was really going to go through with it.'

'Said he had a celebrant he'd paid handsomely enough to not listen to my ravings,' I told him.

'I daresay he's not done then.'

'No, I don't imagine he is,' I agreed, snuggling into Jay's chest where it was warm, where it smelt like home and happiness and safety.

We lay quietly for a while, soaking each other in, just content to be together. I'd really thought for a minute in that basement that I'd never be here again, that I'd never have Jay hold me, to feel his heart beating, to feel the warmth of his body beside me. Thinking of Jay was all that had propelled me to keep going, to fight, to run when running was a ridiculous thing to do. This is why I did it. And for Meg. She wouldn't have fared well once Kevin found out about the baby, she would have been in danger if we hadn't run. If she hadn't miscarried from the stress of it and miscarrying in that dirty basement with no access to doctors was not an option.

'Are you hungry?' Jay asked.

I shrugged.

'Lydia brought you some super soft slippers if you fancy going down for breakfast.'

I nodded, but sank into him a little further. 'In a minute,' I said.

He squeezed me tighter. 'A minute or ten is fine.'

We slowly descended the stairs, the slippers were like clouds but my whole body ached with every step. Jay had offered to carry me down but I refused to be that weak. We met Meg and Al halfway down. Lydia had brought her some slippers too. We hugged. 'Are you alright?' I asked her.

'Yeah, I'm fine. How could I not be when I'm being so well taken care of,' she smiled.

'I'm glad you're being taken care of, you need to be.'

'I am looking forward to going home though, so hopefully this is all over soon.'

'Yeah, me too. Not that I think I have much to go back to,' I said.

'What do you mean?' she asked.

'Well I can't go back to my apartment after the whole space was violated by that creep and I doubt Delia will have me back.'

'Ah, Delia,' she smirked. 'I suppose I better call her and let her know we're okay and what's going on,' she groaned.

After Meg had called Delia who was just grateful we were okay, we went into the dining room and found my family taking over the whole place with a giant round table they used for conferences and big parties, in the middle of the room. I waved hey to everyone. 'Have you met all these crazy people?' I asked Meg.

'Only Lydia who brought me the slippers,' she said.

'Well, everyone, this is Meg, Meg, everyone,' I said and then proceeded to name them all, not that she could ever remember so many.

I was about to sit in the chair Jay was pulling out for me when I looked over to the bar and where my father stood holding two glasses of orange juice and I froze.

'What's wrong?' Jay asked.

I didn't answer him.

'Jaz, you're white as a ghost. What's wrong? I can't take any more scares,' he said, then followed my eyes. 'Ah, I suspected he'd come even though I told him not to.'

My dad walked over carrying his two glasses of orange juice. Suddenly, hope sparked in the pit of my stomach that the extra glass of juice was for my mother. I looked around and there she was, sitting at the table in the corner with the security team, watching me carefully, warily.

Our eyes caught and her face split open in a smile. The most beautiful smile I'd ever seen and although I'd never seen my mother run, she was a proper lady, she near ran to me and her arms were around me, squishing all the air out of me and tears out my eyes.

'Oh Jasmine, I was so scared,' she sobbed into my hair.

'I'm okay, Mum, I promise.'

'Well, let me look at you anyway,' she said, holding me at arm's length.

'I'm alright, Mum. It's good to see you though,' I said, pulling her into another hug.

Dad finally put the glasses of orange juice he was carrying on the table and shook Jay's hand. Jay reluctantly shook hands with my father, his face contorted in a grimace.

'Jasmine,' he said, turning his attention to me. He looked older than when I'd last seen him, his face lined, his eyes shadowed.

'Dad,' I said, more of a groan than any real word.

'I'm glad you're alright,' he said.

'Thank you,' I said, unsure myself if it was for his well wishes or the use of the family resources, which really were under Tom's control now anyway.

Dad nodded, picked up the orange juices and went to sit down with the security team.

'Don't mind him, Love. You know what he's like,' Mum said.

'Sure, Mum,' I said.

'Well, you sit and eat, you need to eat. We'll talk later, alright?'

I nodded, kissed her cheek and she reluctantly walked to the other table while I sat down with the rest of my family to eat the mountain of eggs and bacon, tomatoes and mushrooms that had suddenly appeared before me.

Chapter 17

'When do you think they'll let us go outside again?' Meg asked as she wistfully looked out to the sun-drenched sand and ocean.

'If Jay has his way, never,' I laughed.

It elicited a smile from her too but she still looked outside, craving the fresh air and freedom of space that I was also craving. It had only been a couple of days but we'd been locked in a small dark space, being stuck inside again was messing with our heads. At least we had a window here I suppose. But still, I desperately wanted to feel the warmth of the sun on my arms, breathe in the salt laden air and feel the grass or the sand beneath my feet, I wasn't fussy which, I just needed to feel, something, to know I was alive, to remember the good.

'Jay,' I whispered. 'Can you give us some security so we can go outside?' I begged.

'Hell no, Jaz,' he said, looking at me as though I'd asked to fly to the moon.

'Jay, come on, we need some air, some space. Surely we'll be okay just out there on the grass with some security?'

'What's wrong with the balcony, this one or ours upstairs?'

'There's no grass for my feet to feel, no rays for my arms to bathe in,' I told him.

'Fine,' he conceded. 'One hour, just out there where I can see you and you take Michael, Moe, Al and Bill. No, you take them all, you take Drew and Stevo too and Tom and I will be sitting right here on the balcony.'

'Fine,' I smiled, accepting this was as good as we were going to get.

Sarah, her hair still damp from her morning surf, rustled up a blanket for us to sit on, some iced tea and snacks and a couple of old magazines from the staff room. As I stepped into the sun, it was truly beautiful, the warmth stroking my skin, my skin absorbing its goodness and already I felt better, revived, rejuvenated.

'Nice work,' Meg smiled as we stood on the lawn, our arms outstretched, soaking up the sun's glorious rays, smiles stretching across our faces at the sounds of birds in the trees, the ocean's waves hitting the sand, some children a way down the beach laughing because there certainly wasn't a single person within breathing distance of us. The security team had shooed everyone within 200m away and literally stood on the grass like sentinels surrounding us.

We sat on the blanket and Meg looked up at our sentinels. 'This might not have been quite what I was expecting but I guess it's a small price.'

'Welcome to my world,' I groaned.

'This is how it was growing up? Are you serious?'

I shrugged. 'When I was on my own there was only ever Jay but if we gathered as a family, yeah, this was it. They once knew how to be inconspicuous though,' I said, saying the last loud enough for them all to hear, bringing the smallest of smirks from Michael who stood watching the water.

Meg and I didn't bother with the magazines, we each had a tall glass of iced tea then laid back and breathed in the fresh air, the smells of grass beginning to sweat under the sun's rays filling our noses, breathing in the salt from the water spraying as the waves crashed onto the beach, it was perfect.

I was dozing off when I heard Jay, 'Okay ladies, times up, back up inside,' he said in his stupid commando voice. I hadn't had to put up with that voice in years, not since we'd run. I'd hoped he never had to be that person again but then I'd also hoped I'd never have to be this person again either and some things just came naturally to us both when push came to shove.

I groaned but didn't complain. There was no point. We settled in the dining room right next to the open doors to the balcony with Al and Bill at the next table keeping watch. My brothers and Jay took a break, went to eat or do whatever they did with the rest of the security team.

Mum came to stand before our table. 'May I?' she asked.

'Of course,' I said and she sat.

I introduced her to Meg and she politely enquired after Meg's wellbeing before returning her attention to me.

'This is a beautiful place Jasmine, you've done very well,' she smiled.

'Thanks, but this is all Jay. I live in the city,' I told her.

'Why?' she asked, confused. 'Wasn't the whole point of running away so you could be together?'

'We are together. But no, Mum, the point of running away was to be free,' I told her. 'Free to make my own choices and free to not be dumped in some facility in Italy, free to be with Jay but free to me, to be heard, to be seen, not caged liked an animal.'

'Oh,' she said, taking it all in. 'And did you succeed?' she asked.

'Until I showed up in the paper after Tom's wedding, yes. I'd made a life, Mum. I have, or probably had a job that I liked, that was satisfying, an apartment where people didn't watch every move I made, where I cooked my own food and cleaned and paid my own bills, friends who didn't care I was a Harrington, if they even knew. I lived Mum and it was amazing. But it doesn't matter. It's all gone now. It was all for nothing. Jay won't let me go back to the city, I'll have to stay here under his watchful eye which is no different to Dad's.'

'Jasmine,' she scolded. 'He loves you just like your father loves you. They just want what's best for you, to protect you. They just don't always know how to do that.'

'Well, maybe they should just ask me. I'm a person, too and I'm not stupid.'

'No, dear, no, you're not stupid,' she smiled proudly.

'Then why is it that what I think and what I want is always pushed aside?'

'Because they're men, dear, they sometimes can't see past their own noses,' she smiled.

I smiled too. My mother always did have a forgiving, unique

view on the world. I'd missed her. I didn't agree with her. The 'oh they're men,' argument was flimsy at best. But I missed her.

'Well, I better go and check on your father, he looks a little lost in there without a job to do,' she said, amused.

I followed her eyes into the dining room where Dad was pacing the floor, looking around for something to do but not knowing his place here in the home of his declared enemy.

Mum put her hand on my shoulder as she left and the small comfort warmed me all the way to my toes.

'I can't wait to go home and see my mum,' Meg said wistfully.

'I'm sorry you got caught up in all this,' I told her.

She shrugged. 'It's alright. The being kept here and protected part anyway,' she smirked. 'It takes my mind off the fact that I'm pregnant. My parents are going to kill me and my life is never going to be the same again. I don't even know if I'm capable of being a mother for goodness sake. So yeah, the distraction's not all bad.'

'You're going to be a great mother, Meg. I know it,' I said, drawing her in for a hug.

The dining room emptied out. Lydia and Andrea ate quietly across the room. Sam followed Christian, Ainsley and Henry upstairs so Henry could nap. Michael and Moe were following up a lead in Jay's office with Tom and Jay went to adjudicate a minor scuffle in the front bar so it was just Sarah and another girl clearing the last of the lunch mess and it was quiet and it was nice. People had returned to the grass outside with their families and their picnics. Bill and Al sat at the next table pretending to read the paper, Meg was flipping through

Facebook on her phone and I flipped through one of the magazines Sarah had given us. I was reading something about the Kardashians when something hard and cold pressed against the back of my head.

I slowly turned, fear rippling through me and creepy Kevin smiled as Al clicked the safety off on her gun pressed against Kevin's head. She was stealthier than him and it gave me hope.

'I go, she goes,' he taunted.

We stood in a standoff for what felt like hours but was only seconds, my body desperate to crumble, tears desperate to fall. There was scrambling over by the door, someone asked how the hell he'd gotten past the guy on the door who was checking everyone that came in but he'd clearly changed his hair, added glasses, changed the way he dressed, no doubt had a new ID to go with the new look. It would have been easy if he'd arrived at the same time as a group, mixed in with them. I'd done it myself in the early days of sneaking into a club with a fake ID before I realised no one actually cared. Jay was bellowing orders but there was nothing he could do now so when Kevin waggled his finger signifying I should stand, I stood.

'Jaz?' Meg asked, her voice shaking.

'It's okay. It's going to be okay,' I told her as I looked into Kevin's eyes and he shook his head. It wasn't going to be okay and we all knew it.

'Let her go. You don't want to do this,' Al begged, lowering her gun, trying not to spook a wild animal.

'I do want to do this. She is mine. She is going to be my wife, so you sit your arse back down, lady or me and my fiancée will be off to a better place,' he assured her. 'Come on, walk with me,' he instructed, stepping off the balcony as frightened families abandoned their picnics.

I followed him, slowly, methodically, my eyes glued to his. There was so much security here. He had to know we weren't going to get far.

He walked backwards towards the carpark, his eyes constantly darting over my shoulder to make sure no one was following us. As he did, I looked over his shoulder and saw Michael, partly shielded by a tree. He motioned to me, holding three fingers in the air and then waved his hand, motioning for me to drop. I conveyed my understanding as best I could with my eyes, hoping he saw, too afraid to make any other movement.

Kevin walked me, one step, two, his breathing ragged, his eyes darting left and right.

Michael held up his pointer finger, one.

Then his middle finger, two.

His ring finger came next, three and I dropped. The ear-splitting sound of a gunshot exploded into the air as my mother screamed my name. My hands clasped my ears and I hit the ground, creepy Kevin falling on me.

I screamed, high pitched and loud before shouting, 'Get him off, get him off.' I tried pushing his heavy, dead body off of mine but I was trapped, I had no movement and he was too heavy. Suddenly he was thrown clear and Jay's arms wrapped around me. I broke down, my body shaking, hacking sobs and screeching pleas came from my mouth, from somewhere inside of me, from deep in my very core but sounded as though they came from somewhere else, somewhere far away, somewhere wild and pained.

'It's okay, you're okay,' Jay soothed, rocking me from side to side.

Sirens and flashing lights filled the air and still I clung to Jay as he rocked me, his arms wrapped tightly around me like a vice.

I felt more than saw the police officer come to our side and speak but Jay just shook his head and someone came to lead the officer away.

Eventually Mum and Lydia came to our side, 'Jasmine, come on love, come inside,' Mum pleaded, her voice cracking, on the edge of breaking herself.

I nodded, wiping my messy face with my hands before Mum held out one of Margot's perfectly pressed handkerchiefs and I felt a tiny spark of goodness spread through my body.

Jay carried me up the outside stairs to our apartment. Mum handed me a glass of water while Jay held me to him on one side and Lydia stuck to my other.

'I'm okay,' I finally said.

'You don't have to be, Jaz,' Lydia told me.

I held her hand. 'Thanks. But I am. Sort of. Enough,' I smiled and she pulled me to her not caring that the mess on my clothes would ruin her pretty dress.

'We'll let you rest then,' Mum said. 'Come on Lydia, let your sister rest, she's in good hands,' she smiled to Jay.

When they were gone, I showered under water so hot it burned. I scrubbed and I scrubbed, tears flowing down my face until my skin was raw and my emotions were spent.

Dried and dressed in clean clothes Lydia had brought me. Jay and I lay on the bed looking at each other. Jay stroked the side of my face with his hand, scooping some stray hairs out of the mess of tears and snot on my face before wiping my face with a tissue from the bedside. Then he kissed me, softly. 'Please, don't ever do that to me again.'

I smiled, there had been no choice in the matter but I understood where he was coming from. I never wanted to do that to me again either. My heart had stopped for a minute and I wasn't sure I'd ever get the look of surprise in Kevin's eyes out of my head or forget the feeling of his dead body weighted on mine.

'And before you ask, no, you can't ever leave here,' he smirked, knowing full well he didn't have that much say in my life.

I raised my eyebrows for affect.

'Seriously though, will you stay? Not because I say you have to. Please want to. I don't think I could stand you going back to the city. Not after everything. I want you beside me every night and every morning. I want to see your beautiful face when I wake up and hold you in my arms while I sleep. I need it Jaz. I need you.'

'For now,' I said. 'But eventually, when I'm not so emotionally scarred from all of this, who knows,' I whispered.

'When you're not so emotionally scarred, I want you to marry me. I want you to stay here with me, run the pub with me, or not, do whatever you want as long as you're here in my bed, on my couch drinking coffee every morning. Have babies with me, see the world, live,' he said, his hand tracing my mouth, tapping my nose.

I smiled. 'I think I'd like to be married to you now,' I told him. 'In a while, when everything's calmed down and we're both sane again. You'll have to ask me properly though, so I know you mean it,' I added, smirking.

He laughed out loud. 'So you know I mean it, hey? Because it's not been clear to blind Freddy for the last five years that I'm hopelessly, ridiculously in love with you?'

I kissed him like I meant it. 'I know you love me Jay, but you've never asked me to marry you before. I want you to be sure.'

'Oh, I'm sure Jaz. I've wanted to marry you since the first day I met you but you were only fifteen. When we ran you were 17. I was being a gentleman by waiting, waiting for you to believe in yourself enough, to forgive yourself. The time for being a gentleman and waiting is finally over,' he said, pulling me into a kiss so sweet and sensual, so perfect and filled with love and passion that my toes tingled.

'Well, what can a girl say to that?' I smiled.

'Yes?' he asked.

'Yes,' I smiled, kissing him then finding my perfect place against his body where I could feel his heart beating too fast.

Epilogue

It had been eight weeks since I'd seen my family but they'd returned and gathered en masse in the T-bar drinking martinis as the sun began its nightly descent over the water.

'Oh, Jaz,' Lydia breathed. 'You look beautiful!'

'This is all you Lydia. The dress is really beautiful. It's a masterpiece,' I told her as I twirled this way and that like a child playing dress ups.

'I knew you'd like it. I was driving home with Tom and Alex the last time we were here and it just came to me, I saw you in it and you looked as perfect in my imagination as you do right this minute,' she smiled proudly and she had every right to.

Shoestring straps held up the off-white vintage lace dress with the softest satin underlay. It flowed effortlessly to the ground and made me feel like a princess. I wore my grandmother's pearl earrings Lydia had brought with her, the infinity pendant from Christian someone had dug out of the bin in the desert town with my handbag and I wore the cushion cut solitaire diamond ring Jay had finally gotten onto my finger.

I'd left my out of control black curls do their thing with just a little anti-frizz serum and wore just enough make-up to stop me looking pasty in the photographs. Lydia had painted my nails a soft pale pink and I almost felt worthy.

'Well, we better get out there,' Alex said to Christian and Ainsley. Lydia was flying solo with Andrea having gone back to Paris to visit her family.

Christian squeezed my hand, 'You good?' he asked. I nodded yes and he left with a smile as Tom and Henry stepped forward.

Little Henry gripped my hand and asked, 'Ready Auntie Jaz?' he looked so handsome in his little white tux that it melted my heart. He was becoming an old pro at this wedding thing already.

I nodded, 'I'm ready, let's do it, hey?'

Henry nodded, a huge grin on his face and Tom held out his arm to walk me down the aisle. We'd taken only two steps before my father stepped into the doorway.

'Jasmine, you look beautiful,' my mum gushed, kissing my cheek, careful not to smudge what makeup I wore.

'Thank you, Mum. Lydia is extremely talented.'

'She is. But you make that dress, my dear,' she smiled proudly.

'Dad?' I asked, wondering what he wanted.

He nervously cleared his throat which was disconcerting to see for a man like my father. He didn't struggle with nerves or anxiety. He walked into a room and he owned it, every time. 'I wanted to say congratulations. I'm very proud of you, Jasmine.'

I had to hold my lips together to stop the tears from welling in my eyes. I couldn't remember a single time in my life my father had ever been proud of me.

'You finally have something to be proud of,' I told him.

'Jasmine,' he said, taking my hands in his. 'I have always been proud of you. You have always been the light of my life and my greatest fear.'

I hmphd like a child not a woman about to marry the love of her life. 'I'm sorry,' I said when he gave me that look that begged me to behave. 'It's just a little hard to believe after everything that's happened, everything you did.'

'What I did, I always did for you.' He held his hand up as I was about to protest. 'The day you were born, you had this look in your eye, this look that said no matter what, you were going to take on the world. But you were so tiny and perfect and it filled my heart with so much fear and I just never knew how to protect you. I walked you to kindergarten and school as often as I could just to make sure you were okay. I know you hated working on that soap and in hindsight, it was probably the beginning of the downfall, but I saw the friends you were making and Pete had an opening and I thought maybe it was a good way to give you a purpose, something else to do to keep you out of trouble.'

'You didn't do it so you'd have something to talk about and show off at parties?'

'What? No! I wouldn't use my daughter like that. I introduced you to those people hoping to hell you'd see another path other than the one you were on. You were self destructing so bloody fast. I didn't know how to make it stop.'

'You loved me?' I asked, trying to comprehend what he was saying.

He pulled me into his arms. 'More than my own life. So much I was going to lock my daughter away in Italy,' he said with a laugh on his voice.

'I'm sorry I ran.'

'I'm sorry I gave you a reason to. I'm sorry I didn't listen to you, that I was too pigheaded to listen to you. You were always so strong and smart, smarter than me and it frightened me.'

I laughed. 'Now I think you're giving me a little too much credit.'

'Jasmine, you are the brightest woman I know. Don't tell your sister I said that, but if you put your mind to it, you could have taken over the world and I just didn't know what to do with that. I tried. Hell, I tried everything I knew but clearly I didn't know the right things and I've paid the price for it for three long years. I put your mother through three long years of hell because I was too pigheaded to listen to my brilliant daughter who was always smarter than me.'

I let him hug me, I let him hold me tight and the relief, the years of pent up anger flowed out in my tears.

'Dad, would you like to give me away?' I asked quietly.

'Jasmine, I'd love nothing more,' he smiled as though he'd won a prize.

'Even if it is to Jay?'

'Because it is to Jay. He is a good man. I knew that too. I just didn't want to lose you. I was so damn afraid, I couldn't see straight. But he is a good man and I know he loves you with everything he is.'

'I love him more.'

Tom led Mum away and then as the music started up, an acoustic guitar and a local singer sang one of her original songs, my dad walked me down the aisle to the love of my life.

Jay watched me walk out of the T-bar, his eyes locked on mine, his face grinning with pure joy. Who would have thought the messed-up Princess of Party, Jaz Harrington would have been here, on this beach, living this dream and marrying this incredible human? I beamed like a nutter, I could feel it and I didn't care.

With our declarations of love exchanged, rings placed on fingers and flower petals thrown, we gathered under the big tree in front of the pub with fairly lights twinkling above as the sun finished its descent drinking sparkling apple juice. Jay wasn't ready to put me in the path of too much temptation just yet.

'Jaz, you look beautiful,' Meg gushed as she hugged me.

'And you're starting to show,' I smiled rubbing her stomach.

She giggled. 'I have a feeling there's more than one.'

'Why do you say that?'

'It's either that or I've just eaten waaaay too much of Barb's cake and I don't want to admit that!'

I laughed. I missed Barb's cake.

'When are you coming back?' she begged.

'Oh honey, I'm not. I've been doing a little design work for Christian and it seems it really is in the blood,' I smiled. 'I'm loving it and I get to see Henry all the time and work from home a lot, so I see Jay every day. Delia and I have made peace. I told her it wasn't her fault we were taken a thousand times but she just can't get past it. I'm not sure she ever will and I can't go back to the Chicken Men. I just can't,' I laughed.

'Well, I can't blame you for that,' she moaned. 'It's just not the same without you. No one else laughs at Clary the way you do. Everyone's afraid of her,' she giggled.

'Well, I'm sure Clary is enjoying being the Queen Bee again.'

'Too much. Way too much,' she laughed before Lydia dragged her away.

'So you and your dad made peace, huh?' asked Jay, slipping his arm around my waist and pulling me to him.

'Yep. A little. I'm sure there's a way to go. So many egos and so many misunderstandings Jay and it led to so many bad things. Promise me,' I asked holding his face to make sure he saw me, that he heard me. 'Always say what you mean. Don't assume I know. Don't assume I see between the lines. Just always be upfront, that's all I want from you.'

'That's all?' he asked with that grin of his.

'Weeeellll, maybe not all...' I smiled back before his mouth claimed mine and my husband kissed me like he meant

If you loved The Fall of Jaz, help others find it by reviewing on Amazon or Goodreads.

If you would like to be the first in the know of what is happening in my always evolving world of books, get exclusive news and free content, sign up for my newsletter at tamaramartinauthor.com

Please keep reading for the bonus copy of The Rise of Jaz, originally only released as a free Christmas ebook.

THE RISE OF Jaz

A Harrington Family Christmas

TAMARA MARTIN

The Rise of Jaz - A Harrington Family Christmas

I stepped around the boxes of decorations Margot, our housekeeper, had dragged out of storage ready to begin decorating the house. Christmas was my favourite time of year, no school, lots of eggnog, sparkling wine at every function, parties galore to choose from and it was the one time of year my whole family came together.

The season culminated with my parents, my brothers and sister stopping their chaotic lives to just be, we'd all just be together at the country house for a whole week and this year, we had so much to celebrate because Tom's troubles were finally over, no more clouds of ridiculous accusations, no more whispering in the corners of ballrooms. We could celebrate like Harringtons.

I wanted to get Tom something extra special for Christmas

so went in search of Lydia. My sister knew Tom better than anyone and was a master at gift giving. She had a way of paying attention to people and she could always pick exactly the right gift. And this year, I wanted to give Tom the perfect gift to make him smile, to show him how proud I was of him and to start the next year off just right.

'What's going on?' I asked, walking into the living room to find Tom and Lydia huddled in secret talks. It wasn't uncommon really, they were twins living in a bubble only the two them understood sometimes but I was done with secrets. There'd been too many and they'd been ripping our family apart. It was time for them to stop, for our family to move forward.

'Nothing, Jaz,' Lydia smiled tightly.

But I could see from her face it wasn't nothing, that they were up to something and I'd had it up to my eyeballs with being kept in the dark. Tom had been accused of involuntary manslaughter, which was ridiculous if you knew fastidious, control freak, caring, kind hearted, Tom. But he had and we'd been enduring two years of persecution, he'd been enduring it from the dead boy's family who wanted him dead, an eye for an eye and all that medieval crap, strangers on the street and the vultures with their cameras and the pithy lines they trotted out from behind the safety of their computer screens. We all had suffered in some way.

Some fool had thrown a beer bottle at me as I left school eighteen months ago while declaring my whole fucked up family should be locked up. He'd cut my arm. I'd gotten a Band-Aid and a bodyguard and everyone had moved on.

No one told me anything, not the truth anyway, they watered it down. Mostly I got the same five pieces of information the media dredged up for every story but there was more. I knew it had something to do with my friend, Linc, but no one would tell me what, not even Linc. He'd gone quiet as a mouse and even when wasted, he gave up nothing. So I existed around hushed whispers and false accusations that made no sense and a brother who'd spent the last couple of weeks in a courtroom I wasn't allowed to enter. God forbid anybody tell poor fragile Jaz what the hell was going on. No, best leave me in the dark so I have no bloody idea. But it was over. Tom had been cleared, yet still, the whispers continued and I was sick of them.

I took a long drink from the water bottle in my hand, enjoying the burn of vodka as it slid down my throat. Dutch courage. I was putting my foot down. I took a few steps forward, Tom and Lydia's brows creasing into a frown as one of my traitorous feet caught the other. 'Now look here,' I began.

Tom shook his head. 'Jaz, it's ten o'clock in the bloody morning.'

'So?'

He ripped the bottle out of my hand and sniffed it. 'For fuck's sake, Jaz.'

'What does it even matter to you?' I asked, snatching it back.

Tom sighed, Lydia clutched at his elbow. 'Don't you have school?' he asked, exasperated.

'Exams finished yesterday. Pay attention,' I accused and stormed out of the room as best I could with it swaying.

Then Jay was there catching my elbow, steadying me.

'Jay, come on, man,' Tom begged.

'I don't know how,' he defended, as though I wasn't standing right there and could read through their stupid boy code. They'd served together in the army and like he had with Lydia, Tom had a private way of communicating with Jay. Everyone had a private way of communicating with everyone else but me.

Jay led me upstairs, laid me on the bed, took off my shoes and poured the contents of my water bottle down the sink in my ensuite. I'd have complained, protested but suddenly I didn't have the energy and gave in to the sleep that was tugging at me.

'Jaz,' Jay nudged me awake.

While I'd slept, the sun had risen high enough to pour in to my bedroom, making me sticky and gross.

'You have to get ready, your dad needs you at that charity function tonight,' he said kindly.

'Oh great, so he can parade me around like a fucking dancing monkey,' I grumbled as I climbed out of bed. 'Guess I best find the pink frilly number he likes so much,' I said as I began rummaging in the dresser drawer for underwear.

Jay sat on the bed smirking. 'Feeling better I see,' he joked.

'Oh fuck off,' I laughed, throwing the clean bra I was holding at him.

He caught it, held it up, 'Little much for the old folks don't you think?'

'The old folks won't be seeing it,' I said, raising my eyebrows. 'And neither will you. Go, let me dress.'

He smiled, just a little and put the bra on the bed. 'That beige one would be an excellent choice,' he nodded then left.

I looked at the beige bra in my hand. The nanna bra my

mother had bought me for some ungodly reason. I'd never worn it. Where would I even wear such a thing? It was hideous and plain and I was surprised at Jay. He was always trying to change the way I lived though, 'stop the partying, Jaz,' 'wear the beige bra, Jaz,' 'don't drink the vodka, Jaz.' He was exhausting.

What did he care anyway? He was paid to protect me, not lecture me. It was Tom's doing, I was sure. He was always in Jay's ear about something. Their friendship definitely made the lines between friends and staff blurry. Sometimes I forgot Jay wasn't just Tom's BFF, that he was paid security reporting back to my father. Not that he reported everything. He only ever said what he had to and I was always grateful he had my back. Not that I'd tell him that.

I had long since grown out of the pink frilly number Dad used to love parading me around in but pulled out an equally sweet and demure pink lace Valentino my mother had hung in my wardrobe. A new gown always appeared in my wardrobe ready for one of these events thanks to my mother and her societal rules of couture and they were always saccharine sweet. You only had to glance at my wardrobe to see the gowns my mother bought me, the colours stark against the blacks and greys I bought myself.

I showered off my afternoon nap, ignored Jay's request for granny underwear, instead putting on the pink French lace set I'd bought in June when Lydia and I had gone to Paris for the week. It had been a ploy to get me out of town, although I still hadn't figured out why. Whatever the reason, my wardrobe had benefited and Lydia and I had had a great time just the two of us.

Christian was sitting on my bed when I came out, already dressed and looking dapper in his tux. Sometimes, when he thought he was alone, shadows crept over his face but his face lit up when I walked out.

'You're keen,' I told him as I sat at my dresser in my dressing gown to do my hair and makeup.

'Thought I'd keep you company,' he said.

'Either you're avoiding Dad or Tom sent you in here to keep an eye on me,' I challenged, watching his face for the answer and the lie. Out of my two brothers, it was Christian I knew best. Maybe because I was only twelve when Tom left for the army and had been stuck working every spare minute as an 'actress' before that so we'd missed some of the essential bonding time. Or maybe it was just because Tom was so precise and careful and somehow Christian was the one that got me. Although Christian was more fastidious than Tom, he understood what it was like to live in the shadows of other people's expectations so he was the one who knew me, knew how to keep me grounded when no one else could.

'Maybe both,' he admitted with a smile. That's what I liked about Christian, he didn't lie. Not if he could avoid it, not to me.

I smiled at him in the mirror as I tried taming my curls. Lydia and I had the same wild black hair but she controlled it better than me. I usually didn't mind it had its own way but there were expectations for an event like this so I wrapped it into a knot at the base of my neck and hoped the determined strands looked purposeful and chic.

'So, what's new? How's Uni?' I asked Christian as I began applying makeup.

'Same old. Doing my classes remotely as much as I can so I can work on this new project. I go back to Vegas after Christmas to make sure everything is okay. Well, I was supposed to but I guess now Tom has been cleared and is allowed to leave the country, Dad will no doubt give the project to him and I'll get that renovation job on the Gold Coast.'

'So that's why you're avoiding him?'

Christian smiled. 'If we're not alone, he can't have that conversation, can he?'

'How long are you planning to avoid him?'

'Until I'm on the plane,' he smirked.

'Good luck with that,' I laughed.

'I'll need it,' he agreed as I finished my makeup.

'Okay, you can go now, I have to dress,' I told him.

He smirked but didn't budge.

'Fine,' I mumbled, taking the gown into the bathroom to dress.

I dressed, opened the cabinet, took out the bottle of shampoo and drank a fortifying shot of the tequila that was hidden inside then brushed my teeth and I was ready.

'Here, make yourself useful,' I smiled at Christian as I threw him my phone to take a photo for Instagram.

'I can't believe you bother, especially when you hate all the attention,' he goaded.

I shrugged, 'Insta isn't the same as those vultures hiding in the bushes. I get to control what the public sees, they get to see the real me, not what the journos keep trying to pass off as me.'

'Fair point,' he smiled, patting my hand as we went downstairs.

Town cars waited outside, ready to ferry us to The Rex Hotel, a jewel in the Harrington Hotel crown.

'What's going on?' I asked Jay as Christian and I were hustled into a car. 'Why aren't we going with Tom and Lydia?' I asked as they closed the doors to their car. Usually for an event like this, security would ride in one car and we'd all ride together in the other, leaving Mum and Dad to their own car, it was the only fun part of these events.

Jay shrugged as though it was no big deal but I knew it had to do with their secrets. But he got in the front beside Sam, Christian's security and that was the last of it.

'Do you know what they've been whispering about?' I asked Christian.

He looked at me with raised eyebrows.

'No, of course not,' I smiled. Tom and Christian had never been close, their personalities were just too different and with Christian always living in the shadow of Tom's movie star looks, his sportiness, his brain, the whole war hero thing, it just made everything tense between them.

Christian talked about the Vegas project as we drove and it was nice to see him so animated and alive, he really loved what he was doing and doing it out of the country also meant away from the suffocating scrutiny of Dad and it seemed it was really good for him.

'You ready?' he groaned as the car came to a stop.

'Am I ever?' I grumbled back as Jay opened my door and I was blinded by the flashes of cameras.

Once we'd posed for the obligatory happy family snaps, we were finally free to go inside, away from the vultures with their cameras, dollar signs flashing in their eyes.

Lydia and Tom huddled close as we headed for the doors, still whispering their secrets. I rolled my eyes and looped my arm through Christian's and thanked the universe I at least had him.

Jay kept a professional distance as was the expectation when the family was around. When it was just us going about my life, he had long since stopped bothering to pretend he wasn't there. My father preferred the professional distance of staff. Usually I didn't care much for my father's rules, it's not like he was around much to enforce them, anyway but this was a very public event and right down to my very core, I was a Harrington.

Christian gripped my arm a little tighter as we entered the sparkling ballroom. Someone had spent a great deal of time, not to mention money that would probably better serve whatever charity we were supporting this Christmas, to turn the room into a sparkling winter wonderland complete with snow and glittering stars, the whole bit, no expense spared. I was impressive and beautiful and over the top extravagant.

'You okay?' I asked Christian as we were assaulted with the full sensory overload of the night ahead, the glitzy gowns, the cacophony of noise and the pain of having to be 'on' from this moment forward.

Christian smiled tightly and patted my hand before letting go to begin his night of hand shaking.

No one was interested in shaking my hand, so I scooped

a glass of sparkling from a passing waiter, ignoring the sour faces my brother's shot me. They didn't even try to disguise the look they shared but they were too busy shaking hands with important people so I chose to ignore them and left them to their hob-nobbing.

Lydia tried taking the glass from my hand. 'Shall we go greet some people?'

'If we must. I can walk and drink at the same time though, I've been multitasking since I was two,' I told her, pulling my hand out of her reach.

She had that same pained look as my brothers as we walked across the room to a group of her friends. I really didn't get their constant preoccupation with a few drinks. They had them. They knew it was necessary to survive these events. It was no big deal. They needed to get off their high horses and just worry about themselves.

Lydia's friends weren't exactly what I had in mind for a good time. Her friends were nice enough but they were proper, well educated, well-bred bores. I looked around the room until my eyes landed on a familiar face and before Lydia could stop me, I'd excused myself and was walking away.

Jay, my ever present shadow, followed along the back wall as I made my way over to CeeCee, the daughter of one of my parent's oldest friends. CeeCee, as far as my father was concerned, was an appropriate friend, despite what she did when he wasn't watching. If only he knew. Or maybe he still wouldn't care, her faCther made him look good.

'Oh thank God,' CeeCee whispered with a smile when she saw me. 'I thought I was going to have to converse with boring old people all night long. Now you're here we can have some fun,' she declared, snatching two glasses of sparkling off the passing waiter's tray.

I put my empty glass on the tray and hooked my arm through CeeCee's. We'd been friends since we were five and had been getting into trouble together at these events ever since, helping each other to survive them as best we could.

'Who's this thing even for?' I asked, looking around for some indication.

'The new children's hospital apparently. I bid on the trip to Barbados, you have to come with me if I win.'

'You bid on something?'

'It's for the children,' she smiled. 'And I saw my mother bid, it'd drive her crazy if I beat her,' she laughed. 'Now, tell me,' she said conspiratorially as we moved across the room.

I caught Jay out of the corner of my eye moving with us. He was like a shadow across the back wall. It had been a while since we'd been this far apart. He'd been right beside me a lot lately, we'd been Christmas shopping, to the movies, even at friend's parties, he was often right there or at least within nodding distance. I'd gotten so used to having him there and now I couldn't even see the expression on his face, just his moving shadow, I wasn't sure I liked that empty feeling where he usually stood. That probably needed further thinking but CeeCee was on a mission, it seemed.

'What's the deal with Tom?' CeeCee asked. 'Now the court case is over, do you think he's on the market?'

'I don't think he was ever off the market, Cee,'

'I know but it was all so complicated and I just didn't need complicated but he's not complicated anymore,' she said, stopping to watch him across the room.

Tom was handsome. Women went a little weak knee'd in his presence, almost as much as they did in Jay's. Only Jay frightened them off as soon as he growled at them. Tom had a way when he spoke of drawing them in further. He didn't even realise he had all that power at his command.

I wasn't sure how I felt about CeeCee ogling him, especially after her complicated spiel. Tom had always been Tom and it bothered me that people who were supposed to be friends had been thinking differently about him, not seeing the truth or believing in who he is. But as I took another sip of the sparkling, enjoying the way it seeped into my bones and dulled all the noise, I wasn't sure I had it in me to care. Tom was a big boy, if he didn't want Cee, he'd just say so and that would be that and if she pestered him, Lydia would probably break her arm. So I motioned for her to go, have her shot and stood alone in the middle of the room watching yet another party happen around me.

'You okay?' Jay whispered in my ear.

I nodded.

'Why don't you go sit, they're serving entrees in a minute.'

I nodded and walked away. I found our table and was just about to sit when Dad caught my elbow and off we went for a parade. I sculled the rest of the sparkling and swapped the empty glass for a fresh one as Dad presented me to the first on his list, because with him, there was always a list, a purpose, a plan. After all, what's the point if you don't have a plan? He'd taught me, as though people were projects to be managed.

'You remember my daughter, Jasmine, she was in the soap, Hope Valley,' he reminded people as he introduced me. I hadn't been in Hope Valley for four years yet still it was his crowning glory. He'd angled for months to get me that gig even though I hadn't wanted it and he had used it to his advantage ever since.

Well trained as I was though, like a dancing monkey from the streets of India, I smiled politely, responded when and as expected until they really did begin serving entrees and I finally got to sit in my seat. I looked to the back of the room where Jay watched, his face finally softening, clearly relieved to have me sit for a minute. I hated seeing him back there, working while the rest of us ate our overpriced meals. It didn't feel right.

CeeCee was still doing her best with Tom from across the table. He was nodding politely but clearly not interested. He was too responsible, too army for her. I knew from experience Tom didn't have time for party girl behaviour and Cee loved nothing more than to party. Lydia sat on the other side of Tom, giving me the look of what is CeeCee doing. I shrugged. I was happily ensconced, between Tom and Christian where no one could get to me, where I was safe and comforted, even though they seemed to be tag teaming me. Extra potatoes kept appearing on my plate, a piece of broccoli, another piece of chicken, it was as though they were fattening me up like a Christmas bloody turkey. They thought I didn't know, didn't see but I did and I gave them their victory because the food was really good. My glass of sparkling had disappeared, replaced with a never emptying glass of water and they each did it seamlessly.

We politely clapped through the ceremonies, the speeches

and announcements of prizes and fundraising achieved for the needy children between courses. Neither CeeCee or her mum won the bid for the trip to Barbados, but Mum stood and appeared chuffed when she won a skiing trip she'd bid for in the silent auction, no doubt paying far more than it was worth. A comedian entertained us through desert and then, with no more food to be served, the orchestra returned to the stage and everyone left me to return to their schmoozing and there was no avoiding my father.

'Jasmine, come,' he instructed as though I were the family pet. 'There are some people I want for you to meet.'

So, off we went, parading and impressing the wives of important people. I made for a great conversation starter.

We were on to the fourth pair when I spotted CeeCee out of the corner of my eye waving two bottles of sparkling at me. So, as the conversation gradually and seamlessly moved from me, the soapie star, to whatever it was my father wanted from the poor bloke, I excused myself to go to the ladies. The woman who only moments ago was glittering from having met a real life soapie star looked at me wishfully but going by the grip her husband had on her arm, he was not letting her leave him alone with my father.

'You're a lifesaver,' I declared to CeeCee as we exited the ballroom and blended into the shadows of the garden and onto some bench seats surrounded by roses.

'Why are these things so dull? Even the music is dull,' CeeCee moaned.

'No luck with Tom, then?'

'Nope, not even a spark of interest, what is wrong with him?'

'I don't know, you're blonde and leggy and gorgeous,' I reminded her, as though maybe she'd forgotten.

'Right,' she agreed with a smile.

'At least you aren't constantly crapping on all night about some stupid soap you haven't even been in forever and having to smile and answer the same stupid questions over and over.'

'Nope, because no one cares if I even exist.'

'Oh, I care, Cee, I care,' I smiled.

'That's why I love you,' she said, clinking bottles.

I was halfway through the bottle of sparkling and finally having a lovely laugh when Jay stopped me raising the bottle to my mouth again. 'Jaz, it's time to go,' he insisted.

I looked over to the ballroom doors. No one was leaving so I knew what he was doing. Arguing with him though would have caused a scene and even with the sparkling fizzing beautifully in my veins, I knew better than to make a scene here.

'Come on,' he insisted, helping me up by the elbow.

The garden swam in circles. 'Just a second,' I said, ignoring his pained face. I just had to stand still for a little minute, let my head adjust. That happened to people sometimes. 'Don't look at me like that, I just stood up too fast,' I insisted as he frowned.

'Where are you going? You can't leave now,' CeeCee protested.

Jay kept one hand on my elbow, another around my waist and stoically ignored CeeCee's protesting. He didn't care much for CeeCee. He didn't care much for any of my friends.

'She's right, we have plans to go dancing,' I told him.

'Not tonight, Jaz, you promised your father.'

He was right. Come together, leave together. It was another of my dad's stupid rules and if I wanted to continue living the life I'd become so accustomed to, occasionally I had to follow a rule or two, so he'd been instructing me for as long as I could remember.

The rest of the family were already waiting by our cavalcade of cars. As Jay and I approached, they said nothing, just climbed into the cars they arrived in and Jay guided me into the car beside Christian and went to join Sam in the front.

Christian wrapped his arm around my shoulders and let my head fall to his shoulder.

'You okay?' he asked.

I shrugged. 'I'm tired. All that parading and smiling and fakery, it rips something inside of me and leaves me so tired.

'I know,' he said, squeezing me to him. 'I know.'

I don't know if it was the exhaustion, being held so tight or just the familiar smell of Christian but I was asleep in seconds.

'Hey,' Jay nudged me from the open door when we arrived home.

We seemed to have beaten everyone else home. I noted it as strange and vaguely wondered where they'd gone but my brain was too foggy to give it much more thought.

Christian disappeared in the town car, headed to who knows where. He'd been spending most of his time somewhere else lately but I didn't know where. I overheard he'd spent some of his trust fund on some land, but it was just a rumour and I was afraid to ask him about it in case he said he was leaving me for good.

Jay led me upstairs, helped me out of my dress and shoes and

I climbed into bed in my underwear. It wasn't the first time he'd done so. He tucked me in, I felt him watching me for a minute, then he was gone.

I was only mildly foggy when I woke. Jay had left me juice and Panadol so I took the pills and drank the juice and waited to feel better.

I picked up my phone to find a ton of messages from CeeCee. She'd sent me a photo of her, Indi and Elisabeth posing with big smiles saying *'Wish you were here.'* I read down the rest. *'Where are you?' 'Haven't you ditched the fam yet?' 'Jaz, it's not a party without you'* and finally *'Mitch Campbell is asking for you, oops, he's been snapped up. You snooze, you lose.'*

Mitch was a footballer who had been flirting with me for weeks. I wasn't really interested but it was always nice to be flirted with by a handsome man but he was twenty-five and clearly out of the loop that I was only seventeen. I did a lot of wrong things in my life but ruining someone's career for a bit of bedroom fun was never on my agenda and if he entered my world that would definitely be the end for him. I checked an online gossip page to see who he'd gone home with. Elyse Winters, age appropriate, sweet, tv actress from some arty drama I couldn't be bothered watching. But she was nice and she was smart, he wouldn't be back on the market for a while and even though I thought they were a good match, I was suddenly annoyed my chance had been taken without my consent. Why hadn't I woken to any of my messages? I wasn't that drunk.

I stormed down the stairs hunting for Jay. The house was

quiet, bar for the hum of activity coming from my father's study. He was shouting at someone, not uncommon but what was out of the ordinary was my mother was begging him to calm down. I would worry about their drama later. I was about to storm into the security room where Jay would be when he stepped out and handed me a shirt with a frown on his face.

I'd forgotten I'd slept in my underwear, not pyjamas and sheepishly slid into the shirt. 'Did you do this?' I asked brandishing my phone. But the fight had gone out of me and I couldn't yell at him when he was looking at me with pity all over his face.

'Jaz, we need to talk.'

'Yes, we do, you can't go muting my phone whenever you bloody well feel like it,' I chastised.

'Not about the phone,' he said, leading me to the dining room where Margot had put a freshly brewed latte on the table for me.

Jay pushed the folded newspaper away but not before I caught a glimpse of myself being led by Jay, clearly leaning in to him for support. The headline read '*Can't anyone help poor Jaz Harrington?*' The subtitle saying, '*It was a charity event, after all.*' I choked back the emotion it stirred up. I refused to give in to them, to the vultures that waited in the shadows and the bushes to catch me at my worst. There'd be more online I knew and I cringed. I hadn't felt that bad. I hadn't even realised I'd leaned on Jay. What if I had just been sleepy or we had been snuggling? They don't know, they assume, they take everything out of context and do whatever they like with it.

'What about, then?' I asked Jay, suddenly worried, as more shouting drifted out from my father's study.

'It's Tom and Lydia,' he began.

'What about Tom and Lydia?' I asked, emotion suddenly choking my vocal chords.

'Hey,' he soothed. 'They're okay. They'll be okay.'

'What is this, then?'

'They're gone, Jaz.'

'Gone? Gone where?'

'Gone. On a plane. To Europe. I think.'

'You think?' I shouted.

'Okay, I know. But I don't know where in Europe, I swear.'

'Well when will they be back?' I begged, fear filling my veins.

'They might not be.'

'What? Why? What's going on?'

'Jaz, there's more going on than you know. I'm not going to go into it, Tom made me promise not to, but all I can tell you is they're gone. It's better for you, for everyone, this way and they probably won't be back.'

'What? That's ridiculous. It's over. Tom's stuff is over. He can't leave. They can't leave; they wouldn't leave me.' Tears spilled out of my eyes.

Jay let me cry, held me to him, didn't care that I was crying smudged eyeliner all over his crisp white shirt. Clearly he had a collection stashed inside that security room, anyway.

'It's because of him, isn't it?'

'Who?'

'My father. Who else?'

Jay shrugged.

'What did he do?'

'It's not that simple.'

'Unlikely. It always comes back to him, simple as that,' I said, taking my coffee and going back upstairs.

I came back down an hour later, showered, dressed and demanded we go out. Jay tried to protest, said my family needed me but they didn't need me. I hadn't seen any of them all morning. No one had asked if I was okay. They'd left it to Jay to tell me Tom and Lydia were gone and they couldn't even be bothered to leave me a note. So no, that line wasn't working today, so we left and met Indi at The Gully.

No one knew me like Indi. I didn't even have to tell her what had happened. Tom and Lydia had been spotted at the airport getting the one am Singapore Airlines flight out of Australia so the whole world already knew they'd skipped town so Indi was ready with a line of shots on the bar when I walked in. She was a good friend.

Jay saw the row of little drinks too and begged, 'Jaz, come on, please don't. Come to my place, we can watch Netflix, eat pizza, anything you want.'

'You are not in charge of me,' I reminded him as I wrenched my arm away from him and stormed over to Indi and proceeded to work my way down the row of shots to the scotch and soda that waited at the end. Like I said, Indi was good people, she knew exactly what I needed.

We talked and complained about stupid families, we scoured the Internet for information on Tom and Lydia but mostly it was just me they were reporting on so we drank another shot every time a heinous photo of me popped up from the night before. They called me everything from an overindulged brat to a waste of human life, always under the guise of witty and funny commentary.

'Do they not know I'm a real person?' I asked Indi.

'Ignore them. They're fools. Wasteland fools. You know this,' she said, handing me another scotch and soda. 'What do they even know?'

'You're right,' I smiled tightly, tapping my glass to hers but still my heart was heavy and we eventually left in need of comradery.

'Where are you going?' Jay asked as Indi and I walked passed him to the doors, arm in arm and full of chatter.

'Cascades,' I told him.

'No, we're going home,' he said, opening the car door.

'Absolutely not,' I told him.

'I'm not driving you there,' he argued, attempting a standoff.

'Then we'll get a taxi,' I said, sticking my arm out.

'Jaz, come on,' he begged, holding my arm and stopping me from getting into the taxi that pulled over.

Surrendering to my tantrum, he led me to the SUV with a sigh, Indi giggling beside me. We messaged our entourage, instagrammed our victorious faces and when we arrived, the line for Cascades stretched down the street and our friends were waiting.

We walked passed the line that suddenly came alive like a hive of bees, buzzing as they saw us and walked up to the burly bouncer. He looked me up and down and shook his head.

'Don't you know who I am?' I demanded when he refused to wave us through.

The world wanted to label me a brat, I was more than happy to play the part. That was one of their favourite lines and one they'd exhausted online overnight, not particularly clever really, it was an easy shot when thrown at someone like me. I shouldn't have even looked at the photos, read the reports but once we'd stumbled on them, we were like crack whores. We just couldn't stop the masochistic indulgence. But the more I saw, the more furious I'd become, the heavier my heart had become, the sicker my stomach.

Of course CeeCee was nowhere to be seen in any of the photos. No one cared, she'd spent as much time out in that garden with me, sipping from her own bottle of sparkling. No, they only cared that the great Richard Harrington's daughter was out of control. That the once sweetheart of Australian television with a bright future ahead of her was flushing it all away. They didn't care I didn't want that life. They didn't care about me or what I wanted, they just wanted to sell stories and make their money. Who cared who they hurt along the way.

My father was going to be furious when someone showed him the photos so I refused to go home and if they wanted me to play a part, I would play it. I was sick of them all, sick of their crap. They never showed the pictures I posted to Instagram, the ones that got hundreds of thousands of likes, the photos that sold out dresses in shops, or brought in customers to coffee shops or clubs when I instagrammed I was there. No, they waited and they waited for the worst possible moment, until I was swaggering with a bottle in my hand or puking in the gutter. They could all go to hell. My family, the world, the vultures, they could all go to hell. It didn't seem to matter what

I did, it didn't change anything. They distorted photos if they had to, took things out of context regardless of how it affected my life, my family, my friends. I was done trying. I was giving up, giving in. Who was even going to stop me? Tom or Lydia? No, they'd left me here. My bloody father? He only cared how it looked for him. No, there was no one who was going to stop me now, even Christian had other places to be, other things to do. I was in this alone and I no longer had it in me to care about any of them.

The bouncer before me looked to be in physical pain. The queue of people waiting watched eagerly, some wearing a bad imitation of the Valentino dress I'd worn the night before, snapping pictures with their phones. My friends chuckled around me, loving the drama, egging me on and bloody Jay mouthed an apology.

'Don't you dare apologise for me!' I scolded him. The nerve! Some people just never learned their place, my father always said so, always said you had to be brutal sometimes to show people who was in charge, especially when you were a woman. So I would show them what it was like to be managed by a Harrington, people were just projects waiting to be managed after all, my father had made that clear.

I took a step forward, my finger poised to challenge the insolent fool refusing our entry, show him who was really in charge here. Surely he knew the publicity having me and my friends in his club would bring. Although it always amused me that anyone even cared what I did. But I played it to my advantage when I needed to and this idiot was going to learn the power of a Harrington.

Jay caught my elbow, as I began my tirade, the words not coming out the way they sounded in my head, stopping me from stumbling head first into the pillar on which the arrogant bouncer leaned with a smirk on his face. I wanted to punch that face. How dare he judge me? Standing there, sweating like a hog thinking he was better than me, judging his stupid arse off. He knew nothing, I wanted to scream at him. But it didn't matter, it never mattered, they judged anyway, no matter what I said.

'Jaz, why don't we call it a night?' Jay begged quietly in my ear.

'We? Jay, there is no WE. There is me, my friends and you, my father's employee. You do not get a say in how I spend my time. Come in, don't come in, I don't care. But I, we, me and my friends, are going in,' I declared as a vulture with a camera appeared and the insolent fool guarding the door gave up with an exasperated sigh and shuffled us in.

I might have used the magazine exposure to my advantage, after all they were the fools that kept putting me in there for no good reason, but I still hated every time those vultures shoved a camera in my face, dollar signs flashing in their eyes. You'd think I'd be used to it, my hotel mogul father had been using me to portray happy families since the day I was born, taking me to kindergarten and dance class just because he knew there'd be a camera following. He was just that kind of guy, more political aspiration than warm and fuzzy, that's for sure.

Then came the pulling of strings to get his dancing pony onto the big soap of the time, which lasted until I began self destructing at twelve and they killed me off in some big nationally watched horrifying to-do. The vultures had been watching me long enough now, they always knew when I was at my worst. They never showed the photo of me sitting in Al's Coffee Hut sipping an Iced Frappuccino, no, they waited until I was at my very worst and exploited it, even better if it was a school night.

The bouncer apologised to the manager but she waved him off with the same look of exasperation he wore. We chuckled in our victory as the manager led us to a private area in the heaving club. The music pulsed through my feet and up through my body. The cloying smell of perfume and spilled beer and sweaty people was comfortably familiar. It was the smell of escape, oblivion, anonymity. Not that we were ever anonymous, the stares and the whispers that followed us as we moved through the club proved that but after enough drinking, I forgot and after enough dancing maybe everyone else forgot too, or I just stopped noticing.

A glass of sparkling appeared in my hand and I closed my eyes in appreciation as the sweetness bubbled its way down my throat and the happiness seeped its way into my veins. Jay tried to take it from me but I plainly told him to fuck off. I needed to forget, I needed the world to fade away. I was getting sick of his meddling every time fun was to be had. To prove my point that he was being a royal pain in my arse and had no say at all in how I spent my time or with who, I grabbed the arm of a passing voyeur and led him to the dance floor.

Jay seethed from across the room as I let the bloke run his hands over my body. I don't know why I cared either way what Jay was doing, what he was seeing or if I was bothering him or not. But more and more he'd been fuelling my actions one way or another far too often of late and I didn't like it. I had enough to deal with without having to think of how he bloody felt. I tried ignoring him and his frowning face, giving myself over to the music, let the thumping sounds vibrate through my body, shake away the crap that clung in my head.

It didn't last long before I stole a glance at Jay, almost as though my brain couldn't help itself. He was no longer watching, instead his back was to me while he was talking to one of the club's security who was watching me. I'd finally repulsed him. Jay had finally given up on me and I didn't like it, I didn't like how it felt coming from him. With Jay's back turned, being groped by a sweaty stranger was no longer entertaining so I gave up and walked away. The bloke followed, they usually did, like puppies with no balls. Did they really think wandering behind me with their tongue hanging out was the way to my heart? Fools.

I took another glass of sparkling from Indi. Indi was the daughter of a rock star who, like CeeCee, liked to snort her entertainment as much as drink it. It wasn't my thing, the snorting, the drinking however was my salvation, it filled that hole that always seemed to be gaping inside me, the black gaping hole that ate at me, snapping and twitching until it had its fill.

They both said someday I'd need something more than just alcohol to soothe that beast but I doubted I would, I loved this too much. Elisabeth, a distant royal from some small country no one cared about until she ended up in a magazine doing something outrageous, passed around a tray of shots and I threw one down my throat without even tasting what it was, savouring the burn that followed. As I turned, The Puppy was standing in front of me all starry eyed and wanting, and before I could tell him show time was over, it was time to go back to his people, his tongue was in my throat, a hand on my arse while another groped at my breast.

I meant to push him off but the shot was 30mls too much for my system and suddenly he was all that was keeping me from falling to the floor. I'd rather Jay see me being groped than see his face as he scooped me off the floor. So even though I was losing focus of what was happening, I let the puppy kiss me, let me him grope me even though somewhere deep inside, buried beneath the litres of drink, he repulsed me. I repulsed me. But I let him, anyway. He'd go home with a tale to tell his friends, be king of the world for a day. I'd sober up in a minute and no one would have to know how bad I was.

As I faded away again, I felt the blackness getting thicker, my knees going week and I couldn't hold on anymore. I heard Jay calling my name through the thick dark fog and the next thing I knew, The Puppy was on his arse and Jay had scooped me into his arms.

'It's okay, it's okay, I've got you,' he promised.

'Jay...'

'I've got you,' he said, holding me to his chest. 'Is there a back door?' he asked the manager.

'Yes, but they're out there as well, they've covered all the exits. I'm sorry,' she said and I wondered, even in my blurry fog, if she really was. Free publicity was always good for these places, they didn't care if it was good or bad.

I gripped onto Jay to stop from passing out again as he

pushed through the crowds. These people were getting enough of a show already. I didn't need to be passing out in front of them as well. I held on to Jay's shirt. I held it tight to keep me focussed, keep me from disappearing altogether. He'd get me home, I knew he would, he always did.

I woke with the sun blazing through the windows, my hip aching from the sagging couch cushion. 'When are you going to buy a bloody decent couch?' I asked Jay. 'I'll pay for it if that's your issue.'

'I wouldn't need a decent couch if you didn't need to keep sleeping on it,' he chastised from the kitchen.

'How bad was it?'

He didn't answer.

I looked over and watched him making coffee. Two cups in front of him, the jar of instant in his hand. Even though I'd bought him a perfectly good machine, he still fed me this supermarket crap. Perhaps that was my punishment.

'How bad, Jay?'

'Bad,' he mumbled.

'I'm sorry,' I said, hanging my head as he passed me my coffee.

'You always are, Jaz, you always are,' he grumbled, heading for the bathroom.

The door closed with a thud and I jumped a little even though I had watched it close. I took a sip, not scolding my mouth as I should because he knew me, he'd put in a dash of cold water so it was the perfect temperature.

The cobwebs instantly eased, clarity resuming. It bothered me how mad he got. We were friends, I guess. Even though he was paid to protect me, I spent as much time in his apartment as I did at my own house. Sitting on his couch watching Netflix, eating pizza, especially when I was in bad shape, too bad to take home. His place was closer, and not known to the vultures, that was the thinly veiled excuse we used. But still, his opinion shouldn't matter so much to me. But it did and I hated it when he was mad. I hated that look of sadness in his eyes, the disappointment reflected back to me. It cut me up and I didn't like it. It had to stop. I had enough judgement in my life, enough rules, my father was more than enough for anyone.

Jay thought the bathroom was the only place he was safe from me, the only place I wouldn't accost him but he was wrong. I took a big healing sip of my coffee and followed him in.

The shower was running but he leant against the vanity sipping his coffee thoughtfully. His eyes were downcast, his forehead creased in a frown and his perfectly sculpted body was beautifully naked.

I couldn't turn away from his broad chest, his ridged stomach, those beautiful thighs, the in-between. He was some sort of perfection. A very unexpected form of perfection. I'd seen him shirtless when I'd stayed over before. I always ended up here after a bad night but I'd never noticed, never noticed this.

My breath caught in my chest as he looked up, his dark blue eyes catching mine were more pained than surprised.

I righted myself, stoic to the end us Harringtons. 'I am sorry, Jay, I am.'

'Then stop it, Jaz.'

'I can't.'

'No, you don't want to.'

'Maybe,' I shrugged. I hadn't really thought about it that much. He nagged me all the time about my wayward behaviour, sprouted wisdom filled mumbo jumbo meant for hippies, for people searching for the hidden meaning of life. But there was no hidden meaning, it was just life and I never really thought about stopping, probably because I liked it too much, probably because the thought of living without being numb to the world around me was terrifying.

'Exactly,' he spat, then sipped his coffee, not moving, not covering himself, not even caring, maybe he'd forgotten.

Seeing him like that though, it did things to me I'd never admit, that I'd never tell him. I'd never tell a soul what the sight of him stirred. I could never be that vulnerable, have something to lose, not even with him.

'Why do you even care so much?' I asked, because I always wondered. He was paid to protect me, not to give a shit.

'It's getting late, you have school,' he mumbled, finishing his coffee and stepping into the shower. The school year was over but nothing was over when you were a Harrington, there was always an extra class of some sort to take. This summer it was decided I'd be stuck with a uni level business class but most of it thankfully was online at my leisure.

'Fuck school, Jay,' I said, grabbing his arm and forcing him to face me.

The water beat down on him, beaded on his beautiful body, flattening the few daring wayward strands of bed hair. 'Why do you care?'

'Why? Are you kidding? Have you not figured it out yet?'

'What are you talking about? Figured out what?'

'If you don't understand, then there's no point explaining it.'

'Explain it, Jay. Why?' I begged, unable to control the rising tone of my voice. He frustrated me when he refused to answer, when he treated me like a child. I could take it from almost anyone but not him.

'Because I fucking love you, alright?' he spat, walking out of the bathroom, water dripping in his wake.

I stood watching him, stunned. Why would he do that? Why would he say that?

I followed him into his bedroom, watched as he hunted through his wardrobe for clothes. I threw him a towel.

He let the towel fall to the floor, ignored it, ignored me, preferring to drip on the carpet because he could be a stubborn fool.

'Why would you love me?' I sobbed, suddenly overcome with emotion. Too much emotion.

He stared at me. Those dark blue eyes watched me.

'Why? How could you?' I asked so softly, I wasn't even sure I'd spoken the words.

He dropped the shirt he had in his hand, crossed the room and caught me as I sank to the floor, tucking some stray hairs out of my face, away from the tears I couldn't seem to stop.

I wiped my nose with my hand as he pulled me to his bare chest, as he held me so tight I thought he might be the only thing in the world that would stop me from crumbling.

'Shhh...' he soothed.

My hand rested on his heart, his beating heart, the thumps

pounding as fast as my own. I looked up into his eyes. They were watching me carefully.

'I love you because underneath the bravado, underneath the façade, you are a kind and beautiful human. When you don't think anyone is watching, you have the sweetest laugh and the loveliest heart.'

I humphed. I had a black heart. A Harrington heart.

'Shhh... you asked, I'm telling,' he said. 'I love the way you scrunch your face when you're trying to solve a problem. I love how good you are to Margot, how loyal you are to your friends, even when they don't deserve it. I love how beautiful and fragile and fierce you are.'

I touched his face, his eyes watching mine as I brought my mouth to his, as our lips carefully, softly touched, as electricity raced through my veins with so much power I thought for sure it'd consume me. As he opened his mouth to me, I stopped him, my finger on his lips. 'You are a fool to love me, Jay. You can't love me. I will break you and you are too beautiful, I won't do it.'

'I am a man, Jaz. I can take care of myself and make my own choices. And what makes you think I can stop?'

'You have to.'

'I can't,' he begged, leaning his forehead to mine. 'I know I should. You're seventeen. Your father will kill me. I've tried. I can't.'

I gave in to him then. I let that kiss deepen, let him take me on the floor of his bedroom. I savoured in the touch of his hands and the feel of his mouth on my skin because even though I knew it was wrong, even though I knew this would only end in pain, the kind of pain that could destroy us both, I wanted to know what it felt like, for just a minute, to be the person he saw.

As he took me, as I gave myself to him, revelling in his touch, his mouth on my skin, the way he filled me, moved in me and showed me pleasure I'd never before known, I was lost. Lost in him, to him, all that existed in those moments was him. And it was beautiful, gloriously beautiful.

But who I was was never far away. Sated and happy, he kissed me, slow and languid and I wondered how could he love me? How could I let him? Who I am, the things I'd done, before I'd met Jay, the things I'd done since as I'd tried to fill that unfillable hole that forever gaped inside of me. How could he love me after all of that? I was a foul and vile human being. I'd treated my body like a bloody fun park, only I never seemed to be the one having any fun but still I tried. And now, this beautiful man saw through it all. He should have run repulsed, but no, he lay beside me, having bared his soul in the most intimately exquisite way.

This beautiful yet fearsome man had given himself to me anyway, loved me, anyway. He'd touched me like I was something to be valued. He'd been gentle and sweet, fiercely passionate and he'd filled that unfillable hole and now he opened his arms to me, ready to give more, pulling me to his chest where I felt his heart beating, his skin still slick with pleasure induced sweat and he held me. Just held me. My eyes welled with tears I refused to shed. I didn't deserve this man. He deserved one of those beautiful, well bread bores Lydia was friends with. Someone who would care for him the way he deserved, without drama, without a head so messed up seeing straight was a thing of the distant past. He was a masochist and I was sure at any second he'd realise his error in judgement.

I didn't realise the tears had fallen until he tilted my face to his, kissed my cheeks.

'I don't deserve you, Jay Sullivan.'

'Shhh... You deserve more than I'll ever be able to be.'

He couldn't really believe that but as his strong hands casually moved up and down my arm as though now we were here, in this new place, he couldn't not touch me, I was happy to pretend it was true.

J ay was sleeping when I left. I knew he'd be mad at me for leaving but I needed space, I needed to process everything the happened, all the emotions swarming through my body, to maybe numb them just a little so I could think straight, so I called a car service to take me home.

My parents were out, so I spent time in the kitchen with Margot. Margot knew me well enough to know something was up. I only ever helped her bake when I needed to clear my head but she also knew me well enough not to ask questions so we worked in companionable silence for the most part, only discussing the how tos of cookies and cakes.

Out of the corner of my eye I saw Jay walk past the kitchen doorway but he didn't stop and I didn't look up. I needed space. I needed to process what had happened between us. I couldn't remember ever feeling that much. I needed to decipher what my feelings were for Jay and what was from what he did to me. What those beautiful hands had done to me. I'd fallen apart under those hands, I'd opened the door to my soul, I'd let him see it all and now I was afraid. Afraid of rejection now he'd seen everything. Afraid of what happens next. Afraid of surviving without him. Afraid of what loving him would do to me. Afraid of what I could do to him.

But as the afternoon stretched on and Margot and I moved from cakes to meatballs, I started to gain some clarity, some calm at the very least. That was a start. So when Indi messaged me insisting I go to her place for a few drinks, I decided it would be better than hiding out in my room all night going over the same things in my head. I just couldn't figure out why he would want me but I knew that if I let myself go, if I really gave myself to him, I'd be utterly destroyed when he left because I was sure that at some point he would leave, everyone left at some point. It didn't matter why they did, it was inevitable that something or someone far more important would drag him away and I didn't think I would survive him going.

Drinks at Indi's was a come as you are affair so when it was time to go, I went to the security room, beckoned Jay and we left. I'd decided by then I'd probably blown it all out of proportion anyway, that my emotionally starved and stunted brain had latched on to more than it had been but as soon as I sat in the car beside him, I knew I was wrong.

Jay was more than I imagined I'd ever have. The way he touched me, the way he groaned my name, the way he held me, the things he'd made me feel. I'd slept with more men than I should have, boys, men, I wasn't always picky or a good judge but none of them had ever made me feel. It was more than I knew what to do with.

'Why did you leave?' he asked, not messing around with small talk.

I shrugged. 'I just needed to clear my head and you were asleep. I didn't want to wake you.' The memory of his perfect, peaceful face flashed in my mind and a stab of pain struck my chest.

He nodded as if understanding my inner turmoil but I doubted he had a clue. I just didn't know what to do with all these feelings. Thankfully, Indi lived nearby and we pulled up before Jay could quiz me any further because I just didn't think I had the words, or at least not the words he wanted to hear.

'I thought this was just drinks?' Jay asked when I opened Indi's front door to find her enormous living room full of people, snorting, shooting and practically fucking in some extravagant display of indulgence.

'So did I,' I told him as I was accosted by Indi. 'I thought this was just a few drinks,' I quizzed her.

'A few drinks, an outrageous party, same, same,' she smiled. 'You seem tense, let's get you a drink,' she insisted, dragging me away.

Jay was left by the door. He was my security, not my date and if it looked like anything else, someone, friend or not, would be leaking it to the gossip pages. You couldn't trust a group like this. I wasn't even sure I'd have trusted Indi with the information even if it was just us, no matter how much I needed some girl talk. That's just how my world worked and whatever happened with Jay romantically, I couldn't bare to have him taken from me and if my father got wind of what happened this morning, he'd be gone so fast, my head would spin for a week.

But the more I drank, the more liquor Indi plied me with while we laughed and danced out on the patio, the further away the morning became. This was what I needed, to dull the feelings, to dull it all, put it in a box. I'd felt something for the first time and I'd blown it up into this big massive thing but even as I thought it, the memory of his mouth on my skin hit me, the look on his beautiful face as he came, the words he whispered, the way he said my name, his voice husky and low, the way he'd held me, the way his heart beat, the way he'd said he loved me. Tears welled in my eyes, it was too much. I needed to erase the memories before they grew wings they were never meant to have, so when Indi had somehow disappeared and been replaced with some guy whose name I had never bothered to remember, I let him lead me into the pool house.

While people were snorting and shooting their entertainment outside and Jay was inside breaking up a fight and making sure people didn't die, I let this guy touch me, strip me, but as his mouth moved over my body, I was neither partaking nor protesting, too busy hating myself for not living up to the person Jay saw when he looked at me but as this bloke whose name I couldn't remember was about to enter me, his breathing sharp and ragged, needy, I thought of Jay. I thought of all we'd done that morning, all I'd felt, the beauty of it and I pushed the sweaty, foul body of the stranger off me, curled into a foetal ball and cried. While he called me names as he regained self control beside me, I cried for the person I was. I cried for the person Jay saw. I cried for what I could have had if I didn't have a blackened heart. I cried for the pain on Jay's face when he opened the door and saw what I'd done, what I'd broken, what I'd destroyed because I didn't know how to do anything else.

Jay scooped me into his arms as I sobbed, great heaving sobs of grief. 'I know,' he soothed.

In the lift riding down to the basement carpark I put my hand on his pained face. 'Please hate me,' I begged.

He half smiled at me. 'Is that what that was about?'

I shrugged, sobering at the speed of light.

He shook his head. 'The least you can do is be honest with me, Jaz.'

'It was too much. This morning. The words. The sex. Oh God, the sex. I didn't know what to do with it.'

'With love? You didn't know what to do with love? Because that's what that was, Jaz. This morning. That was me loving you. It felt like you were loving me back. But maybe I was wrong.'

'Maybe you weren't,' I mumbled.

'Then what the fuck, Jaz?' he asked furiously as he all but threw me in the car.

'I didn't know what to do with it. I was scared.'

'Scared? Of what?' he asked as he drove out of the carpark like an angry rally driver.

'What it meant. Where it would go. The pain when it ends.'

'What if it doesn't end?'

'It always ends.'

'It doesn't have to.'

'Come on, Jay, we both know no one loves me for long. Hell, no one even likes me for long.'

'Only because you push everyone away.'

'I'm a Harrington. It's what we do.'

'No. It's what your father does. You don't have to be the same.'

'It's his blood running through my veins, his DNA holding me together. It's who I am.'

'No, it's not. It's not who Tom is or Lydia or even Christian.'

'Tom and Lydia? They're exactly like him. They fucking left me, Jay. In the middle of the night, they left me here.'

'No, Jaz. They're surviving him the only way they know how. You know that.'

'Do I? They didn't say goodbye. They didn't leave a note. No explanation, nothing. Just one day he gets cleared of all charges and the next they've vanished. I'm their sister. They were supposed to protect me but they left me here.'

'There's more to it than that and you know it.'

'No, I don't because no one has said a word. Not since it all began. It doesn't matter anyway. It doesn't change anything in the end. Doesn't change what's inside me. It's all him and that's just the way it is.'

'No. It's not. You get to choose. You don't have to be like him.'

'But it's all I know.'

He pulled over to the side of the road. Pulled my face to his. 'Then let me show you another way,' he begged. 'Please, before you kill yourself, let me love you, Jaz.'

I wanted it so badly I ached. Every muscle, every cell in my body ached for his love as my skin ached for his touch. Could it even be true? Could I be any different? Could he really love me? Could he love me enough?

'Please,' he begged again, his mouth brushing mine and right then, in that instant, I was his and I knew, somehow, in my messed up head, I knew I'd never want for anyone else but him. That all this time, it had been him and I'd been fighting it, fighting the want and the friendship. All those days and nights on his couch watching tv and eating pizza, all those times he saved me from myself. I'd been self destructing in my fight but I had no fight left and I gripped onto him so tightly, pulled his mouth hard up against mine desperate for him. To be close to him.

He pulled away, a smile on his fearsome face, because he looked that way, both compellingly beautiful and fearsome at the same time. But right then as he grinned, as he panted with want, he looked so perfect, so innocent and I was terrified I was going to ruin him.

'If you keep that up, I'm going to take you right here in this car on the side of this road,' he panted.

'And that would be bad because...'

'No. We're not going to do that, Jaz. I'm not that guy. I'm not one of those guys,' he said, raising his eyebrow just so. It turned some people to water but I was used to it.

'Fine,' I whined, sitting back in my seat.

He smirked.

'I didn't do it, you know,' I quietly admitted.

He looked at me questioningly.

'Before, when you found me, I know how it looked but I

didn't do it. I couldn't. I thought of you and I pushed him off. I couldn't go through with it.'

'Why were you in there?'

'I thought if I replaced the memories of you with something else, I'd be able to deal with it easier. It was just too much feeling. I didn't know what to do with it. But I couldn't. What we did, I liked it and when it came down to it, I didn't want to replace those memories. Whatever happens next, I didn't want to forget what happened this morning.'

He smiled. 'Good. Let me take you home.'

Which home, I wondered? My home where my father would be locked away working in his study? Where my mother would be working on her social calendar and Margot would be cleaning the kitchen or preparing for bed? Or was he taking me to his home where he would order pizza and we would curl up on the couch watching Outlander and drinking beer?

'What?' he asked, glancing at me curiously.

'Which home?'

'Your home. You haven't been home two nights in a row. Your parent's will notice.'

I nodded. They didn't notice these things themselves. People were paid to inform them. But I guess that counted for something.

'Don't sulk on me, Jaz. After what you did tonight, you need to clean yourself up and get some sleep.'

I nodded. He was right and the shame flooded through my body. The shame of what I'd done, what I'd almost done, what I'd put him through. I was an awful, awful person. I couldn't fathom how he could love me but I'd find a way to make it right, to be that person he saw.

'We start fresh in the morning.'

I looked at him hopefully.

'Fresh. Tomorrow,' he promised as he pulled up in front of my house.

He saw me inside but only as far as the door and then he was gone.

In the morning, I lay on the couch eating cereal and watching cartoons. Jay was in the security room drinking coffee with my father's security team. Just like always.

He was already there when I woke. I knew it, I'd found Panadol and juice beside my bed and I could feel him. I'd asked Margot anyway when she'd brought the coffee and cereal to the couch. 'Did you need him?' she'd asked curiously but I shook my head. Clearly if he was in the security room, my parents were home, otherwise he didn't bother keeping his distance and often sat on a chair and watched cartoons with me.

Now I found myself wondering what he was doing and what he was thinking. I was going to drive myself mad if I didn't find a way to stop it, to control my wayward thoughts but I couldn't help it, I'd seen him at his rawest. I'd seen his soul and I'd liked what I'd seen and I wanted to see it again. Now we'd hashed things out, now my head was straight. I kept going back to the same thoughts, him naked, on top of me, every beautifully taut muscle flexing, the way his face went just so in that moment right before....

'More coffee, dear,' Margot offered, ripping me from my thoughts.

I had to stop, think about something else. I checked my phone. Surely there was a party or something being planned that could distract me? But I got no further than the first two posts on Facebook before I messaged him, 'I need to see you.'

'No. Just do your thing like normal, we'll go out at lunch time, like usual.'

'I have nowhere to go,' I told him.

He replied with a winky face. A bloody winky face. I would give him a bloody winky face. I wasn't twelve and I didn't like being kept and managed. I'd promised to let him love me, I didn't promise to behave. I didn't feel like sitting around the house watching cartoons while he drank coffee in another room. I wanted to see him, to feel him, just for a minute, to remember it was all real. I needed it like I needed air. Something. I wasn't even sure what myself. But I couldn't sit still, so if he wouldn't come out to play then I was going to have to force him out.

I dressed in my skimpiest bikini, a fluorescent green number I'd bought for a pool party at Indi's, then put on a pair of cut offs and a tank top. There were cameras in all the main living spaces of the house and I knew exactly where each one of them was. I mightn't have known much about love and being loved or relationships and their rules but I knew about men. I knew about turning them on, frustrating them, and mostly, I knew about Jay. I knew, or I hoped I knew, what would draw him out of his foxhole to take me somewhere else.

If I'd been thinking straight, I'd have thought things through better, remembered at least one or both of my parents were somewhere but I wasn't thinking straight. I hadn't been thinking straight since he'd done beautiful things to me on his bedroom floor. When I stayed still long enough, I could still feel him inside me and I was so glad that I hadn't let whatshisname from the night before take that away from me. I just needed to see him, to remember it was all real, just a glimpse of his beautiful face would be enough.

I gave him a last chance. 'Come out, come out wherever you are!' I messaged him

'Jaz???????'

'???????'

'Stop it.'

'Stop what?' I asked as I leaned against the kitchen bench, my bare legs stretched out in front, a smirk on my face.

'Don't...' he pleaded but still there were no doors being opened or closed, no Jay.

I walked over to the couch, bent over it to reach for the remote and turn off the television knowing exactly what view he'd be getting on his little monitor. It wasn't fair, he could sit there in his little box and watch me for as long as he liked but I didn't get to see him even for a second.

My phone buzzed with a message. 'Jaz...'

I sent him a stupid bloody winky face, put my phone on the bench, then took off my tank top as I walked towards the patio. I kicked off my shorts, kicking them to floor and walked perfectly in line with the camera in that teeny tiny bikini.

Outside, I dived straight into the pool, swam halfway down then hoisted myself out, pausing a second as the water dripped from my body. Casually, I glanced up at the camera that had caught my movement and couldn't help the tiny smirk on my face. If he was going to sit in the safety of his box and watch me, I was going to give him a show. I sat on the pool lounger, reaching behind to undo the tie and then he was there, wrenching me out of my seat.

'What the fucking hell are you doing?' he ground out.

'What does it look like I'm doing? I'm about sunbake,' I smirked, taking him in, feeling his energy, memorising his face, his smell, getting my momentary fill as though he were some new designer drug. My whole body seemed to exhale from the sight of him, the touch of him and I savoured the feeling.

He quickly did up the tie of my bikini. 'There are six blokes in that room ogling every fucking move you make. They don't even realise they're doing it. But God, look at you,' he said, shaking his head. 'I was practically hard as a rock watching that show.'

'And now?'

'And now I'm angry because you were about to flash six unprepared middle-aged men.'

'They've seen my boobs before, Jay, they were in a bloody magazine a couple of years ago for goodness sake.'

'And we sued their arses for distribution of child pornography. I will not have you sitting here flashing them now, not any more, do you understand?' he demanded, putting on his scary voice that was very rarely directed right at me and far more powerful than the gun he kept in his waistband.

'What, never?' I asked.

'Never. Unless we're alone. From now on, only I get to see

those, you got that? No more of this or that other crap you've been pulling.'

I nodded, somehow feeling triumphant.

He handed me my phone. 'Look at it as though you just got a message then go inside and get dressed. We'll leave in 45 minutes.'

'Fine,' I agreed, trying not to smile now I'd gotten my own way like the brat I was.

He sighed, exasperated and walked away. I went and showered, rinsing off the salty water from the pool, put on a pretty sundress and my favourite espadrilles, threw a change of underwear and a new toothbrush in my tote and walked out. It would have been suspicious if I didn't behave normally, so I walked to the security room, opened the door and summoned him. 'We're going. Now.'

'Yes, Ma'am,' he joked.

We drove past my cute little Audi in the Volvo SUV my father provided. Jay's own jeep sat parked in the unofficial staff carpark with Margot's Mazda and whatever else my father's security team drove. I wasn't allowed in the Jeep and the SUV was safer against the vultures with their cameras than my cute little Audi. I sometimes wondered why my father bought me the Audi at all.

'Where are we going?' I asked as we drove away from the house.

'My place.'

'Okay. Will there be Outlander?'

He smiled. 'If you like.'

'And pizza?'

'Maybe.'

'And beer?'

He sighed.

'What?'

'You have to stop drinking.'

'Why? Because you can't love me otherwise?'

He sighed again, almost a groan. 'No. It won't stop me loving you but you need to love yourself, too, Jaz and you can't do that if you're constantly drunk.'

'I'm not *constantly* drunk,' I whined.

He gave me that look that said he knew better.

'Fine, no beer,' I conceded. I certainly didn't need to be having a discussion on how much I drank when I finally had him sitting next to me, when I could finally see and feel and smell him.

He smiled, held my hand, raised it to his mouth and kissed my knuckles and I couldn't remember ever feeling so much tenderness and I knew there wasn't anything I wouldn't give this man if he asked. I wasn't telling him that of course. I'm not an idiot. But knowing it changed me, changed something in me, in who I wanted to be. For him I'd be a better person, for him I'd be the person he saw when no one else bothered to look.

While my parents spent the week in Sydney doing whatever it is they do, having meetings, attending a fancy function, I stayed at Jays until my system had been cleaned. He fed me green smoothies, held me through the worst parts until the pain eased, until it was better, until everything slowly became clearer and the world became a different place.

I'd realised in all those unfamiliar, sober, clarity-filled days, he'd been my best friend for a long time and I'd treated him like rubbish but I was making up for it, doing my best to show him he was someone, my someone, the only one who gave a shit, the only one who saw through my crap, who saw me, not the IT girl, life of the party that got them on the front cover of a magazine but a person to be valued, to be loved.

I shoved pizza into my mouth, my legs stretched onto Jay's lap as we worked our way through an Outlander marathon. It had been a tough few days as my body detoxed. They'd been rough, dark, frightening. I'd begged for the pain to be over and Jay had held me until it passed. He whispered kind and beautiful words and I promised him I was done with my old life, old ways, old friends. Laughing with him, being loved by him, they all became more important than all the other things I'd been filling my life with. Parties, sex and drinking, they'd all filled the empty hole my father had created with his demands and expectations. They'd all made the life I'd been living bearable, but I didn't need them anymore. I needed Jay more and I needed to be the person I was becoming when I was with him. I liked that person he was brining out in me, the person with thoughts and dreams, who laughed and cried and felt. This was the life I wanted, a life with him.

'How long before we make it known the old Jaz Harrington is dead and buried and never coming back?' I couldn't imagine returning to my old life when my parents came home, sneaking around or pretending Jay wasn't important to me, wasn't the most important person in my universe.

'Your father will kill me if he finds out,' Jay said quietly.

'You're not afraid of my father are you?' I challenged.

'I'm afraid of what your father will do to you, to us, if he finds out.'

'I'm seventeen, I'm not a child.'

'To him you are.'

'Besides, he's known me to date older men before, he's even introduced me to them, encouraged it. What does he think happens on those dates?'

'But they were for his gain. None of them were employed to protect his daughter.'

'He'll lose it, won't he?' I asked, understanding.

'To put it mildly,' Jay smiled.

'Then what do we do? I'm not faking my old life forever. I'm not ignoring you,' I said, snuggling into him as though someone might take him away. 'And what if I start behaving and he sees no purpose for you anymore? What then?'

'You're 18 in less than a year, maybe I'll marry you,' he joked, tapping my nose then trailing his finger along my jaw as his mouth met mine and moved deliciously, igniting that beautiful fire that began way down in my toes.

We hadn't slept together while I was detoxing and now it seemed he was ready to make up for it and I was more than willing to go along for the wild and beautiful ride.

It was like everything was brand new, like I was seeing everything with new eyes. I suppose I was. I was sober, I'd been sober for days and the things his touch did to me, his mouth, his hands, set my skin on fire, everything was more intense and he knew it.

As his mouth moved over my skin, as my body came alive beneath his touch, I could feel him smile, feel his own body react to mine until neither of us could stand it a second longer. The want and the need took over and it was like our souls joined in some hippy ceremony from a romance novel but it was real and it was beautiful.

'Would you really want to marry me someday?' I asked as I rested my head on his bare chest, the gentle beat of his heart thrumming familiarly against my cheek.

'Someday, Jaz, someday. Maybe Christian will have that new Vegas hotel he's working on up and running and we can run away together,' he laughed.

'I'd run away with you, you know.'

He kissed the top of my head and held me tight. 'It won't come to that.'

We both knew we had no control over anything if my father found out but we pretended, just for a minute that maybe we did, that our lives wouldn't be full of stolen moments.

In an effort to prove we had any control over the coming weeks, Jay brought my mouth to his before his hands roamed over my body, knowing their way now, to the pleasure zones, the comfort zone, knowing all the hidden tricks of my body and he exploited them with a satisfied grin until I fell apart. He followed me, allowing me that rare glimpse into his soul, his vulnerability.

'So, what really happened on the soap?' Jay asked as we ate

cold pizza in his bed, soaking up all of the minutes that remained.

'What do you mean? You know this, the whole country knows I self destructed.'

'I know what the magazines said and what Tom said, but what really happened?'

'I don't know. Tom had just left for the army. Christian keeps me grounded, Tom gave me direction. I was a bit lost in a world I didn't want to be. I was at a cast party celebrating something, someone passed around glasses of sparkling and I took one and that was it, love,' I smiled. When he scowled at me, I added, 'I hated it, the limelight, being some darling of television, having to go there and work instead of dance or spend time with my friends. It was all Dad. He made it happen. I was his prop. It gave people a reason to speak to him at parties. He'd parade me around like a doll, you've seen him, I hated it. I still do. I just wanted to be invisible and that first drink, that first time, it just made it all fade away. Then one afternoon after I'd begun sneaking vodka into nearly everything, I started fooling around with my fifteen-year-old tv brother in the dressing room and I liked it. The approval from someone else, having the power to say yes or no, to make him feel things, to make his body do things. It was just another vice to add to my growing list of things that made life better, bearable.

'Jeff, the director, said I was a great kid but he knew I didn't really want to be there and who wants a drunk thirteen year old to worry about? So he said it was best for everyone if I left and I hugged him so hard. He even agreed to kill me off so my father couldn't force me to go back. It had the whole country outraged when my character died but it was the best day of my life.' I smiled. 'But by then, I was so used to sneaking vodka into my water bottle and I was afraid of what the world would look like without it. I liked being numb too much to give it up so I didn't and before long, I stopped bothering to mix anything with the vodka and I needed more and more to be numb and here we are.'

He stroked my hair, kissed me softly but said nothing, the emotion on his face saying everything.

'I'm sorry you got dragged in to my family's mess. First Tom's shit, now me.'

'But if Tom hadn't been in trouble, if the whole country hadn't wanted his head on a stick, you wouldn't have needed protection and we'd have never met.'

'You could have left once he'd been cleared.'

'You were out of control. Your mum begged your dad to keep me.'

'Really?' I asked, surprised my mother had asked my dad for anything, even if it was for my wellbeing.

'She mightn't stand up to him in public, but she does, trust me. That was one hell of a fight and she wasn't backing down, stood toe to toe with him in the living room.'

'I'll have to remember how much you lot see on those cameras,' I joked, my brain rapidly flipping through years of inappropriate behaviour.

'I'd appreciate that,' he smirked and I wondered how much they'd seen of me over the years and held back an involuntary shiver of shame.

W hen my parents returned, so did reality. Jay and I carried on as best we could. We attended parties, Jay controlled my drinks, lemonade in champagne glasses, shots that were filled water instead of vodka so no one would notice I wasn't drinking and start asking questions. Then as soon as everyone was distracted, we'd disappear and spend time at his place until I had to go home.

In the clubs, I stuck to the dance floor as much as possible. Lacey was the only one of us who was just out for a good time and was so emotionally well adjusted she handled her few vices with ease. I stuck with her and did my best to stay out of trouble, relying on Jay to intervene when I needed and always disappearing into the night once everyone was too drunk to notice I was gone. But mostly we lived off stolen moments, glances across the room, holding hands while we drove alone. It was better than nothing I told myself.

A s Jay's tongue worked my nipple, his groin hard against my hip, I reminded him of my parent's Christmas party Saturday night.

His spare hand started ministering between my legs. 'I am not talking about your parent's fucking Christmas party right now.'

His finger dived inside me and I threw my head back, groaning from the pleasure of it.

'Okay?' he smirked.

'Ahuh. Fine. No party,' I stumbled breathlessly.

His mouth dived onto mine as his hands worked their magic right up until I almost... 'Not yet. We're not going to be together for a few days,' he moved until his tip was at my core. 'Look at me, I want to see you,' he commanded in that husky sex voice of his.

As I melted into his dark blue eyes, he watched my face as he entered me.

I watched the look of ecstasy cross his and nothing could have ever been more perfect than in that moment.

'I love you, Jaz Harrington. I'll love you until the day I die,' he declared before we lost ourselves in each other.

My parent's Christmas party was an annual nightmare only tolerated by copious amounts of booze. They held it at their country house, filled it with a who's who of the social scene, politicians, actors, actresses, important journos, business moguls, sportspeople, you name them, they were there, parading the halls, sipping their fancy champagne and talking crap.

We then stayed at the country house until after New Years as a family. It was the only week of the year guaranteed to have us all in one place at the one time. This would be our first without Tom and Lydia and I still didn't really know why. Why they'd gone, why they'd left me. The trouble was over. They should have been celebrating. We should have been celebrating Christmas together without that dark cloud of accusation Tom had been stuck with. The building collapse hadn't been his fault. Everyone knew it. But it was either him or Linc and Linc's dad had more power and influence than ours, so the first fingers were pointed at my brother. But of course he was cleared. He was a good guy. He'd fought for our country. He didn't cut corners. This should have been the time when we all came together, we should have been happy, but he'd run and he'd taken my sister with him. As soon as I walked in, their absence screamed in the quiet and I stumbled for a second, Jay catching my arm.

'You okay?' he asked.

'It's just strange, them not being here. Tom and Lydia. Have you heard from them? Heard anything?' I begged.

'Nothing,' he said sadly.

The house was sparkling with fairy lights. Silver stars hung from the ceiling, fat golden tinsel was strung artfully and the enormous Christmas tree filled the corner looking glorious as always. Margot looked forward to decorating the country house every year. She did a lovely job of the city house, but she could go crazy out here with the annual party and she made the most of it. We had been allowed to help when we were children, as long as our parents were out but it had been a while since these rooms had been filled with laughing children. There wasn't much laughter anymore and the rooms echoed with the absence of Tom and Lydia. Those two filled a room with joy. I don't know how but they did. They were our glue, our light and without them we were falling apart.

Arriving usually meant eggnog as we unloaded our gifts around the tree and caught up on the last couple of weeks and reminisced to the sound of carolling in the sound system overhead. But today the room was empty and quiet. No eggnog, no laughter, no reminiscing. I wasn't even sure what I was supposed to do in this new version so I just dumped my bag of gifts under the tree and kept walking.

Christian leaned against the bar on the other side of the

room, a glass of scotch in one hand. He raked a frustrated hand through his hair as my father talked to him. Because you didn't speak with my father, you stood quietly and listened. I felt a stab of pity for Christian but there was nothing I could do to ease his pain, so I left them to their discussion.

Jay carried my bags up the stairs behind me and I knew these were probably going to be our last moments alone and pain already stabbed at my chest, my stomach in knots with not being able to be with him or speak to him with too much familiarity. I was going to have to watch my every action, my every word and all I wanted to do was curl up on the couch with him and watch cheesy Christmas movies.

Jay put the bags at the end of my bed and stood for a second as though trying to commit my face to memory. 'I'll be downstairs if you need me,' he said, his voice as pained as my heart.

I nodded sadly, afraid to speak in case I cried because at this point it could go either way if I opened my mouth.

'It's just a week or so, your parents go to Italy on the third,' he reminded me but the third seemed a million days away and I wasn't sure I was going to be able to last that long. Jay was keeping me together, keeping me sober, making me human and loveable. I liked who I was with him and I didn't want to be without him, without even the stolen moments because there were too many eyes in this house. 'We'll be okay,' he promised. 'You'll be okay. Just no topless sunbathing, please, my heart couldn't take it,' he begged with a grin.

I nodded. 'No topless sunbathing. I can do that,' I grinned, the pain easing a little.

He kissed me hard then left with wishes in his eyes and I flopped on my bed and lay there staring at the ceiling like some foolish lovesick girl from a sad romcom until my mother came knocking. 'People are arriving, Jasmine, could you dress please?'

I nodded and she left.

A red dress with a lot of tulle hung in a garment bag in my wardrobe. It wasn't worth the fight to defy Mum when it came to her societal rules and it was a beautiful dress. As I took it out of the garment bag and checked the label, I realised it wasn't a designer I knew, but one of Lydia's. LAHLAH was printed in pink sensible letters on the label, her initials, Lydia Anne Harrington. We'd always joked that LAH so easily became LAHLAH and the childhood memory that seemed so far away made me smile. It also made me realise how much she'd given up to run away with Tom. She'd been working her way through design school and working with a famous designer, but she'd thrown it all away to run away to Europe with Tom. And seeing the dress, how incredibly talented she was, I finally understood that whatever was going on, whatever they were keeping from me must have been huge. Bigger than me, bigger than childhood dreams. Designing had been Lydia's dream since she could speak, even though it took her a long, defiant time, to get to it. It was all she'd ever wanted to do, all she'd ever dreamt off and had tortured me and our Barbie dolls with her endless creations. I wished, like I'd wished so many times, she'd confided in me, let me help her. But I suppose I could barely help myself and I suddenly realised it was me who had let her down, it was me who hadn't been there for her and Tom when they'd needed me because I was too busy drowning myself in a bottle and now it was too late, there was nothing I could do.

I sent Lydia an email for whatever it was worth.

The dress is beautiful, thank you. I wish you were here. I miss you. I miss you both. So much is happening, everything has been thrown upside down and turned inside out in a good way. I wish you'd both come home and let me show you. At least let me know where to forward your gifts. Let me know you're okay, that you're alive, please, something. But if nothing else, please take care of yourselves and each other and know I love you both. Merry Christmas, the country house is empty without you both and I hate it but I love you, always, Jaz.

I slid into the dress, zipped it and admired it in the mirror. It fitted perfectly, as though Lydia had measured and cut it just for me, which she probably had and I smiled. I knew Jay would be weaving his way through the room so I took extra care with my hair, letting the wild black curls hang loose the way he liked, put on an extra squirt of perfume and when I couldn't delay it any longer, I made my way down the stairs.

My father waited at the bottom of the stairs with a scowl on his face. Not his usual everyday scowl but the one he saved for when he was really pissed off and I tried to think of anything I'd done recently that could have made him angry. It wasn't hard to anger him but I'd been so well behaved, laid low at Jay's, not had a drop of alcohol in the last couple of weeks so I thought for sure I was safe. Maybe he was waiting for Christian? But I spotted Christian across the room looking dapper in his tux speaking with Margot. Then I saw the magazine in Dad's hand and my stomach sank to my toes.

'Jasmine.'

'Dad.'

'My office. Now,' he somehow seemed to bellow without raising his voice. It was a skill of his and with the living room already full of guests spilling out onto the patio, a scene was the last thing he'd tolerate so I nodded.

I followed Dad away from the partygoers, down the hall towards his office. I caught Jay's eyes and saw the concern on his face. I shrugged. We couldn't have been caught. I was already at Jay's a lot and even though we used our thinly veiled excuses, Dad knew why, so seeing me going in or coming out of his building, if the vultures had even found out where he lived, in a magazine would not arouse suspicion and we'd not been affectionate in public. We'd been careful.

Inside, Dad slammed the monthly magazine onto his desk, face up and on the cover was a photograph of Jay carrying me out of the club, Cascades after Tom and Lydia had left, limp as a rag doll. He'd had no choice that night. The vultures had covered every exit. Jay had saved me like he always saves me. But worse than the cover photo, there was an inset photo of me barely coherent with The Puppy kissing me in Cascades with his hand up my dress for everyone to see.

'I'm sorry,' I said before Dad even bothered shouting at me. 'I promise, I'm doing better.'

'This is not better,' he shouted.

'Dad, I promise, I've had nothing to drink since then.' It was close enough. It wasn't time for semantics.

'I don't believe you, Jasmine. It's too much. This can't go on.'

'I know. I promise, I've stopped. Ask Jay.'

'I will be speaking with him. Don't you worry about that.

He is paid to protect you, not stand by while strange men put their hands up your dress for everyone to see. What were you thinking? NO, don't answer that,' he spat, his hand in the air. 'You weren't thinking, you're never thinking about what you're doing, about how it looks for everyone else. How am I supposed to go to a meeting next week when everyone has seen my daughter being groped by a stranger on the front cover of a national bloody magazine?'

'I'm sorry,' I sobbed.

'Sorry or not. This ends now, do you hear me? You do not leave this house until I say so.'

I looked at him horrified. He was going to lock me in this bloody house.

'Not a step out that door, do you hear me?'

'Yes,' I whispered, because there was no point arguing with him when he was like this. Then he stormed out and left me there alone.

Jay knocked on the door a few minutes later as I was wiping the last of my tears. He handed me my tote bag, which he knew had a full makeup supply. This wasn't the first time I'd needed supplies.

'What was that about?' he asked.

I indicated my father's desk with my head as I fixed my face in my compact mirror.

'Shit,' he mumbled as he picked up the magazine. 'How bad?'

'Really bad. I'm not allowed to leave this house until he says so.'

'Wow.'

'He'll forget though, right? In a couple of days, he'll forget?'

'Maybe. Either way, it'll be okay. Don't worry about it. You're sober now so you'll be fine, he just needs to see it.'

'Not if I'm stuck here, I won't be fine, I'll go mad.'

'It's just a week and they'll go to Italy. You'll be fine for a week, read a book, get in some R&R.'

I nodded. He was right. I would be okay for a week.

'You look beautiful, by the way,' Jay smiled before he led me back to the party.

We dispersed at the end of the hallway, Jay went back to work and I stood beside the towering Christmas tree with my champagne glass of lemonade realising everyone was a giant bore when you're sober, and not really sure what I was supposed to do with myself.

'Jaz,' smirked Ceecee. 'What say we head outside and get this party started?' she asked with a smirk, brandishing a bottle of sparkling.

'Thanks, Cee, but not today, I'm afraid.'

'What do you mean?' she asked, genuinely confused.

'Cee, I'm in a whole world of trouble right now. The last thing I need is to be pissing my father off anymore than he already is,' I smiled.

'Righteo then,' she shrugged as though my presence was really neither here nor there for her. 'I'll see you later,' she said, holding the bottle of sparkling aloft and heading out to the patio and disappearing around the corner and I wondered if she'd always been so vacuous. She didn't even care what was going on with me, if I was okay, just where the party was. Maybe Jay was right. I was loyal to my friends even though they didn't always deserve it. Where was CeeCee's loyalty in return?

I watched her go, knowing what would happen around that corner. I'd shown them the spots that were out of the camera view where they could drink and snort and fuck without a worry. That was my world. It was all I knew. I didn't know what to do in this sober world. A waiter passed with a tray of drinks and I wondered if I'd be okay with just one? It'd loosen me up. Take off the edge. I looked around for Jay and he was standing on the other side of the room, an invisible sentinel to anyone but me. He was watching me carefully and I couldn't stand the thought of the disappointment that'd show in his face if I reached for one of those drinks so I let the waiter pass.

I saw Christian talking to some people I recognised on the patio so I went out there, hooked my arm through his and joined the conversation. He patted my hand, made sure everyone knew each other and then continued his conversation.

As the people left, Christian asked, 'You okay?' but before I could answer, we were joined by Cameron Taylor. 'That'll be my cue,' Christian ground out through his teeth before disappearing towards the drink cart.

Cam was drunk, roaring drunk. He stank and his words slurred and I wondered how anyone had ever even tolerated me.

'Not the same without Linc, is it?' he slurred wistfully.

I shrugged. Linc had disappeared off to the states to be with some blonde bimbo just after Tom had gone to court. He wasn't my favourite person right now, just another fair weather friend, a deserter, a member of the old crew now.

Cam offered me the bottle of scotch he was holding and I

shook my head. He raised his eyebrows, in question, in surprise and I shook my head again.

'Don't tell me our magical starlet, The Princess of Party, Jaz Harrington has gone on the straight and narrow?' he asked, amused.

I shrugged.

'Ah, come on,' he said, taking a long drink from the bottle. 'We all know better than that,' he grinned.

I realised he'd slowly been edging me backwards towards the wall and I was trapped. We'd edged into one of the darker corners just out of sight line from the cameras. Ordinarily the cameras would still have caught the movement but with so many people around they were in stationery positions and just as I realised how much trouble I might be in, Cam pushed himself against me, pinned me with his legs, strong as an ox, his thickset body doing the rest.

'Come now, Jaz, I know you better than that. What's got into you? Surely not Daddy?' he asked with a laugh, taking another drink. Then he pushed the bottle towards me and when I didn't take it, shook my head again, he grabbed my jaw, forcing my mouth open and poured the scotch in.

I spat it to the ground. 'You stupid pig. I said no,' I spat, trying to push him off me but he wouldn't budge and I wondered where the fuck was Jay.

I kept struggling against him as Cam took another drink but before swallowing, he attached his mouth to mine and spat the scotch straight in. I had no choice but to swallow and then dry reached, from the scotch, from his tongue in my mouth,

I wasn't sure which but scotch spurted all over his face as he finally detached himself from me.

'You fucking bitch,' he groaned, swore, ground at me harder. I struggled against him as he tried to grope me, grabbing at my crotch and my breasts, tears flooding down my face.

I'd promised Jay no more. I'd said no more drinking, no more men, no more drama and here we were so soon and it was as bad as always. I struggled and I struggled, screaming and pushing and then all of a sudden he was flung from me and Jay wrapped his arms around me, making soothing sounds as I cried into his chest. He kissed the top of my head and my father bellowed, 'You bloody better not be.'

We both looked over at my furious father pushing his way through the crowd.

'Get out,' he spat at Jay.

'Dad, what are you doing?' I asked as he tried wrenching me from Jay.

'Get out! Get out! Get out!' he screamed at Jay like a madman.

'What? Why?' Jay begged.

'You think I don't know? You think I don't see?'

'See what Dad?'

'I've seen the way he looks at you, Jasmine. Tom told me to ignore it. That Jay was a good guy. That we could trust him but now, now this.'

'This what? He just saved me from bloody drunk Cam Taylor trying to grope me.'

'Then... You don't comfort someone like that. You don't kiss them like that if you're not... You...you bastard! I trusted you with my daughter. She's only seventeen for crying out loud. Get out! Get out of my house!' he bellowed like a crazy man, losing all control of his usual boardroom calm.

Jay took his arms away from me, his face as pained and fearful as my heart as the rest of Dad's security team moved forward.

I howled, I begged, 'No! Please, no!' I grasped at air as I reached for him, fell to my knees, begging but no one would listen and then he was gone, not even looking back and I howled. I wailed like an animal, as though my soul had been torn until Christian gathered me to him, scooped me up, walking through the hordes of stunned party goers and took me to my room.

D ays passed. Margot brought me food but I barely ate it, I was too sick in my stomach and I couldn't leave my bed. My worried mother sat on the corner of my bed Christmas morning, the sound of carolling drifting up the stairs and begged me to come down. 'Why? Tom and Lydia aren't even here. Why are we bothering to pretend our family hasn't disintegrated? What's the point? What's the point to any of it, Mum?' I sobbed into my pillow wondering when I'd be all cried out.

'He did what he thought was best, Jasmine.'

'He would have to know me, to know what's best. If he knew me, even just a little, he'd know Jay is what's best for me. I'm sober because of Jay. I'm a better person because of him. I love him,' I cried.

Mum held me to her. 'I know, dear, I know.'

Eventually she coaxed me downstairs in my pyjamas to open

presents with her, Dad and Christian. We went through the motions, none of us really there, our seemingly perfect family now shattered into a million pieces, then I went back to bed. No one had even bothered to fake any cheer. Grateful hugs exchanged for gifts we'd spent hours choosing was as festive as we managed.

After a brief and quiet knock, Christian came in and sat on my bed.

'I have something extra for you,' he smiled, handing me a small box.

'But you already gave me a beautiful gift,' I said, happy with the trip to Vegas he'd given me so I could spend some time with him after he went back.

I opened the small box he gave me to find a sweet necklace with an infinity pendant and a black stone in the middle. 'It's Onyx, for strength,' he told me as I ran my finger over the smooth stone. 'No matter what happens, Jaz, it's you and me to infinity,' he smiled.

It was a joke of ours, one developed after hours and hours of watching Toy Story as children and it had become our motto when things got tough. Emotion filled my throat. I couldn't find the words to tell him how much it meant to me, how special and thoughtful it was.

'I have one more. It was already under the tree but I managed to pocket it before Dad saw it.' He handed me the small gift wrapped in gold with a shimmering purple bow and said, 'I'll leave you to it.'

The gift card attached read, 'You have my heart, now, always and forever.'

I unwrapped the box, tears rolling down my face wondering if I'd ever see him again, ever know that kind of love again, ever feel what it was to be loved like that, unconditionally, despite my flaws, in spite of who I was.

Inside the box was an exquisitely fine silver bracelet with a single heart charm. It was perfect.

I had to see him. The desperate need to see him forced me to shower. I dressed and I went downstairs.

'Where are you going?' Mum asked from where she sat at the dining table with her appointment book.

'I need to see him,' I said, rummaging in my bag for my keys before realising we'd come in the SUV and my car was still in the city. I was stranded.

'Jasmine, your father has asked you to stay here. He'd rather you didn't leave and has given strict instructions you are not to see him again.'

'And we're all supposed to just bow down to the almighty Richard Harrington like he's some eighteenth century Duke? What everyone else wants be damned?'

'Jasmine...'

'What, Mum? You know I'm right. But you just sit there and nod and bow and do whatever the hell he asks no matter the damage it does. I can't take it anymore,' I cried.

'You won't have to take it much longer, then,' Dad said too quietly from the entrance.

'What is that supposed to mean?'

'You'll be coming to Italy with us. There's a facility there.'

'What kind of facility?' I asked horrified. There was nothing bloody wrong with me.

'One that deals with all this kind of hysteria,' he said, waving his hand around like my entire being was some sort of ailment to be treated.

'Hysteria? This is not hysteria! I love him!'

'You don't know what love is. You're a seventeen-year-old drunk, Jasmine!'

'I am more than a drunk,' I said, in that same quiet angry voice he used. 'I am more than you see. I am more and he saw it. He's the only one who saw it. You can't make me go.'

'Yes, I can,' he said, eyebrows raised in challenge and I wondered what lengths he'd gone to now. What strings he'd pulled to have that much power over me. I wasn't yet an adult but I was legally able to leave home so surely that gave me some rights over my choices? 'You are going to Italy and you are going to the facility and that is final,' he declared.

'For how long?' I asked, suddenly more scared than I'd ever been.

'Until I say so,' he bellowed, leaving the room.

I fell to my knees. I knew what this meant. Those photos in the magazine. Dad realising Jay and I were sleeping together. It was too much. It had pushed him over the edge and he was doing the only thing he knew how to do, locking me up and throwing away the key. Until when? Until I was better? Until I forgot about Jay? Until Jay moved on and married someone else? I gasped for air. It couldn't happen. I couldn't go to the other side of the world for an indeterminate amount of time while Jay married someone else. I couldn't, I couldn't bare it.

Mum patted me on the shoulder, 'Come Jasmine, don't make a scene.'

'A scene? Mum, there's no one here but us.'

She glanced up to a nearby camera. 'No one, not even Margot needs to see our business.'

Margot had seen more Harrington business than any Harrington. Margot had done most of the raising, most of the loving, most of the caring. Margot saw everything and if Mum thought she didn't, if she thought this was too much for Margot to see, Mum was a bigger fool than Dad.

It was Christian who eventually led me back to my room. 'I can't go to Italy, Christian, I can't.'

'It'll just be for a while,' he consoled. 'Think of it as a lovely Italian holiday.'

'You didn't see him, Christian. If I go, I'm not coming back. Not until there's nothing to come back to.'

'Hey,' he soothed, wiping at my tears.

'I need to see him, please,' I begged.

'Okay,' he smiled.

'Okay?'

'Yes. I can't bear to see you like this, Jaz. In this much pain. I think I prefer drunk Jaz,' he said, humour in his voice.

'Drunk Jaz was easier,' I agreed with a tight smile.

'They'll be in the city for New Year's Eve,' he said.

'They'll leave security here though, lots of it, I bet.'

'I know. You leave them to me,' he smiled. 'You and me to infinity, remember?' he said, gently tugging on the chain I'd already put around my neck.

I nodded. 'No matter what, you and me to infinity, always,' I agreed as I let myself sink into his arms.

T he air was brisk for New Years Eve, the sky clear and full of stars and possibilities and as the fireworks exploded in the distant sky, I ran. I ran across the garden where we'd once played as children, between the frangipanis, around Margot's prized roses and through the orchard, the fallen summer fruit squishing beneath my feet, the bright, nearly full moon above lighting my way. I ran to the creek, to the dinghy where I'd been sneaking my most prized possessions for days.

I'm not sure if this is what Christian had in mind when he arranged for Jay to meet me on the other side of the creek but I'd left him a note with my apology. I couldn't go to Italy. I couldn't be held captive a day longer and I couldn't, wouldn't live without Jay.

As I was about to climb into the dinghy we'd once used to go up and down the creek catching tadpoles as children, I looked back to the house. Lit up, it was pretty. It had always been pretty, my favourite of the houses. As soon as I stepped into the dinghy that would be it. I would be disinherited with nothing but the ziplock bag of money in my coat pocket. Jay would never work for my father again, for anyone. His reputation would be ruined. My father would make sure of it. We would have nothing.

I stepped into the dinghy, anyway. I only had a short time before security noticed I was gone. I rowed to the other side and climbed the hill and there, leaning against his jeep waiting was Jay.

Jay's beautifully fearsome face broke into a grin when he saw me. Tears fell down my face in relief as his arms wrapped around me and finally I could breathe, finally everything was okay.

'What's all this, then?' he asked, indicating the sheet I'd fashioned into a sack to carry my things. 'You look like Tom Sawyer,' he smiled.

'Take me away, Jay? Can you take me away?'

'To where?'

'Anywhere.'

He suddenly understood my meaning. 'Jaz... Are you sure? That's a big thing. It changes everything. I don't want you to regret anything.'

'I would never regret being with you.'

'But this?'

'This is the only way, it's all that's left,' I told him.

'Then let's go,' he smiled.

Acknowledgements

Thank you to everyone who supported me through the creation of this book. The continuation of Jaz's story began before The Rise of Jaz and was very special to me but one of the hardest books I've written. Cathleen Ross, you're amazing, thank you for busting my butt. Kristyn McQuiggan, thank you for making sense of my ramblings and sharing your creative genius.

To my support crew, Amanda, Carly and Kelly, thank you for always believing, for the wine and the laughs. To my RWA family, particularly Kaye and Brooke, thanks for sharing the ride.

To Patrick, Hamish, Bella-Rose, Serena and Jaxon, thank you for making me believe in humanity and perfection and giving me so much joy, no matter the dark.

To Mum who pushes my books on everyone, thanks, you're a gem. To Andrew, thanks for dreaming with me. To all my family who buy and read and support, thank you, you're amazing!

To everyone who has shared The Harrington Family's journey, thank you so much for taking the ride with me, it has been beautiful. This, however, is not the end!

www.ingramcontent.com/pod-product-compliance
Lightning Source LLC
Chambersburg PA
CBHW030622110726
47901CB00002B/280